"Elizabeth?"

She stiffened.

His eyes were glazed over all of a sudden, his tone different now. She waited on bated breath as he uttered his next words in the huskiest, sexiest voice she'd ever heard.

"I want to kiss you."

Her body hummed with desire at his words, and as much as she wanted to straddle his huge body and have her way with him, she did not move.

Do it. Don't do it. God, please, do it.

"But if I kiss you, I won't be able to stop, and your intimacy problems will be a thing of the past."

She could only gape at him.

"Thank you for checking on me, but if you want to remain a virgin, you need to leave."

"Ramo…" she uttered.

"I mean it, Elizabeth." He nodded toward his waist and she saw the thick bulge straining under the denim.

Nodding, she stood and grabbed her sweater Pausing at the door, she was just going to say goodbye, but he said, "Goodbye, Vitale."

Praise for Julia Laque

Tortured Kiss

by

Julia Laque

Tortured Series, Book 3

Tortured Kiss

Cover Art by *Debbie Taylor*

The Wild Rose Press, Inc.
PO Box 708
Adams Basin, NY 14410-0708
Visit us at www.thewildrosepress.com

Publishing History
First Black Rose Edition, 2019
Print ISBN 978-1-5092-2643-6
Digital ISBN 978-1-5092-2644-3

Tortured Series, Book 3
Published in the United States of America

Dedication

For Matthew, my long-lost brother.
Thank you for finding me.
Julia

Prologue

"Nervous?" her father asked as he shut her bedroom door. "It's almost time. Your grandmother told me to bring you down in three minutes and not a moment sooner."

Anxiety shot through Elizabeth, leaving a burning sensation in her chest where her heart had begun to pound in rapid succession. Placing a hand on her chest, she caught her eyes widening in the reflection of the vanity mirror in her bedroom and could see her father standing by the door, his presence making her nerves multiply.

Was this really happening?

Her father paused by the door, as a werewolf he could easily sense her nervousness and tension. "Please try and relax sweetheart," her father soothed. "Please...I..." Alonso Vitale trailed off, lowering his gaze. In an instant, his passive façade melted into apprehension and guilt. Well...it wasn't every day you married off your only daughter to a Were from another pack.

She gave her father a weak smile and made to grab for her compact, knocking down her perfume, which caused several items to fall on the floor. Cursing silently, she went to pick up the mess she'd made, but her father got there first. He reached for her trembling hands and gripped them firmly, his brow tight with tension.

As alpha of the Graybacks, Alonso Vitale had his hands full to begin with; protecting the pack in a city like Chicago had many obstacles. The Graybacks were a large pack, but not as big as the Blacktails, which covered much of the Chicago area. But they were big enough to make an impression on other packs trying to root themselves in the city.

The debate between the Graybacks and Blacktails on rights to the territory had gone on for centuries. To end further animosity and heaven-forbid, a war, Elizabeth's father approached Adam Perez, the Blacktail alpha about forming an alliance. Along with threatening wolf packs, there was a mounting vampire population to contend with. Both alphas, although reluctant, knew that standing together would keep their enemies at bay. There would never be peace in the city if they kept fighting over territory.

They were the largest packs in the Midwest, neither could be forced out without starting a war. It not only made sense to form this alliance with the Blacktails, it was strategically smart. At least, that's what they kept telling each other. After that brief and tense meeting with the Blacktails, things had moved swiftly.

And here she was now, staring at herself in a mirror wearing an off the rack wedding gown about to marry a complete stranger.

She glanced back up at Alonso. Her poor father looked the worse for wear. Losing his daughter to a Were from another pack seemed a helluva lot worse than being overthrown by the Blacktails or any other pack, but she couldn't bear to see her father suffer. Shaking off any building trepidation, she took a deep breath and surveyed herself in the mirror, content at what she saw.

Her dark hair was pulled back from her face, which drew attention to her dark eyes. Her best friend, Sophia had gone light with the makeup. At age eighteen with her olive complexion, Elizabeth hardly needed a lot.

"I'll be fine papa," she said cheerily, hoping he bought her small fib. "Just had a quick vision of me tripping and falling flat on my face, so be sure to hang on to me. You know how clumsy I can get." She got up and smoothed the front of her satin gown. "Hey! *You* should trip and fall. Take the focus off me," she declared, wide-eyed with mirth. "Better yet, split your pants bending over or something."

Her father seemed to brighten at her joke, glad she was in good spirits. Then his eyes registered her apparel and glossed over. "You look beautiful baby."

She beamed thankfully. "Ready?" she asked, grabbing for her bouquet. "Don't want to keep what's-his-face waiting."

Her father gave her an exasperated look, but what could he say? In truth, she *was* marrying a complete stranger named Ramo...something... *Oh no.* She couldn't even remember his last name. *Crap!* She should know this. It was going to be hers in a few minutes. Wait...was she changing her name? These were the types of things one thought about before marrying. With the agreement finalized only last weekend, she hadn't had the time to ponder it.

Her father looked uneasy again. Making jokes was probably not a good idea. She really didn't blame her father for making the alliance. In fact, she'd suggested it. Even told her father this is what they did in a monarchy way back when. She'd read all about them in her historical romance novels.

Sure, it was impulsive, but when Alonso spoke with the Blacktail alpha they'd both agreed, especially considering the new pack forming in Wisconsin. They were on good terms with a couple of packs in Indiana, but then there were the Darkwolves, who'd always given them trouble...

Perez! That was his name.

"Look at me, baby," her father intoned, knowing her mind had wandered.

She met his stare.

"If you want to back out, you can. I'll come up with an excuse and you and I can go see a movie or something. She laughed at that, loving the thought of doing something so normal like going to see a movie with her dad rather than altering her life completely.

"Papa, I've said it before...do people really know who they're married to? My marriage may not be under the best of circumstances, but so far it's managed a solid alliance." She rolled her eyes as she continued, "Some couples just marry for selfish reasons like, *love*."

Her father smirked again, always enjoying her dry jokes.

"My marriage is securing the safety of our pack and that makes me feel good."

He shook his head in defeat. "You have no idea how proud I am of you."

She hooked their arms and gave his bicep a squeeze. "Let's get this show on the road," she replied, hoping she looked as calm as she sounded.

While she'd agreed to the marriage, it sure as hell scared her. God, she was so young and he...Ramo

Perez...he was older and a bit intimidating. They'd only met once. He was handsome, for sure, in a dark and frightening sort of way. Sophia had been terrified of him. With his skull trim, dark eyes, and lip ring, Sophia told her he looked like a crazed killer. Her father had certainly shown his dislike at the sight of him. He'd expected the Blacktail to look like his cousin, the alpha.

She had assured both her father and her friend the tattoos and lip ring didn't bother her in the slightest. They knew she didn't scare easily. In fact, she thought the tattoos were kinda hot.

When they were introduced in the living room of her father's home, he'd barely met her eyes, only giving her a shake of the hand and a curt nod. She had been nervous too, she'd thought derisively. A reassuring smile would have been nice. She had played their awkward meeting over and over again in her mind, trying to decipher how he was feeling.

Music broke through her thoughts and her stomach knotted. She felt her father pat her arm but could not be distracted at the moment. The instant they rounded the corner into her father's spacious living room, her eyes went straight to her future husband.

Although she didn't think it possible, Ramo looked even more dangerous dressed up so elegantly. His exotic features and piercings contrasted well with his dark gray suit. The black tattoo that peeked out of his collar on the back of his neck teased her, as if inviting her to take a look at what was hidden underneath all that clothing.

In those few seconds before he looked her way, a torrent of emotions raced through her. First, he looked so damn handsome she wanted to pat herself on the back for being so lucky. Then, she noticed his stern expression, the hard set of his jaw, and instantly began to worry.

He didn't want this.

Hell, did she want this?

When he finally turned his head toward her she could have sworn she saw a hint of surprise flit across his face. What did that look mean?

It was basically the first time he'd really looked at her and she would have given anything to know what he was thinking. When she reached out to read his emotions she was hit with the same trepidation she was feeling and a pleasant surprise. His amazement grew as he gazed at her.

"Honey," her father whispered next to her.

"Mmmm?" she glanced at him.

Alonso stared questioningly. Only then did she realize she was holding him back slightly as she stared. Hitching in a sharp breath, she turned her gaze back to Ramo. She couldn't move. Shit. How long had she been standing there?

Eyes narrowing briefly, he shifted forward slightly, his lips parted. It looked as though he actually wanted to go to her, obviously sensing her hesitation.

Coming out of her trance, she gave him a small smile and surprisingly he returned it, taking her breath away. Her heart skipped at how gorgeous he looked with that devilish smirk.

Before she knew it, she was at his side, and the Were adjudicator had begun the nuptials. All the while, Ramo stared at her with an encouraging smile. She felt light-headed and breathless throughout the entire ceremony. When it was over and his lips met hers for a brief second, he pulled away, giving her a quick wink before leading her down the small make-shift aisle.

She felt as though she were a leaf in the wind, letting the elements sway her in the direction it chose, having little to no control of her limbs.

They were in the small foyer now, being congratulated by the few guests coming out of the living room. Every face that beamed at her was a complete blur. She dutifully smiled and said thank you, shaking hands and hugging everyone with an odd paralyzing feeling humming through her.

She'd done it. She'd actually married a complete stranger from another pack.

Oh God.

Her stomach rolled and she thought she might be sick. Biting down hard to keep down whatever was in her stomach, she closed her eyes, inhaling deeply through her nose and exhaling surreptitiously out her mouth.

Feeling a hand press lightly at her back, she stiffened, knowing damn well it wasn't her father who stood to her right, because the instant the contact was made, she felt a tingling spread over her skin, and the hair at her nape rose. The hand rubbed ever so gently over the thin satin and her heart stung. Ramo's soft caress warmed her insides and calmed her nerves like nothing ever had. A cup of hot chocolate on a cold winter's day couldn't have done the exquisite job her husband's hand was doing right now.

Husband.

Her husband.

Opening her eyes, she glanced up at him furtively.

He was speaking to his alpha in quiet tones. She wondered how old he was. He looked about twenty-six, she guessed, but as werewolves stopped aging in their twenties, he could actually be a hundred years old for all she knew.

In which case, what the hell would they have in common? She was only eighteen in her first year at the University of Michigan. The only topic of conversation she was good at nowadays was Piaget's theory of cognitive development and *The Bachelor*.

She'd had a couple boyfriends in high school, but nothing serious. Guys at her school were just curious to see what it was like to date a werewolf. The idiots thought Weres did some kinky secret thing in bed, but as soon as she'd hit the brakes when things got a little hot and heavy they'd turn into assholes.

What did he expect from her? Shit, she had no idea how to be a wife. Her mother had passed during childbirth and her father never remarried, so she had no frame of reference on the home front. Would he be disappointed that she didn't know how to cook anything but ramen noodles? Would he be annoyed she had no experience in the bedroom?

Nausea hit her hard again and she swayed in her heels. Ramo gripped her around the waist and the contact this time only made her think of what was supposed to happen tonight.

He leaned toward her and whispered huskily in her ear, "Go to the kitchen and get some water." Then released her to shake hands and talk with her grandmother, who, she suspected was providing a cover for her to escape into the kitchen when she grabbed him by the face and kissed each cheek, speaking loudly in

Italian to a stunned and bemused Ramo.

Moments later, she slowly sipped water at the sink as the guests who stayed after the ceremony had shrimp and champagne in the living room. She and her father had decided on a small, brief reception as there were a few Blacktails in the house with Graybacks. They thought it wise not to have a lengthy gathering. She could already feel tension rising outside of the kitchen.

"Feeling better?" a grim voice asked behind her.

Pivoting carefully, she gave Ramo a small smile. "Yes. Thank you."

He nodded quietly, his mouth a hard line.

"And thanks for making it easier," she said, pointing toward the other side of the kitchen door, indicating their swift marriage ceremony. She was really thankful he'd been so chill about the situation. It was easy just to let him navigate her through the process when he smiled at her in that sensual way.

He just nodded again mutely and put a hand in his pant pocket.

They both shifted a bit where they stood, an awkward silence ensuing.

Playing with the glass in her hands, she looked up at him and was taken aback at his gaze. He watched her with an odd assessing look in his eye. "You…you look nice," he uttered quickly, his compliment sounding obligatory." "Listen…I'm sorry this had to happen." He looked around the room as though he'd rather be anywhere but here.

Setting the glass in the sink, she linked her hands together. "No need to apologize. All for the cause, right?"

Their eyes locked and in that instant she knew

something bad was coming. Guilt oozed out of him. Guilt, anger, remorse and…was that desire she sensed? Her stomach knotted as she waited for him to speak.

"I'm going out of town. I need to take care of some things at home…"

"Home?" Did he mean the new condo? It wasn't out of town. He'd bought them a condo in Lincoln Park. During semesters she'd live in her dorm in Michigan, and at the condo during the summer. She was going to move into the new place during winter break.

"Wilmington. The Fighters have a meeting and I need to be present."

"Oh…" Wilmington was fifty miles south of Chicago. What did this mean? "You're leaving now?"

His wordless nods were beginning to irritate her. It was strange for a guy like him to look so solemn. She had a feeling he was outspoken, naughty, and having to restrain himself looked like it was stressing him out.

"Don't look at me like that," he said suddenly.

She blinked. "What?"

"Like you're trying to figure me out," he answered bitterly.

Where was this brusque attitude coming from? What happened to the sweet man who'd rubbed her back just minutes ago? Shaking her head, she stammered. "I don't know what…"

Shaking his head, he straightened. "I gotta get out of here."

He was about to push the swinging door when she spoke up. "Are you coming back? Tonight?" she asked in a small voice.

His hand was on the door, his back to her, but he'd turned his head. She stared at his profile, at his perfectly sculpted jaw. He shook his head. "No." He moved again, opening the door.

Alarm bells rang loudly in her ears. "Wait! You're just leaving me? You're not coming back?" She felt nauseous all over again. This couldn't be happening. Was he really leaving her? No. She must have been confused.

His voice cut through her like a chainsaw. "I didn't want a *fucking* wife. You'll be fine without me." With that, he left, the kitchen door swinging ominously in his wake.

Chapter One

Present Day, Ten years later...

Cool wind stung her eyes, the sound of it roaring in her ears as she ran. Elizabeth could hear a few of her pack members nearby, taking in the full moon's effect and exercising their constrained limbs around the city. The mayor of Chicago had designated certain areas where werewolves could run during the full moon.

Most of the pack chose to run around Lake Michigan to take in the view and stay close to home. She and a few others needed to feel earth underneath their paws, not cement. She chose the Sag Valley Forest Preserve. Not the best place for Weres to stretch their legs, but at least it was quiet.

Running during the full moon always gave her a rush. She could breathe better, see clearer, feel the breeze that whipped through her fur as if she were flying. The invigorating sensation made her feel alive and she knew tomorrow morning she'd feel like a million bucks. Her muscles would have that delightful soreness she got after a workout and a steam at the gym she rarely visited.

The full moon and moon heat, the day before the full moon when werewolves mated, were like a national holiday. It was their chance to shine, to let the animal within free, literally. Werewolves were not allowed to phase on other days in the city unless they had special permission from the mayor or under supernatural circumstances, which meant a vampire was undoubtedly up your ass.

There were boundaries outside of the city where werewolves could phase the rest of the month, but she never had the time to travel, or rather, she only allowed herself the chance to phase on a full moon night when her body didn't give her a choice. Otherwise, she'd probably skip the run altogether and get some grading done.

Shaking her mane, she pushed herself faster, refusing to think of work and the progress reports she hadn't started on her fifth graders or the…

Damn it! This is your night to yourself. Enjoy your run, she told herself.

Switching directions, she hoped the new path would help her focus on taking in the exhilarating run and the outdoors.

Heavy pants came from about thirty feet to her left. She smelled the familiar scent of her alpha, his pounding footfalls just a tad faster than her own. Male Weres had the advantage of extraordinary height. Females were tall too, but they rarely got as tall as her six-foot-four-inch alpha.

Owen was not only tall, but extremely well built and in his wolf form reached seven-feet-four-inches as werewolves were man-shaped wolves and could walk and stand on their hind legs. They only four-footed it when they ran or when they were about to pounce.

She imagined her students seeing her in her wolf form. Lord knew she'd wanted to phase in a rage when they were acting out. They knew what she was and had asked her thousands of questions on the first day of school. She'd obliged them, letting them know she was just like them with a tiny difference. They'd had a good talk, but she knew they would be terrified if they ever saw her phase.

Deep black fur covered her body, which reached to six-feet-eight-inches when she phased. The snout and fangs of her wolf face would ensure every student never missed a homework assignment again. Her furred paws were as big as basketballs, the claws as sharp as an Exacto knife. Her students had loved these details and had begged her to show them how her normally black eyes could change to yellow, but she'd refused. She did get a kick out of staring her troublesome students down and watching them panic, just waiting to see if her eyes would alter.

Her amused thoughts were interrupted again by Owen's deep puffs of breaths. She could actually see the hot smoke from his snout rise in the air where he was running. Feeling his frustration, she cringed inwardly.

Male Weres were often irritable during the full moon when they were denied the previous night. The moon heat was the night before the full moon when a werewolf's urges were way too powerful to abstain.

The entire pack knew he'd been alone last night as he was pushing himself harder than he ever had. He'd texted her earlier before she'd phased to let her know he wanted to see her in the morning to discuss a few things. It was strange, but the tension he was emanating was making her nervous. Perhaps they should reschedule when he'd had time to cool off a bit more.

What could he possibly have to talk to her about at

the crack of dawn anyway? Didn't he know she valued her sleep? Just thinking about everything she had to do tomorrow made her want to throw a snowball at her alpha for asking her to meet.

Heading back to the main road, she thought now was as good a time as any to call it a night. The streets of Chicago were predictably empty at this time during a full moon.

Opening the back door to her place, she padded into the dark hallway. It was fairly quiet in her apartment. With her grandmother just downstairs, the only real noise was from the two toddlers above her who were up for their three AM parent torture. The traffic outside had become white noise to her years ago.

If it hadn't been a Sunday, she would have run straight till sunrise. As it was, she needed to get some shuteye, especially if Owen wanted to see her in just a short while.

As she was still in wolf form, she didn't bother with pj's. Awkwardly, she turned on the kitchen faucet and lapped at the cool water. Exhaustion burned her eyes as she traipsed into her tiny living room.

Crashing on her overstuffed couch was easy enough after her workout. She'd managed to snooze for a couple hours before the doorbell woke her out of a dead sleep. Letting out an exhausted, frustrated breath, she moved to the door in a sleep-ridden daze, knocking her shin into the coffee table.

Opening the door with one eye open, she squinted at the tall image of her alpha. Owen's eyes widened and his lips thinned. His tense expression confused her.

"Elizabeth," he muttered through gritted teeth and looked away, staring up at the doorframe.

"Mmm…Oh shit." Realizing too late she was stark naked, she reached for the black trench coat hanging on the wall hook by the door and threw it on, totally awake now. "I'm sorry," she managed, blushing profusely as she crossed her arms over her front.

Lord knows this didn't help their situation. She hoped he didn't think she was teasing him in some way. It's not like he hadn't snuck a peek when she'd had to phase to human out in public. It was an occupational hazard as a Were. She didn't like it of course, never having been comfortable with her body, but what could you do?

Most werewolves in their pack were respectful enough to look away, but others took pleasure in ogling all the nakedness. She'd usually phase back when she was home or would at least keep an outfit nearby to quickly change into, but other times she was forced to cross her legs and arms and deal with it.

Owen looked relieved she'd covered up, but when his eyes met hers she saw the frustration lurking in their depths. He reached out to grip the sides of the door. "You can't do this, Elizabeth. You can't continue to deny me and then flaunt yourself like that."

Embarrassed, she said, "I wasn't flaunting. You woke me out of a dead sleep. I was just out of it. I didn't mean…" God, why was this so hard? It really wasn't her fault. She'd fallen asleep before phasing back, and hardly noticed she was human again.

Feeling guilty for her lapse in judgement, she wondered once again why he even wanted to date her. She was flattered for sure as he was a catch. Blonde and blue-eyed with manners like a nineteenth-century gentleman, Owen could have anyone he wanted. There were several of their pack members who would love to be with him, but he'd pursued *her*, even knowing she was technically married.

She did like him though, but after several moon heats without release, she wondered how much more their relationship could withstand.

He straightened and waved a hand in the hair. "It's fine. I'm sorry. I just...I don't know...I'll get over it." She backed away as he stepped into her apartment and closed the door. Giving her a weak smile, he said, "Let's start this over." He gripped the belt of her jacket and pulled her to him. "Can I have a kiss?" he murmured softly.

She smiled in answer as he leaned down, kissing her gently and this time, she actually felt something. There was excitement in her belly, nothing earth shattering, but it was the perfect set up. They were alone in her apartment and it was as if the entire city still slept except for the two of them. Sunlight filtered in through the kitchen window as it rose in the sky adding a sense of peacefulness to their quiet moment. They were both so busy; it was odd to get these moments together. It felt nice.

Wrapping his hands around her waist and neck, Owen continued to kiss her softly. He smelled of coffee and aftershave and as soft and wonderful as his lips felt, she suddenly wanted a cup of coffee really bad.

Focus, Elizabeth.

Hugging him to her, she opened her mouth to let him in, giving him only a fraction of what he actually wanted. Her body responded, and her lips moved more urgently. It wasn't like she didn't like sex or all the other stuff, in fact, she was quite curious about it. There was just this sense of dread, which always halted things for her, telling her what she was doing was wrong. She hated when that happened.

When her back hit the kitchen counter and his hands moved down to her ass, alarm bells sounded in her ears.

Really? Again?

The familiar ringing in her ears was like an annoying clock alarm. Her body began to hum, her heart rate accelerating and not in a good way. She was beginning to panic and if they didn't stop soon, she'd be in the middle of a full-blown attack in a few seconds.

Sensing her nerves spiraling, he pulled away, all too acquainted with her anxiety attacks. "I'm sorry. I thought you..." He broke off, backing away as he looked around the room, not knowing what to do next.

Owen seemed apologetic and irritated all at once. She smiled at him nervously waiting for her heart to stop pounding because she knew he could hear it. For once, she wanted him to take charge, tell her to get the hell over it and do the deed. At this rate, if she didn't get her shit together, they were never having sex. And that would really suck.

Trying to lighten the mood, Elizabeth asked if he wanted coffee and moved around to the other side of the counter to put some space between them as she clicked on the coffee maker.

"No thanks. And I think you should hold off on the coffee for a bit."

She paused at the cabinet where she kept her coffee, knowing he was right. Coffee wasn't going to help her heart rate right now.

Glancing at the clock, she noted it was almost 7.

She needed to get dressed soon for work. Leaning against the counter she gave him her full attention. "What did you want to talk about?"

The look on his face startled her. He was staring at her, but she had a feeling his mind was somewhere else. Too late, she realized she had just woken up and had no makeup and her waist-length hair was a tousled mess. Running her fingers through her thick strands, she spoke. "You're staring. What is it?"

Shaking his head, he said, "Let's just talk later. I'll come by tonight with dinner. Okay?"

She furrowed her brow. "What?"

"Nothing…" He was heading toward the door, becoming tetchier by the second.

"Owen. Don't." She came around the counter over to him. Reaching for his hand she said, "I'm trying. Really." She stepped in closer. "You've been so patient with me and I really appreciate it. I don't want things to be awkward between us. Please. Talk to me."

Staring into her eyes, Owen looked like he had a million things he wanted to tell her. Squeezing her hand in his, he reached up with his other and pushed her hair away from her face. "You know I'm crazy about you, right?"

Damn. He was so wonderful. She vowed to work through her issues and give him the attention he needed. He deserved more from her and she was determined to give it to him. Attempting a seductive smile, she whispered, "Tonight?"

His eyes heated and he nodded.

As she walked him to the door he paused and turned to her. "We're going to be making some changes in the pack…" He seemed distracted again, looking everywhere but at her. "We'll talk more tonight."

"Okay," she said, standing on her toes and quickly kissing him on the mouth. She really wanted to discuss whatever what was on his mind, but if she didn't hurry, she was going to be late for work. *Again.*

Forty minutes later she flew down the stairs with her coffee travel mug, purse, lunch bag, and teacher tote. When she hit the first floor, she knocked twice on the door to her left with her coffee mug as she rushed by. "Love you, Nonni. See you later," she called through the door.

Her stomach groaned at the smell of bacon and eggs wafting out into the small foyer. On the rare occurrence she woke up early she'd eat breakfast with her grandmother. As she was usually late, most days she'd have to suffer with a granola bar on the train.

Racing down Addison with her load, she cursed the city and its weather. Although the February morning wasn't too cold to her as her body ran at hundred-and-five-degree temperature, she couldn't stand trudging through the snow on the ground. Especially when she neared the train station and it became wet and dirty mulch. She lost count how many times she'd wiped out.

As expected, she slipped when she crossed over the Kennedy expressway and almost dropped her purse. When she managed to get onto the blue line platform without further mishaps, she leaned against one of the white pillars, resting her school tote filled with papers she hadn't finished grading at her feet.

She glanced around at the local commuters, all with Monday morning expressions and sipped her coffee. As great as her body felt for the exercise she'd given it last night, she was extremely exhausted. She'd have to skip the run next month or perhaps call off work the next day.

Rubbing the back of her neck with her free hand, she straightened slightly on the pillar, the hairs at her nape tingling as her body went on alert. The platform filled with people ambling to get onto the train that was pulling in. Ignoring the loud roaring in front of her and the vibration underfoot, she raised her nose to the air and was sure she could smell a Were nearby.

As a member of the Graybacks, she knew every werewolf in the city and yet this one smelled unfamiliar. Concentrating, she looked around surreptitiously trying to gauge if she and the people around her were in danger from some rogue werewolf.

The wind picked up and she got a good whiff of him. She was certain it was a man. The musky scent in the air was all male.

Just as she spotted a tall figure far off down the platform, the doors to the train slid open and everyone shuffled forward to get on and find a seat. As she moved through the throng onto the train she lost sight of the man. Managing to get a seat, she peered out the window in the direction where the stranger had been, but there were too many people to tell if he was still there.

She sat back against the cool, hard seat and wiggled her nose at the familiar pungent smell of old metal and grimy floor. Could there be a rogue werewolf in the city? If so, what were his intentions? As the train lurched, she wondered if she should let Owen know she'd spotted a werewolf not in their pack lurking around town. He had been lurking hadn't he? There was no scent of him whatsoever on the train.

The Blue Line pulled away and she watched through the foggy window as the platform sped away from her, more commuters making their way to catch the next train. Stiffening slightly, she caught sight of a dark figure watching her. They were too far away, and she couldn't make out his face, but she knew he was staring at her. Even as the crowd around him weaved back and forth, obscuring her vision further, every instinct told her he was on that platform for *her*.

Chapter Two

Standing like a dumb shit on the crowded platform, Ramo Perez stared as the back end of the Blue Line grew smaller and smaller. A man shoved his shoulder as he tried to get by, uttering a frightened apology as he got a look at Ramo towering a good two feet over him. Well, he was just standing there in the way, wasn't he? He gave the man a quick nod, then looked around wondering how he'd gotten on the Blue Line platform in the first place. Coming slightly to his senses, he shook himself and turned to head back onto the street. He shot up the stairs as if the solution for his mind fuck was back at his car.

Slamming the door to his Audi Q7, he settled into the seat and fished around for his phone, looking up the address for the bar he was supposed to be at. When he located the address, he punched it into the navigations system on the dash. Yanking the seatbelt around his chest, he took off down Addison and toward the expressway, accidentally hitting the seat massager. Having just purchased the car before moving to the city, he was still getting use to all the gadgets. He let the massager go, though, basking in the comfort.

Hitting traffic on the 94, he leaned his head back a little and thought about what had just happened. He was supposed to be on his way to meet with the Grayback alpha, but his car had somehow driven him to this side of town.

After learning his...*wife*— He shook his head, still not believing he was back here where she lived—had not moved into the condo he'd bought her ten years ago, he'd done some investigating to figure out where she was these days. It appeared she'd sold her father's place years ago and was living in a three flat on Addison just above her grandmother. Curiosity led him to scope it out, if for no reason than to check it off his list of things to do.

One: Meet with the prick alpha.

Two: Say hi to wife he left ten years ago.

Three: Create an army.

He'd driven past her house this morning with every intention of just checking out the area and noting the building to visit on another occasion, when suddenly a dark-haired woman raced out the front door and down the stairs laden with bags and a thermos of coffee. Slipping when she hit the bottom of the stairs, she'd muttered a curse and continued down the street, the flaps of her black jacket billowing in her wake.

Barely aware of his actions, he'd pulled over and cut the engine with his eyes glued to the back of her head. As he slid out of his car, he watched her stop for a second, tuck the coffee between her knees and tie her hair into a ponytail. Her thick black hair bounced as she rushed down the street, and he hoped she'd turn around so he could get a better look at her face. He'd only managed to glimpse an olive profile with high cheekbones.

Slipping again as she charged down the street, he wondered why the hell she was walking and not driving to wherever she worked? He made a mental note to email his contact for more information regarding the mysterious Elizabeth Vitale.

Guilt swelled deep in his stomach. Elizabeth wouldn't be mysterious if he'd taken the time to get to know her all those years ago or stuck around to be an appropriate husband.

She'd made her way onto the platform and leaned her back on a pillar with an exaggerated sigh. He'd stopped a fair distance to observe her silent monologue. He had a better angle of her face and observed with comic interest how her body language and facial expressions told him what she was feeling. The way she leaned on the pillar as if she'd collapse if she didn't, clearly showed him how exhausted she was. Her heavy-lidded dark eyes had circles under them, and she chewed the inside of her cheeks as though she had a million things on her mind.

Her delicate, straight nose crinkled, and her lax position stiffened suddenly. Sensing her vigilance, it was obvious she'd detected him, but for some reason he remained where he was, not bothering to hide or walk away. Some stupid part of him wanted her to see him.

Smirking, he watched as she straightened and looked around with a terrible interpretation of nonchalance. The girl must be a horrible poker player. Even the humans surrounding her could see she was trying to find someone.

Tossing her bag back on her shoulder and spilling some of her coffee, her thin trench coat slipped open and he could see full breasts straining through a dark blue shirt. She bit her bottom lip as her gaze scanned in his direction and he noticed how supple they were. Her black, long hair made her olive complexion pop, contrasting amazingly with her dark eyes.

Only one thing came to mind as he watched her train speed away.

His wife was fucking hot.

He exited the expressway, his mind still a muddled mess. He felt as if some invisible force had smacked him in the face on that platform and he was still reeling from the effects. This wasn't good. He didn't want to be attracted to her. He couldn't be. But, shit…

He remembered leaving a young beautiful girl ten years ago, but as time passed, her face began to blur. All he could remember was her dark hair. He thought of her as she walked down the makeshift aisle, feeling genuinely pleased at how gorgeous she was. Although, as pretty as she had been, he knew he did not want to be tied down, especially with an eighteen-year-old.

Now he was back where she was, and his job was to make nice with her pack and help them to form Fighters. His cousin's words echoed in his mind. *You have a duty to fulfill. The two of you hold this alliance together, without which, our defenses will be nothing against the Nightwalkers. Your separation cannot continue.*

He had left all those years ago telling himself he'd be back to give their marriage a chance. He decided he needed a year to get used to the idea. Then he told himself he'd wait till she was twenty. He wasn't keen on a teenage wife. Too weird. She had school though, and so he decided allowing her to finish her degree would be the wise thing to do before he came back to insert himself in her life. After three years, then five, he couldn't do it. Cowardice made him stay put. He knew she'd hate him for what he'd done, so what was the point in coming back at all?

Circumstances change though and their race was in danger of the witches' new weapon, Nightwalkers, mutated jackals whose bite was venomous to Weres. With all the crap that went down in Wilmington, he was under orders to make nice with the Graybacks. What's more, his alpha wanted him to claim his wife now he was in the city. Smirking as he got off at the Division exit, he was sure his boss didn't mean to sound all cave man. In all his years of experience with women not one of them expressed an interest in him "claiming" them outside of the bedroom.

Once he spotted the sports bar on Division, it was a matter of finding a parking spot on the busy street. He loved the city, but parking was a bitch. He'd lived in Wilmington so long he'd forgotten how annoying it could be to park your car. It was too early for valet, so he had to circle a bit. Finding a spot, he headed across the street to the two glass doors, pushing them open to find a surprisingly immense bar.

There were tables and chairs, which covered most of the wide-open dining area and to the right, a long bar stretched all the way toward the back wall. A row of booths separated the bar area from the tables and more booths lined the wall on the left. Wide screen TV's were scattered about the area and he knew the place must get pretty crowded on game days. Decorated in subtle, modern furnishings, it was an inviting place and he found himself jonesing for a beer and chilling on one of the cozy looking bar stools.

As it was, the place was empty at eight in the morning except for a werewolf wiping down bottles behind the bar. He'd noticed him before he'd entered the bar, noting the tense shoulders and abrupt movements as he worked. It was obvious to him, the guy had sensed him too and didn't like it. Stopping near the hostess podium, he raised his chin and cleared his throat.

The man nodded, but never looked up. Dark haired and clean shaven, he figured he was the Grayback's beta. Betas were usually the silent type, and given the way his emotions screamed power, he was sure this was Hunter's right hand man. Adam had told him the beta worked with the alpha and considering this guy could barely look his way, tensions were going to skyrocket when he got started with his training.

He'd expected animosity from the other pack, so he didn't take the beta's indifference personally. He was just going to have to get used to the cold shoulder while he was here and in truth, couldn't care less.

Stacking a bottle of Glenlivet on one of the glass shelves, the guy called over his shoulder, "Follow me," and headed toward the back with the rag in his hand.

Walking along the row of barstools, he attempted to set his temper aside and focus on the reason he was there. They didn't have to be friendly to work together. As long as they remained cool, calm, and collected, he wouldn't have to rip their throats open.

Bottle Boy Beta led him down a short hallway into a back office near the bathrooms. Before he could even step in, he felt the alpha's emotion of fury hit him like a sharp gust of wind. Ignoring the ever-growing rigidity of the situation, he followed the tool into the office.

Owen Hunter sat behind a small desk in a brown leather chair wearing a button-down navy shirt and khakis. The blue-eyed, dirty blonde looked up from the laptop open in front of him, his palm still on the wireless mouse. His elbows rested on either side of the MacBook under wide, bulky shoulders. They were practically built the same and he was sure that if the alpha stood, they'd be eye to eye.

"Morning," the Grayback alpha said in a clipped tone.

He nodded once.

"Shut the door Joe," he uttered to his beta, then in his direction, "Have a seat."

He sat down and crossed his legs ankle to knee, leaning one arm on the back of the swivel chair. His goal was to discuss business and nothing else, but Ramo felt himself slipping into the cocky role he was born to play. In a bored voice, he teased, "You two look like I just smacked your grandma. Chill." Smirking, he looked around at all the sport paraphernalia.

It was well known to the Blacktails, he had diarrhea of the mouth. It was a pleasant feeling to have a different audience; one he took even more pleasure in annoying.

"So why are we closing the door?" He glanced behind him at Joe, the beta. "Privacy?" He asked, his eyebrows raised as he took a seat. "Because you do realize we're the only ones here." He knew the move was made to intimidate him and it didn't work.

Owen stared at him for a moment then chose to ignore his comments. "I assume you know the terms Adam and I discussed." Without waiting for a response he went on. "So long as you're here, you will respect me and Joe as if you were a part of this pack. Disobey, and there will be consequences. So don't think you can conduct yourself like a lone werewolf because you're not."

"I have pack members in the city you know. Never gone rogue and I don't plan on it either."

"I'm sure this was already covered with your alpha, but while you're here you will work closely with the Graybacks. Since you will be training them, I expect you to be around them as much as possible, which includes the full moon. We need to be able to trust you and we cannot do that if you're only running with the Blacktails."

Ramo smiled roguishly as if Owen were an amusing child pretending to be all grown up.

"We came up with a list of werewolves who we feel will do well as Fighters, however..." Owen surveyed a sheet of paper on a clipboard. "We're going to open up the option to my entire pack. With the exception of young Weres who are still aging, anyone will be allowed to put forth their name if they choose."

"How diplomatic of you."

"There will be a meeting here tomorrow night. The entire pack will attend, and they are aware you will be working with them. The Graybacks are under orders to treat you as one of their own. Notices were sent out a few days ago."

There was an unexpected lurch in the pit of his stomach. Did this mean Elizabeth knew he was here?

"Do you have any questions so far?" Owen asked humorlessly, his hands in a steeple over his mouth.

"Yes. Can I get some coffee?" he asked, looking around at Joe.

Again Owen stared, his nostrils flaring. Sitting up straighter in his chair, he slammed his laptop shut and leaned forward over his desk. "Are we gonna have a problem?"

"Not unless I don't get coffee…" Ramo answered as if he didn't understand why the alpha was getting so heated.

Owen narrowed his eyes. "You've built yourself a shitty reputation over the years. In fact, I'm surprised Adam sent you of all people. Danny Amato could have trained my pack considering he lives here." Owen referred to one of his pack members and fellow Fighter, a cop who lived in the city. "So why the hell did he send me a cocky, low-life, whore?"

The growl was instantaneous. His shoulders crouched slightly, his animal instinct ready to attack. He quieted himself, refusing to let this prick incense him. From the corner of his eye he saw Joe take a step forward. Stopping himself from launching at the bastard was proving difficult, but this is what he'd expected. Calming, he cleared his throat. "You forgot architect. I'm a cocky, low-life, whoring *architect*."

This further annoyed Owen to his pleasure, and as he stared back, his expression no longer cheerful, he played with his lip ring, knowing *it* and the tattoos on his arms and neck were the reason for the "low-life" comment. He was used to the assumptions made about him. Who could blame them? His height and build notwithstanding, his Randy Orton crew cut seemed to offend people and the perpetual morning shadow didn't soften his looks either.

"Are you up for this or not?" Owen demanded.

"I don't really have a choice now, do I?" he answered, looking around the room, seemingly bored. Owen knew damn well why he'd been chosen. It was his marriage that was holding this alliance together and only he would be "welcome" among the Graybacks. No matter how begrudgingly they accepted him, they had no choice. Marrying the former alpha's daughter had assured peace between the packs but asking another member of the Blacktails to train the Graybacks would be pushing it.

There was disgust in Owen's voice as he spoke. "I'm placing my pack members' lives in the hands of a degenerate. Vitale must have been insane to ally with you."

He stiffened slightly, meeting the alpha's glare. He wondered when he'd bring this up. "Go ahead," he goaded, his tone more subdued. "Spit it out."

Owen's jaw twitched and an anxious feeling mingled with the man's fury. He wondered what the alpha was nervous about. "What are your plans in regard to his daughter? Elizabeth has been through a lot since her father passed, I don't want your presence here to cause her any further stress."

Chewing over this info, he said, "The alliance has withstood these past few years. I'm back now and I intend..." As he spoke he noticed the alpha's clenched fists on the table. "...to reacquaint myself with my wife and to maintain an amicable relationship for the sake of our packs."

Owen snorted. "That crap sounded rehearsed. Did Adam make you memorize that?"

Angry now, he said, "Look, don't worry about me and Elizabeth. What goes on between us is our business. You and I..." he indicated the two of them with his index finger. "...are here to discuss recruiting Fighters and how best to train them. I may give you a lot of shit, but when it comes to fighting I'm as serious as a fucking heart attack."

Owen leaned back thoughtfully in his chair. "At least we're in agreement about one thing."

"Good." He stood and caught the alpha's glance at the tats on his biceps. "I'll be here tomorrow morning with the agenda." He turned to leave. "Thanks for the coffee by the way," he muttered snidely to Joe as he opened the door. The beta just mean mugged him in response.

"You were wrong about something, though," Owen said.

Ramo turned to look at him in the doorway. "Oh yeah? What's that?"

"Elizabeth," Owen said as he stood, staring him dead in the face. "She *is* my business."

An odd feeling slid down Ramo's spine and he felt Joe tense next to him.

"She's not only a valued member of the Graybacks, she..." The alpha looked momentarily uncomfortable but recovered fast as his eyes practically gleamed when he said, "Well...you should know...we've been dating for the past six months."

Whatthefuck?

It was like getting hit on the head with a frying pan.

He stood frozen with his hand on the door replaying what Owen just said over and over in his head, trying to make sense of his words. Did this man just tell him he'd been fucking his wife? Albeit, estranged wife, but still...*wife*. What the hell was he supposed to do with this information?

He hadn't expected her to remain faithful to him, but before now he'd never given it much thought. There was a second when he'd driven up to Chicago he'd wondered if she'd been with someone in that way, but he didn't let himself think on it too long.

Too late, he realized he'd been standing there facing the alpha with a stoic expression. What did one say to the boyfriend of their wife? "Okay…uh…I don't…" He stammered stupidly. "How does this…" He let out a harsh laugh, running his hand over his scalp. "So…how does this work?"

Crossing his arms over his chest, Owen said, "That's up to Elizabeth. She's the only member who's unaware of the job you will have in our pack. I'm going to speak to her first and explain the situation."

Narrowing his eyes at the alpha, he pursed his lips, listening to Owen tell him how he was going to handle Elizabeth. How *he* was going to let her know he was here in the city. There was no reason for it, but this simple fact pissed him off. Like he needed this fucker to talk to her first before he did as if they were in high school. Resentment toward Adam, his alpha built in his chest. He felt set up. How was he supposed to make nice with Elizabeth and keep the peace with the other pack when she was *with* the fucking alpha?

Owen kept talking. "I know this is unprecedented, but I thought you should know since on paper you're married, but, we all know it's not a real marriage. So we didn't see a problem with…" He paused a second then cleared his throat, "…well, you know." He smirked.

"You make a habit of hitting on married women? No single ladies in the city catch your eye? Just my wife?"

Owen snarled, "Don't call her that."

Brows raised, he said, "Are you fucking kidding me? You're acting like a mated Were when technically, she belongs to *me*."

Stepping around the desk Owen got up in his face, growling. "She doesn't belong to you. You married her and left. You're nothing to her. There's a little piece of paper with your names on it and it's the only thing keeping us from ripping your pack apart. But let's get this shit straight. You will leave her alone. She's mine and doesn't want anything to do with you."

"Have you mated?" The words were out before he could stop himself. Werewolves were only mated if they impregnated a female Were or a human woman. If she had children with the alpha, they had a very serious problem. Fuck training new Fighters, the two packs would go to battle. There was no way he'd let that shit go. "Does she have children?" He demanded as though he needed to clarify his first question and he took a step closer, feeling every muscle tense in his body.

"You think I'm stupid? Of course not."

He tried to hide the relief he felt in his expression, but knew Owen felt it.

Scowling, Owen said, "You don't even know her. Probably have no clue what she looks like now. Why do you care about a woman who most likely despises you?"

He grimaced. Having no desire to stand here while Owen lectured him on his lack of husbandly duties, he opened the door. "Whatever. Have at it. You can date my *wife*. Tell her I said hi." With that, he left, wondering what the hell the next few weeks were going to bring.

Chapter Three

The end of the day for an elementary school teacher was like winning the Hunger Games. It was how she looked and felt anyway. The day was filled with challenging obstacles such as, standing on your feet all day while ignoring the urge to pee, directing and redirecting students, reprimanding students, small rewards and feelings of failure; unannounced fire drills, fights and crying students, vomiting in the classroom, and irate parents demanding the impossible. But, at the end of the day Elizabeth hoped she'd reached the majority of her students and would head home to toast her survival with a glass of cheap wine.

The lack of sleep the night before made the commute home excruciating tonight. Her body was not only sore and run down from last night's full moon, but also from the day she'd had. She never felt tired when her students were in the classroom, but the minute they were gone it was as though they took her energy with them. To top it off, she was behind on grading papers for their progress reports and she still had to read a chapter and write two reflections for her graduate class before Wednesday.

Dragging her feet off the train that evening, she hoped her grandmother had some leftovers for dinner. She had no wish to eat ramen again. With her appetite, the tiny meal just didn't cut it. Walking down Addison laden with all her bags, she remembered Owen saying he wanted to talk with her. Groaning inwardly, she felt instantly guilty. It wasn't that he bothered her. It was the fact she was always tired. Thankfully he was pretty understanding with her workload. She just wished they didn't have to talk when her eyes stung, and her body craved food and rest.

Wondering if she'd have time for a quick nap before he came over, she suddenly felt someone watching her. Her spine straightening, she faltered in her step, chastising herself for being so careless and aloof as she trudged down the street like a zombie. It was only about six-thirty, but it was dark, and she was alone and probably looked vulnerable.

The February night whipped her hair about, and she caught the same scent she'd smelled earlier on the platform.

The rogue Were.

What was he doing? Looking around, she only saw the unshoveled walk behind her, yet the distinct scent still lingered in the air.

Moving a bit faster whilst trying not to slip on the slushy ground, she thought of phasing to scare whoever it was watching her, but without just cause, she could get arrested and there was no way she wanted a record for something so stupid. What's more, the thought of turning while she was dressed in one of her favorite pair of black pants, which actually fit her well was a bummer. She shook off the dumb thought as her safety was more important than clothes and cursed as she slipped on the snow.

Hitching her bags further on her shoulder, she fumbled for her cell phone in her coat pocket. The second she found it, she heard footsteps crunch in the snow behind her. Panic setting in, she quickened her stride, but the presence behind her loomed ever closer.

Infuriated at being stalked, she gathered her courage and spun around to confront the rogue werewolf, slamming into a rock-solid wall. The impact knocked her off her feet and she landed hard on her ass in the cold, wet, mulch.

"WHAT THE FUCK!" she yelled, her body whirring with fury and dread. Was she about to be attacked? Shaking the hair out of her eyes, she realized it was her stalker's chest she'd hit.

"Why the hell are you walking alone late at night? Where's your fucking car?" The man's voice rang out, penetrating her ears and mind as if mere words had magical powers.

She blinked.

In the act of reaching for her phone three feet to her right, she froze and stared up at the dark image above her. "Wh...what?" Her jacket hung open over her left shoulder, her bags splayed across the mulch, hung precariously in the crook of her arm and her beloved pants were soaked.

No matter how foolish she felt sitting there in the middle of the sidewalk, she couldn't move. She gazed, fixated at the man hovering over her. Taking in the skull trim and lip ring, she ignored her precarious position on the ground.

There was something strangely familiar about him. Concern for her radiated from his body. It was this and the outstretched hand, which told her she was safe; calming her racing heart. But who was he? And why did she think she knew him?

Disoriented, she stared transfixed at his piercing brown eyes. They shone bright among all his dark features. He only wore a pair of distressed jeans and a black t-shirt with a stick figure humping the word *it*. Stepping closer to her, the streetlamp illuminated his face and she got a better look...

BAM!

It hit her in an instant and she felt as though someone poured a barrel of ice, cold water on her head.

"You?" she whispered.

Heat flushed her cheeks and not in a cute blushing sort of way; in the way her head began to throb as though she were going to pass out. "No," she said inaudibly. She felt her skin vibrate and her vision blur. *Jesus Christ.* He could not be here. This couldn't be happening.

She backed up from him on the ground leaving her bags in the snow and stood on wobbly legs. There was too much to process. Her husband was standing right in front of her and she was severely close to a full-blown anxiety attack.

Why?

Why was he here?

Swaying, she closed her eyes and tried to steady herself. The heat in her face was making her dizzy and her hands and feet were becoming numb.

"Oh shit!" he said, reaching out and grabbing her arm to steady her. "Are you all right?"

The contact jolted her out of her wave of dizziness, and she yanked her arm out of his grip. "Don't touch me!"

He must have noticed the fury in her expression because he backed away, palms up. "Sorry, you just looked…"

"Shut up!" She reached down for her bags and when he went to help her she held up her hand. "Don't!" Leaning her hands on her knees for a moment, she took a deep breath hating how he watched her become so undone. Then she grabbed her things, straightened her coat and ran a trembling hand through her hair. "I don't know why the fuck you're here but stay the hell away from me."

"Elizabeth…" his voice was deep and smooth as he took a cautious step forward.

The use of her name coming out of his despicable mouth infuriated her. "I mean it. Do your business, then get the hell out of my city." Her voice trembled and she sounded like someone else. Turning, she walked slowly toward her apartment, never once checking behind her. Although she knew he was there and hoped to God she never saw him again.

*****

Real smooth asshole.

Sliding back into his car, Ramo started the engine but didn't put the car in gear. He sat with his hands in his lap staring at the building Elizabeth had just disappeared in. What was his problem? It was bad enough he'd knocked her down, but then he didn't even say anything to her. He'd just stood there and stared at her. It wasn't like she would have let him get a word in edgewise, but he could have tried harder.

Cursing, he replayed the whole fiasco over in his head. He expected her to be angry with him but seeing it firsthand didn't sit well. The horrible sensation of guilt and regret burned his insides. He'd clearly hurt her, and God knew if she'd ever forgive him, but he intended to try and make amends. It was not only the right thing to do and the direct order given by his alpha, but it was also something he *wanted* to do. He could not go on living knowing he'd hurt someone that badly. It was too late as far as she was concerned, but he was determined, nonetheless. Looking into her incredible face made him feel like a light had been clicked on in his brain.

Jesus, did she have to be so pretty? It was going to make it difficult for him to be around her. He'd left a young wide-eyed girl ten years ago and he returned to discover he was married to an exotic beauty.

Who was dating her alpha.

The annoying voice in his head echoed. This plan was not going to go well. It was bad enough he was stuck in the middle of another pack who would, no doubt, already despise him for being a Blacktail and ditching one of their own, but now he was going to be giving orders during training. Meanwhile, his estranged wife is dating someone else. Fucking Great!

His eyes narrowed as an SUV pulled up and parked across the street. The man in question got out of his car carrying a plastic bag and sauntered up to her building.

Owen opened the glass door, which apparently didn't lock and went in. Just...moseyed on up to *his* wife's place.

Fuck!

He still didn't know what he was supposed to do or think about this. There was no reason to be jealous, but shit they *were* married. Chastising himself, he had to remember he hadn't exactly been faithful to his dear spouse either. What did he expect; that she'd be waiting for him in the condo he'd bought them with a home cooked meal on the table after ten years? She had every right to move on with her life.

Then why was he gripping the door handle of his Audi as though he were going to bolt out of the car?

****

Elizabeth stood on the other side of the counter across from Owen, who sat with his tacos still wrapped in aluminum foil in front of him. He watched her silently as she dipped her tortilla chip into guacamole for the tenth time. It was a horrible habit, but stress eating was one of her many vices. She loved food, but when she stressed out, she reached for the junk. It was the reason for her ample ass and thick thighs.

After listening to Owen talk about the threat of witches in the area, poisonous jackals, and an explosion of an old home that led to the current situation they were in, she'd begun eating quietly.

Taking a sip of her pop, she looked up at him calmly, wiping her hands on a flimsy white napkin. "So he's staying? He's here to stay?" she asked numbly as though her first question needed explaining.

"Yes."

"And he'll be working with us? Teaching us to fight?" she asked, her head nodding.

"Only if you want to join. There's no pressure."

Her nodding increased its tempo. "Okay. We'll get back to the fighting part." Leaning her elbows on the counter, she wrung her hands as she spoke. "What does this mean for me? Is he expecting to…"

"No!" Owen said forcefully. "I mean…it's up to you of course, but he is required to reacquaint himself per Adam's orders, whatever that means, but we don't expect you to live together as husband and wife." He reached for her hands and steadied them, "It doesn't mean you have to let him into your life. Perez will be our trainer and that's it. Nothing has to change, Elizabeth." She heard the worry in his voice and for the first time in twenty minutes, realized this obviously affected him too.

Furrowing her brow, she asked, "How do you feel about this? I mean...what does this mean for...us?"

He dropped his gaze as he spoke, contemplating the little white napkins on the counter. "I don't like it, but we have the pack to think of. As for us..." he let the words drift in the air.

Stunned beyond belief, she stared at the man she'd been dating for months; who'd told her he loved her; who'd been waiting for months to have sex with her only now to be confronted with this.

Flipping her hands over, she gripped his. "Owen, I don't care what the alliance says. I'm your girlfriend. We have a good thing going here and I won't let him come here and disrupt our lives. I can separate the fact we're married from *us*."

Owen met her eyes and she hated the worry she saw in them.

"I'm not saying it's gonna be easy, but you and I can do this." She came around the counter and put her arms around his neck.

Leaning his forehead against hers, he pulled her close by the waist and murmured, "I hate this."

"I know," she whispered back. "But you have nothing to worry about. He's virtually a stranger to me." She pulled away to sit on the stool next to his. Still rattled but hungry, she grabbed a taco and unwrapped the foil. Hands shaking slightly, she tried with all her might not to show Owen just how upsetting this situation was.

Her. Husband. Was. Back.

The son of a bitch who left her at the altar had the audacity to return to the city and stick himself in her life. She had no idea how she was supposed to react to this knowledge, but she knew Owen was worried and there was no reason for him to get upset. Acting as though it didn't matter was the only way he'd feel better about the situation.

"Are you sure you're going to be okay? I don't want you upset." Owen finally reached for his food, opening his taco distractedly.

"I'll be fine," she said too quickly. Then, "Really, I'll be okay. Just wished I had a heads up before I saw him."

Owen froze with his taco in hand. "What do you mean? This was the heads up." He gestured about as though it were obvious. "I told him I was going to let you know first before you saw him. Are you telling me he came here?"

She stared as Owen's eyes turned yellow, the vein in his forehead throbbed as he waited for her to respond. "He didn't come here. I…ran into him on my way home from the train." She left out he'd been watching her this morning. Owen didn't need to know this little tidbit.

Dropping his food, he wiped his mouth with a napkin and stood, hands at his hips. "What did he do?"

"Nothing, Owen. It's fine."

"Elizabeth. Tell me what happened," he demanded.

Squirming, she rolled her eyes. She hated when he spoke like this because she couldn't tell if he simply wanted an answer as a friend or demanding one as her alpha. Regardless, she had no choice but to answer him. As her alpha, the force to do as he told her was so strong it would pain her to disobey.

"I bumped into him on the street and fell." She felt stupid for reminding him how clumsy she was.

Owen looked her up and down, and she knew he was assessing if she was hurt or not.

"He asked me why I was walking home alone and where my car was." Her brows pinched, wondering why it would matter to him. "It took me a moment to recognize who he was and when I did, I told him to stay away from me. Told him to do his business and leave. But, now I know his business is with us."

Owen's gaze never faltered as he chewed this over. "That's the first thing he says to you after ten years? Where's your car?"

Ugh! She was ready to change the subject. Looking forlornly at her uneaten food, she said, "He bought me a car after we were married and three years ago the Blacktail, Danny Amato, you know, the cop...well he showed up with another brand new one. I donated the first car to the Salvation Army and the other to my grandmother's church." Finishing her explanation, she looked at him and winced.

Owen's eyes were still yellow, and it looked as though he were biting his tongue. "You never mentioned the cars."

"Why would I? I didn't keep them and it's not like we were together when I got them, so there was no point."

"You told me he was completely out of your life. Purchasing cars for you doesn't sound like he's out of your life," Owen visibly seethed as he started to pace her small living room.

She should have realized he'd be upset about any connection she still had with Ramo. It was in a werewolf's nature to be overbearing and territorial.

Stopping to face her, Owen asked, "Has he contacted you at all over the years?"

"No," she answered calmly. "Not a phone call, letter, email...nothing."

"Any other big purchases? Your college tuition, an island?"

She tensed and knew he'd sensed it.

"What?"

Damn it! The guy had only been in town a day and already he was causing havoc. "A condo."

Owen cursed and glared up at the ceiling.

"It was supposed to be *our* place after we were married, but I never moved in. Honestly, I don't know what he did with it and I don't care."

They were silent for a while as Owen contemplated her kitchen counter. "You know...I knew you were married, and I understood why you did it. I'm not faulting you for that. In fact, it was a noble thing to do, but...now that he's here..." A low rumble began to build in his chest, and he looked away from her again as if the sight of her would cause him to phase.

She stood slowly and walked to him, putting a hand on his throbbing chest. "Owen, it doesn't matter. Please. I don't want this to come between us." Wrapping her arms around his waist, she urged, "Look at me."

And when he did, she smiled warmly and felt him calm some, his eyes fading back to brown. "How can it not? When I look at the prick all I see is a big blaring sign that says, 'YOUR GIRL IS MARRIED!'"

"Stop it. We've been separated for ten years and I didn't even know him when I married him. You know this marriage doesn't mean anything to me. *He* doesn't mean anything." She squeezed him tighter. "This is weird, yes, but our focus is us and the pack. That's it. We'll get through this and in a couple of days it'll be like he's not even here."

His arms came around her and he held her close. Nuzzled in her neck, he said, "I love you Elizabeth. This is so fucking hard, because I love you."

"I know," she said, then without thinking, blurted, "I love you too."

He stiffened in her arms.

Oh shit!

Why did she say it? It just came out. God, she hadn't even given it much thought. Even when he'd told her weeks ago, she'd been shocked and could only thank him like an idiot. Did she love him? She cared for him deeply, yes, but was she in love with him?

Too late, he had pulled back to look her dead in the face and what she saw made her cringe. "Do you mean it? Elizabeth, tell me you're not just saying it to appease me."

"Of course not," she said instantly; again, without thinking. Was she just saying it to make him feel better? If there ever was a time to validate her loyalty to him, it'd be right now; with her husband back in the city. Damn it. Owen didn't deserve this. She didn't deserve him. "I do, Owen. I love you."

His mouth was on hers in an instant, hard and insistent. Thankfully, he stopped himself before he got carried away.

They finished their dinner with Owen in much better spirits after her surprising declaration. As they ate, they discussed the Nightwalkers and who he considered to be worthy and able Fighters in the pack.

It had been a long and tiring day and to end it with a bang, she told her alpha she loved him and had no idea if she actually meant it. But no matter how hard she tried to focus on Owen and what her true feelings were for him, she could not stop thinking about Ramo Perez and his intense brown eyes.

****

The condo on Lincoln Park West was a two-bedroom, two bath rehab. He'd purchased the model unit, fully furnished in his haste to get things over and done with ten years ago. When he'd bought it he expected Elizabeth to move in after her first semester at school. Knowing he wasn't going to be living in it, he'd made sure to hire a cleaning service to come in every other week and paid the utilities and assessments monthly. What he didn't expect, was to come home to the condo, empty and never been lived in.

The cabinets and closets were empty, and the fridge was bare. If it weren't for the model's furniture, he'd be sitting on the floor. He'd assumed the utilities were being paid, but if he looked at his statement regularly he probably would have noticed she never called to set it up. The paperwork he'd left for her had all been neatly piled on the desk near the window in the same spot he'd left it years ago. The fact she'd refused this place didn't exactly surprise him, but it did piss him off. It was a much better place than where she was living now. Why the hell hadn't she just taken advantage of his money and lived there for free?

Sitting at the dainty desk in the living room that overlooked the park across the street, he read the email he'd received from his PI. The more he read, the angrier he became.

The email described what Elizabeth had been up to for the last ten years, financially and socially. After finishing college she landed a teaching position on the south side of Chicago. A year later, her father was killed in a fight with a member of another pack in a bar in Indiana.

After living in her father's home for a few months, she could not keep up with the mortgage and utilities and sold it for way below market value. She used the money to pay off her student loans and bought the three-flat she currently lived in. Her grandmother lived rent-free on the first floor and Elizabeth rented out the third to a human couple and their kids. She was elbow deep in bills and took out another loan to pay for her grad school tuition. In short, his wife was living paycheck to paycheck when she didn't have to, and it infuriated him.

For the past five years, she'd worked to pay the mortgage on a building, which obviously needed some serious tuckpointing along with new boilers and window treatments. Things of which, she'd neglected due to cost.

What's more, her grandmother had started aging at four hundred ninety-two and was suffering from osteoarthritis. It wreaked havoc on her joints, and she had trouble moving around unless she moved very slowly.

Werewolves were resilient, but unfortunately, once

the aging process begins, time starts to take a toll on the body. Her grandmother was forced to retire from the store she'd worked at since it's opening in 1925.

The email went on to describe her social habits. Described as a homebody, she occasionally ventured out with friends for dinner and drinks. She'd gone on a few dates but hasn't been in any long-term relationship up until recently. Six months ago, after a Grayback meeting, Elizabeth was seen having dinner with Owen Hunter and sharing a kiss in the corner of his bar later that evening. They go out for dinner every weekend and he comes by at least once or twice during the week after work. His stomach clenched when the email went on about her moon heat habits.

Ms. Vitale stays home alone during the moon heat. It has been reported that Mr. Hunter ended his relationship with his past heat mate and has spent those evenings alone as well for the past six months.

Joy flickered down his spine. He had no right to relish this information, but he was glad they stayed apart during those nights.

What did this mean? Were they having sex? Just because they weren't together on heat nights didn't mean they weren't. They might just be overly cautious since those were the days a female werewolf was fertile.

Whatever the reason, he was glad of it.

Scratch that.

He. Did. Not. Care.

Shutting off the laptop, he got up and was about to storm the fridge when he realized it was empty. Turning on the television instead, he stood in front of the flat screen and surfed through the basic cable channels not taking anything in.

He really didn't care she was with the alpha. Really. Why would he care? He left her ages ago and he didn't come back to rekindle anything. He was there to do a job and that was it. Once he was done, he was going back to Wilmington to his perfectly uncomplicated life of work, women, and beer.

The only reason he was feeling so heated was because he was among another pack and it was just plain weird his wife was seeing the alpha. He really didn't blame her. She had a right to date whoever she wanted. It's not like they had a real marriage but being here and knowing what was going down put a bad taste in his mouth.

His stomach lurched guiltily at the image of her glaring at him with hatred in her eyes. He'd caused the look of hurt and confusion. Her nearly black eyes seared in his brain and then he remembered the dark circles under them, and her disheveled hair and he thought of the bills she hadn't paid and the work she was doing to better her education and take care of her grandmother.

He thought about all the things he'd learned about her so far and he was surprised to find she was a smart, hard working woman with a big heart. Why did this surprise him? Because she was from another pack? He'd built this image of her in his head and made her out to be an insipid young girl without a mind of her own, but she was far from it. Now he was hoping she was mind-numbing boring because on the surface, Elizabeth Vitale was pretty fucking amazing.

Chapter Four

Elizabeth woke up the next morning feeling mildly well rested, but as if she were living someone else's life. Her body felt oddly numb and she went through the day as though an invisible force was in charge of her limbs. Fighting to keep her mind focused on her job, she ignored the reason for her preoccupation.

Thinking about him wasn't going to make him go away. It wasn't going to help her work so there was no point in harping on the fact they were going to see each other again that night. Hating the distracted state she was in, she stayed on the blue line for a few extra stops and headed to the YMCA on Irving Park.

Her membership to the gym was going to expire soon, but she had other reasons for visiting the establishment. Cutting through the weight room after she flashed her card at the guy behind the counter, she went through a door next to the abdominal machine.

A narrow stairway led up to the rooms for rent and she climbed up to the second floor. Mold filled her senses and the smell of garbage made her gag. It wasn't the most ideal place to stay, but it was the best they could do.

Knocking on the last door to the left, a young man opened it quickly and let her in.

"I didn't think you'd come today," he said in his southern drawl, his eyes alight.

"I told you I'd visit as much as I could." She placed her bags down and stared at the young Were like a doctor would assessing a patient's injuries.

Jordan was eighteen years old and was already six feet five inches tall. He was thin for a werewolf but considering what he'd been through it wasn't surprising. He wore tattered jeans and a fraying t-shirt she'd bought him second hand. With his dark hair and tanned skin, he would grow up to be quite handsome if he didn't get himself killed.

"Your leg looks better," she noticed. "Did you work today?" She had managed to get him a job at the YMCA as a janitor. She knew he hated it, but it was an honest living and he would be able to save some money and build up a reference for another job.

"Yeah. Just finished my shift." Sitting on the bed, he looked up at her. He put up his hands and said, "I swear. You can ask the manager."

"I believe you," she said offensively.

"Then why are you staring at me like that?" he mused.

"Huh? Oh. Sorry. It's been a long day." She walked over to the window and sat on the radiator thinking it was more appropriate than sitting next to him on the tiny twin bed. She liked Jordan, but she really didn't know him. As she looked him over she thought about when she'd first seen him.

Two months ago, after running straight through the night one full moon, she'd found Jordan in the woods, phasing back to human form with a horrible bite on his leg. He'd told her he'd defied his alpha in Savannah, Georgia and his beta had attacked him when he'd tried to run.

She'd wanted to contact the alpha to alert him of his pack member's whereabouts, but Jordan had begged her not to. He'd told her they'd kill him on sight. His words and the desperate look in his eyes stopped her.

She'd urged him to return to Georgia or at least let her call a member of his pack to come there, but he was quite adamant. She told him if he stayed he'd be considered a packless Were, which was illegal under werewolf law, but he didn't care. She'd brought him to the Y and paid for his room for the week till he could recover from his wound, all the while urging him to return to his pack. To let him stay was dangerous for both of them. If Owen knew she was helping a rogue Were, he could kick her out of the pack.

"Elizabeth?"

"Mmm?"

"You're staring again. What's wrong?" he asked, his expression concerned.

"Damn it. I'm sorry. I just have a lot on my mind." She shook herself then looked at her bags next to the tiny table that held the television. "Shit! I didn't bring you anything to eat."

"No, it's fine. I was going to walk to the Golden Nugget in a minute."

Narrowing her eyes, she said, "You have to be careful when you go out. I know for sure a Grayback lives in one of the townhomes down the street."

He waved his hand in the air as if it weren't a big deal. "I'll be careful. So tell me what's going on with you. You seem...distracted."

Over the past two months they'd become friends. She'd never had any siblings, but she cared for him like a big sister would and worried constantly he was going to get caught. Hoping he'd see reason, she even offered to go with him to Savannah and persuade the alpha to punish instead of killing him. No matter what she said, though, he outright refused.

She wondered what Ramo would think if he knew she was aiding a packless Were.

Wait. Where the hell did that thought come from? She didn't care what her estranged husband thought.

Shrugging out of her coat, she threw it on the bed next to Jordan and before she knew it, she was pacing his tiny room, telling him about Ramo.

When she was done, he sat, dumbfounded. "Wow. I had no idea you were even married. After all this time, you never mentioned...Well, I can see why. What a douche!"

She let out a harsh laugh. "Yep."

"And you just told him to fuck off?" She nodded, biting her bottom lip. "But he's staying, and you have to see him again?" More nodding. "Then you can't let him get to you."

Her eyes shot to his. "What? How can I not?"

Folding a leg on the bed to face her better, he said, "Easy. Pretend like he's just some other guy, an acquaintance you met ten years ago. You have to separate the man he is now from the man you married in the past. You keep harping on the fact he's your husband then you're going to drive yourself nuts."

He smiled at her and his tanned face had too many lines for one so young. Every time she thought of telling Owen about him, she'd think of how friendly and kind he was and couldn't do it. "Trust me, I did it with this girl in high school and it drove her wild." He finished in his Georgia twang.

She squinted her eyes at him. "I'm not trying to get his attention, but you do have a point." Resuming her pacing, she thought this over. For a teenager, he made a lot sense. Guessing, as an outsider, he had an unobstructed viewpoint. Nevertheless, it was a good idea.

If she kept blowing up every time she saw him, he was going to think she cared. Maintaining an aloof front would show him she could care less whether he was there or not. And she didn't care, right? Just because the urge to smash his face in overwhelmed her did not mean she had feelings for him. They were strangers.

"You're making me dizzy," he said, smirking.

"Oh. Sorry." Picking up her bags, she said, "Look, I have to go. There's a meeting tonight so if you want to stretch your legs, all the Graybacks will be in one place." Once those words were out of her mouth, she felt like a traitor. Body tensing, she froze as if all the Graybacks were about to bust down the door and seize her. When nothing dramatic happened, she eyed him warily.

Feeling her apprehension he got to his feet, his face a mixture of hurt and anxiety. "Elizabeth, you know I'd never hurt you or your pack. That's not what I'm about. You helped me so much. How could you even think I'd use that information to hurt you?"

"I don't," she said too quickly. "Really. I just wish you'd consider going back or at least allowing me to speak to Owen. There has to be something in the laws which…"

Jordan shook his head vehemently. "You don't know what he's like." She assumed he was speaking of his alpha. "You don't know what I did. If he finds me,

I'm dead."

"And that right there scares me too. You won't tell me what you did and yet I'm supposed to take you at your word that you're not dangerous." Shaking her head in frustration, she turned to leave, but he came toward her and gripped her by the elbow.

"Don't. I'm not dangerous, so please don't think I'd do anything crazy." His eyes were round and filled with fear.

Trying to soften her gaze, she said, "If you don't tell me what you did soon, I'm going to have to tell my alpha. I can't go on like this."

Lowering his gaze to the floor he nodded slowly. "I know it's not right to put you in this position and God, I don't want you to take the fall for this. Just…give me some time. Okay?"

Feeling like she was digging an even bigger hole for herself, she gave him a small smile. "Okay."

As she walked back toward the train station, the knot in her stomach only increased. She was playing a dangerous game taking him in this way, but what other choice did she have? It wasn't fair werewolves were bound to one pack and were considered loose cannons if they were thrown out.

What were they supposed to do? It was no wonder the kid was nervous. His alpha wanted to kill him and if Owen found out, he'd be honor bound to call a summit where they would undoubtedly send him to SPONA, the supernatural prison. He was just a kid for Christ's sake.

Climbing the stairs to the platform she tried to think of alternatives for Jordan, but tonight's meeting loomed over her like a gray cloud. Thankfully, she had her plan in place as far as Ramo went and redirected her thoughts to completing her homework for class before the meeting.

She stopped at the store across the street from her place and picked up her grandmother's prescription. By the time she was home she felt exhausted but forced herself to get to work. Sitting on the couch, she took out the article she was supposed to read for class tomorrow, and then positioned her laptop next to her. As she sipped her coffee she propped her feet on the coffee table to get comfortable.

And fell asleep.

****

Buzzing woke her from the deepest sleep she'd had in days. Reaching lazily for her cell on the sofa cushion, she saw Owen's name displayed on the lock screen. Entering her passcode, she checked her texts. She had five messages from her alpha.

Closing the bar early for the meeting. Come early. I want to spend a few minutes with you before we get started. Love you.

Are you close?

Where are you?

Elizabeth? You ok?

The meeting is going to start in ten minutes. Where are you?

"Shit!" Jumping off the couch she grabbed her jacket and purse as she Ubered on her cell. She stuffed her feet into her boots by the door and looked around to make sure she didn't leave anything electronic on. Flying down the stairs and out the door, she texted Owen.

I'm so sorry. Fell asleep. OTW.

Checking her phone to follow the little black car on the Uber app, she saw her driver was a minute away. Sighing with relief, she straightened her white shirtsleeve through her open trench coat and made sure she didn't have any spills on her gray slacks.

A car turned the corner with the headlights on and stopped in front of her. Getting in, she gave the address to Owen's bar and sat back to survey her makeup situation. Peering at her reflection in her compact, she thought it wasn't too bad. She added a little concealer under her eyes to hide the dark circles and applied lip balm in a neutral color. Dabbing on a little blush to get some color back in her cheeks, she decided it was the best she could do in the backseat of a dark car.

Checking her phone again, there were no more messages, which meant the damn meeting had already started. Quickly, she checked her bank statement since an Uber charge wasn't on the budget for the week and cringed. Thank goodness Friday was pay day.

As they neared the bar, she combed her fingers through her hair, noting it was time for a trim. By the time she got out and headed for the glass doors, she was only about five minutes late. Hoping Owen wasn't too irritated with her, she rounded the vacant hostess stand and faltered.

Oh God. In her mad rush to get here, she had completely forgotten about Ramo. Ramo, who stood side by side with Owen in front of the bar while the other pack members sat scattered in various seats at the tables. Silence fell as everyone turned to face her, the late one.

"Glad you could make it, Elizabeth. Have a seat."

She heard Owen's composed voice speak, but for

some god-awful reason her eyes were on Ramo. Tonight he wore jeans, a pair of white and gray Chuck Taylors and a gray t-shirt which simply read, *Nah*. Beneath this in smaller font read, *Rosa Parks, 1955*. The look was laid back, but she could tell his jeans weren't cheap. Just looking at the perfect fit and texture and you knew they were of good quality.

If it weren't for the man wearing the shirt, she would have laughed. Her students would get a kick out of it since it was black history month and they were reading about Rosa Parks.

Noting Ramo was staring back, she reminded herself to stay aloof and gave him a stiff smile, then nodded to Owen, who scowled back. Taking the seat closest to her at a table next to a Grayback couple she was well acquainted with, she angled her chair, noisily to face the bar and gave *Owen* her rapt attention.

"So in answer to your question, Miles, yes, for the mean time our meetings will be held here. They'll have to be after hours because I still have a business to run."

Although Elizabeth stared directly at Owen, she was never so aware of someone as she was of Ramo. It was as if he dominated the room, dwarfing every single person, including her boyfriend, which was silly because they were practically the same height.

No! Don't start comparing.

Ramo had nothing on Owen. Her boyfriend was the freaking alpha, with a strong and brooding air about him. Whereas Ramo, well, he was arrogant and seemed way too confident standing...

Ugh. I said don't compare. Focus!

"...Perez of the Blacktail pack. Now, I know you have questions as to why we're hosting another pack member, but before we get into that, you'll need to be updated on what's been happening. Therefore, I'm going to turn it over to Perez who knows firsthand what we're dealing with." Owen gave Ramo a clipped nod and sat down on one of the bar stools, crossing his arms in front of him.

Ramo seemed to study something on the floor till he looked up and the cocky expression he'd been sporting was gone. He was all business now.

"Evening," he started, then spoke solemnly, his voice smooth and stimulating. Every single eye was on him and not just because he was a virtual outsider, but because Ramo's presence, his voice pulled you in as though he were trying to hypnotize rather than give a mere update. "Last summer my alpha's sister was kidnapped and tortured for several months by the head witch or high priestess, as they are referred to, of her coven. I know you are aware of this as we made several inquiries to find Serena's whereabouts.

The purpose of her imprisonment was to use her for her blood. Serena, along with two other members of our pack were brutally cut and drained for a spell. The high priestess, Cassandra aimed to use werewolf blood to create mutant jackals called Nightwalkers. Somehow, she managed to make their saliva or canines poisonous. We know for a fact their bite is venomous to Weres and vampires."

There were collective gasps and curses, several of her pack members shifted uncomfortably in their seats, but no one interrupted.

"We were able to infiltrate the coven and wipe out the place with the remaining Nightwalkers left inside. Cassandra was last seen in the building, but we have reason to believe she may still be out there as she had teleporting capabilities. There may even be more covens aiming to overthrow us due to the more recent attacks on your pack members." He paused then, and she felt the sorrow for her lost pack members pour out of him.

"My deepest condolences for your loss." Clearing his throat he went on. "We have to assume there are more covens forming more Nightwalkers. This is why I am here. We…" He turned his head slightly to Owen, but never met his gaze. "…thought it would be best to form Fighters, much like our Blacktail Fighters. I helped Adam Perez form our protection group years ago and now I'm going to help Hunter form his. As for where the Nightwalkers and witches are located, we are still looking into it. It's been tricky since witches have slipped under the radar for years, but we're learning new things every day and your alpha knows everything we do."

Owen broke in when several hands went up, "Any questions regarding witches and Nightwalkers can be addressed to me. Perez is here to teach us battle tactics only."

Several of the male Weres asked Ramo questions about the battle at Sweetin Home. She watched as he addressed her pack members with respect, no hint of animosity or hostility, which usually laced through a werewolf when speaking to another pack. Looking at his profile as he listened to questions, she noticed the stubble growing on his jaw and how his cheek sloped inward just below his high cheekbones. It was like seeing him for the first time.

She remembered him having a hooped lip ring in

the corner of his right bottom lip. Now he sported a stud there, the two tiny silver balls getting lost in his supple lip. And was his hair always so short? She swore he had more when they married.

Her vision blurred as she stared at the flecks of gold in his chestnut eyes, numb with the realization he was here, standing just a few feet away. *Her husband.*

A husband whom she did not know.

How in the world was she going to do this? How could she act normal around him when she felt everything but normal right now? Could she really ignore she was married to this man; pretend he was an outsider when it was their marriage that connected their two packs?

Squeezing her eyes shut, she took a deep breath to get a grip, to fight the myriad of trouble having him here could make. When she opened them, she found Owen's gaze on *her*. There was worry lurking there and she sensed the fading envy he'd felt as she'd gawked at Ramo.

Shame filled her and as if the whole pack knew what was on their minds, a male Were asked the inevitable question. She cringed as Grayson, the nosey, big mouth she'd went to high school with called out, "Aren't you married to Elizabeth?"

Her heart jumped to her throat as the pack first stared at Ramo and then her as though watching a tennis match. She couldn't look at him now, instead, she looked at Owen who had bristled at the question, his face flushed with embarrassment. Even though Grayson had asked Ramo, it seemed everyone waited for Owen to answer the question. God, she knew this was going to be awkward, but it was beyond that for her alpha. Everyone knew they were together and here he was, hosting his girlfriend's husband.

Ramo glared at Grayson with narrowed eyes. "We are allied, yes."

Heads turned to focus on the Blacktail, and she felt Owen's slight sense of relief he didn't have to answer his pack member's question.

Ramo continued, "Our union has protected our two packs for several years from usurpers and vampires. The bond our packs share is well known across the nation, not just the Midwest. I know for a fact the Darkwolves were hatching an attack on your pack just days before our...union. Once word spread...well...I'm sure you noticed you're still a pack."

He glared daggers at Grayson. "What's more, the Blacktails have the backing of the Vampire King of North America now." Growls echoed throughout the bar. "It's not ideal, but it was useful at the Sweetin Home and for the mean time, we, Weres and vampires, have a common enemy."

The Graybacks seemed to ponder his words as Owen grabbed a tablet off the bar with pursed lips and handed it to Ramo.

Dismissing the topic as if Grayson had simply asked about the weather, Ramo announced, "I'm going to take names of volunteers and enter them myself. This way, I can learn and identify the Weres I'll be training. You're under no obligation to put your name forth, but if you think you can handle the training and are willing to fight, then by all means..."

She watched as both males and females gave their names while Ramo typed them into the touchscreen along with their weight and height in human and werewolf form. Owen stood beside him with his phone to give Ramo each volunteer's contact information, which Ramo added to his digital document.

"An email will go out with an application. Please fill this out as soon as you can." Ramo spoke as he typed away. "Again, all applicants are welcome, but if you cannot handle the training, you will be asked to withdraw your name."

When all was said and done there were nine volunteers, seven men and two women. Owen looked impressed with his pack even though he was one of the seven men to put forth their name. He was commending them when a woman on the opposite side of where she sat raised her hand and waited to be called on as if they were in class.

"Yes, Destiny?" Owen asked.

The woman looked nervous to be speaking in front of everyone. "My question is for Mr. Perez…Can you…I mean…What are they like? The Nightwalkers? Are they highly skilled? More powerful?" She looked so nervous to speak up.

Destiny listened with wide eyes as Ramo delicately described what they knew about the Nightwalkers and she remembered who the woman was. Destiny Jensen married to Ethan Jensen. They had three small children, triplets around five years old. She remembered meeting the children two full moons ago, just before their parents had phased in front of them.

It was the first time the two boys and girl had witnessed it and watched in gleeful amazement as their parents ran circles around them making them laugh and jump excitedly. All of a sudden she understood just how dire their circumstances were. Thinking about those three innocent children, totally unaware of the danger they all faced made her shudder. Their mother wasn't frightened for herself, she was terrified for her children.

Without a thought, her hand shot in the air.

Ramo hesitated before addressing her, his eyes thoughtful on hers. "Question Ms. Vitale?"

He actually looked a bit nervous speaking to her, and did she detect annoyance when he'd used her surname? Really? As if she'd take his name?

"I'm volunteering," she answered a matter of fact. "Five foot six. A hundred and forty-five pounds." *Give or take a few*, she thought guiltily.

Ramo froze with the tablet in hand, his gaze unwavering on hers. By the bar, Owen unfolded his arms, rising from his seat. The look on both men's faces was enough to make her squirm a bit. She felt the rising trepidation coming from them and her face reddened. If either of them embarrassed her in front of her pack she'd kill them.

She looked to Owen with eyebrows raised. "Well…add my name." Looking to Ramo, "It's Elizabeth," she enunciated sarcastically.

There were a few soft chuckles around them, but her gaze never faltered, daring him to deny her.

Pursing his lips, Ramo glared as she honed her senses on him, reading him as if he were holding a neon sign. He wasn't angry she'd teased him just now. He was actually worried that she was serious. His head jerked around to Owen, giving her boyfriend a '*check your girl*' expression. Owen only spared him an, '*I got this*' glance, stepping closer to where she sat. "Elizabeth, are you sure you want to do this?"

She felt her eyes widen at him.

Putting his palms up, he said, "I'm only questioning you because you have quite a lot on your plate as it is. This will take a lot of dedication."

She wanted to punch him in the face. They'd done well to hide their relationship from the pack in the beginning, then when word got out, he was mindful of not treating her any differently than other pack members lest they grow to resent her.

But now, now he wanted to pull the over-protecting boyfriend card in front of everyone, including Ramo? He hadn't questioned the others about their schedule. She wasn't the only one with things to do. Why was he questioning just *her?*

Straightening in her seat, she said, "If anyone knows about dedication, it's me. I have every right to prepare myself and defend my pack." Giving Owen one last scathing, *'this isn't over'* glare, she addressed Ramo. "That's Elizabeth Vitale." She sat back and crossed her leg over her knee, her face flushed with anger, but determined all the same.

Ramo no longer glared, he was thoughtful again and his pensive expression unnerved her. Nodding mutely, he added her name on the touchscreen.

Owen addressed the pack again, closing the meeting. As they couldn't train in the bar, he was working with the Chicago Park District to secure a location with ample space for fight training and phasing. After agreeing upon a date and time for the new trainees, she felt her phone buzz in her purse alerting her she had an email. Ramo had set up a thread to contact them in regard to training. As the pack stood to leave several of them checked their phones.

She didn't know why, but she didn't want to see his name on her phone, didn't even want to read the email. It gave her a funny feeling in her stomach just to know that she had a message from him. *God!* Why? Why did she care? She couldn't be this immature. He was her trainer now. Telling herself, she'd read the damn message later, she stood and gathered her things.

Most of the pack had filed out of the bar already, but she stayed behind to talk to Owen. Despite his behavior a few minutes ago, she still felt bad for not arriving earlier to be with him. He was talking to a couple by the bar as she approached, turning her head around casually searching for Ramo. A moment ago he'd been putting his tablet away. Where was he? Had he already left?

Oh well. She didn't care. The less she saw him, the better.

Jake and Vivenne, a cute couple she and Owen often double dated with kissed her on the cheek and left through the glass doors.

Alone now, she turned to Owen with pursed lips. She wasn't as upset as she had been moments ago, but knew she had to stick to her guns.

Smiling at her sheepishly, he said, "I know, I know. I'm sorry. I couldn't help it." Grabbing her hand, he pulled her closer to him, playing with her fingers. "But, honey, are you sure? It's just us right now. You can be honest. Were you just volunteering to stick it to Perez?"

Her head shot back as if he'd slapped her. "Owen, give me a little credit. In all honesty I think our whole pack can benefit from this, why shouldn't I?"

Nodding quietly, he surveyed her mouth, neck,

cleavage. "Okay. Look, I'm sorry I put you on the spot like that. I just worry, you know?" His fingers moved through hers in midair, across the tops to her palm over and over. "If anything happened…"

Cough.

Stiffening, her breath hitched as she sensed Ramo's presence coming from the bathroom in the back. Reluctantly, she turned in his direction. He strode toward them with a small duffle bag loose in his right hand. The expression on his hard features was unreadable, but she couldn't miss the uncomfortable vibe coming from him.

This shouldn't feel strange; standing with her boyfriend, holding his hand in front of Ramo, but damn if it didn't. She so wanted to be cool and nonchalant around him, but it was these awkward moments that pissed her off. Damn him for throwing her world off its axis.

Smiling roguishly, he said, "Sorry to interrupt. Mind if I have a chat with my wife?"

She gasped as Owen growled, his grip on her hand tightening.

Scowling, Elizabeth snapped. "You've got a lot of nerve…"

Ramo rolled his eyes and waved his hand dismissively. "Relax. It was a joke." Shrugging, he said, "Hey, I'm gonna be here awhile so you might as well get used to how obnoxious I am."

She glared at him in exasperation. He had no right to be facetious with her. Ever!

"So can we talk?" No longer businesslike, Ramo had turned into this overly confident man.

Remaining aloof was proving harder than she

thought. She chewed the inside of her mouth. "Actually, now isn't a good time. Owen was just about to take me home."

Ramo's left eye twitched at her response, his gaze flicking to Owen and back.

"Whatever you want to discuss with Elizabeth, you can discuss with me," Owen stated.

"Uh…no offense, but that would be really fucking awkward seeing as how you're my wife's boyfriend."

Oh Jesus! She knew this was wrong on so many levels.

"And I think Elizabeth can speak for herself," Ramo added as he grabbed his bag off the barstool. "We're gonna have to talk sometime, Vitale." His expression softened a bit as he stared longer than he should have. Then, nodding, he strode out of the bar.

Chapter Five

Upon entering her apartment, Elizabeth threw her discarded articles back in her school bag and changed into her pajamas. They weren't really pajamas, just an old t-shirt and panties. She couldn't stand sleeping in pants, her body temperature ran too hot.

It wasn't until she was under the covers and the light off that she looked at the message she'd received. It was simply a notice of their first training, but seeing *his* name did something to her she could not describe.

Frustrated with herself for letting something so simple as a message affect her this way, she plugged in her phone and turned on her stomach to let sleep claim her. As she replayed the evening's events in her head her phoned chimed.

Opening one eye, she stared at her phone with her cheek to the pillow, wondering who it could be. It was probably Owen saying goodnight, but the hairs rising on her neck told her otherwise. At once, she felt nervous, dreading the idea it could be Ramo messaging.

She wished she hadn't given him her number, but as a trainee it was not a choice. But would he cross the line and message just her? She couldn't move, but the desire to check her text messages had never been stronger.

Lifting herself on her elbows, she reached for the phone. A number she did not recognize glowed on her screen with the text reading, —*Can we talk?*—

Her heart lurched with sudden excitement. Why, oh why did his message do this to her?

—*Now? I'm in bed.*—

Responding with trembling fingers, she waited for a message back.

She watched the little dots move back and forth as he responded. He was either texting a long message or he didn't know what to type.

—*Yes. Now.*—

What the hell?

Staring at the boldness of his message, she jumped when she heard the soft knock on her front door.

"You've got to be kidding me?" she muttered, sitting up on her bed.

"Not kidding, Elizabeth." She heard his hushed reply all the way from her bedroom, knowing he'd heard her as well. One of the perks of being a Were was having profound hearing. "Just give me a minute," she heard him utter through the door.

Irritated at his intrusion when she needed to be up early tomorrow, she got up and threw on a pair of yoga pants. Opening the front door, she tried not to stare at the way he casually leaned against the doorframe. She quickly let him in and shut the door, crossing her arms over her unsupported breasts. Some women could go braless, but at a D cup she was not one of those women.

She turned to face him. "What do you want?" Trying hopelessly not to stare too closely, she avoided the concern etched on his features. He wore the same clothes he'd had on earlier, but the stubble at his jaw was significantly darker. His eyes took her in, from the tips of her toes to her tousled hair, taking a second glance at her arms covering her chest. "Well?"

Even though he and Owen were nearly the same size, somehow Ramo engulfed her tiny apartment. It was as if he suffocated the room with his presence. She flushed, realizing they were entirely alone. She shouldn't have let him in.

Ramo walked around her small living room, looking out the front window, then ambling into her tiny kitchen. She watched him with narrowed eyes through the buffet window as he casually opened her fridge, shut it and then look through her cabinets.

"What the hell are you doing?"

"I'm hungry. Got anything to eat?"

"No! This isn't a restaurant. Either tell me why you're here or get out." What was his deal?

As if he didn't hear her he said, incredulously, "All you have is Ramen and Kraft Macaroni and Cheese. You eat like a frat boy." He shook his head as he came out of the kitchen. "You know those noodles are fried right?"

Her brow furrowed at his nerve. She wondered if he'd been this cocky ten years ago because all she remembered was the heartless man who stood in her father's kitchen and told her he didn't want to be married to her.

Glaring at his strong jaw as he inspected her apartment, she shuffled her feet, wishing she'd pick up more often. A box of Cheez-its sat on the small coffee table and her cozy socks she'd kicked off the night before were thrown on the floor. The kitchen counter was piled with magazines and mail and some papers she had yet to finish grading. "You're kind of a slob, huh?" he stated, with a smirk on his face, taking in the dirty dishes in the sink.

"Screw you. I wasn't expecting company in the middle of the night." Far beyond irritated, she demanded, "What do you want?"

"Kiss your grandmother with that mouth?" he joked, strolling around the living room again.

"Who do you think I get it from? Last time, why are you here?"

She followed his wide, muscular back as he surveyed the pictures on her side table. She stopped when she got too close. His natural scent filled her senses and she took a step back. She didn't want to know his scent.

It was way too personal even though she was a wolf and their sense of smell was strong by nature. It was far too intimate to take notice of one's fragrance. Besides, the smell of musk, woods, and dryer sheets weren't such a big deal.

She rubbed her nose looking away.

Turning to face her by the front window, he placed his hands on his hips. He stared at the floor for a moment. Then, in a gentler voice he said, "I wanted to make sure you were okay with all this. I know my coming here was unexpected, and I..." he searched the room for words, shrugging his shoulders. "I don't know...I was just checking, you know?"

She didn't know how old he was, but at the moment he was acting like he was a high school teenager asking a girl to a dance. "How old are you?"

Her question seemed to throw him off. "What...I...I'm ninety-three. Why?"

Shrugging her shoulder, she walked to the couch and sat down, curling her legs under her. "Just curious."

She felt his confusion, which oddly, satisfied her. "I'm doing fine, by the way. It's weird of course, but I'll get used to it."

"You didn't seem fine last night."

"Wasn't expecting you last night. I'm...prepared now." Her voice sounded calmer than she felt.

He looked at her uncertainly, his head cocked slightly to one side. "I wasn't expecting you to be so easy going."

She huffed. "Why not? Did you think I'd scream and curse you out? Demand to know what the hell you've been doing for the past ten years? Well, you were mistaken. I don't care Perez. You are my trainer and I'll treat you like I treat everyone else. Nothing more. Nothing less."

His searing gaze was unwavering. The corners of his eyes dipped down slightly under thick, heavy lashes. She didn't know if it was his eyes or the man alone that unnerved her. He was staring as though he couldn't read her emotions, which was silly. Stepping closer to her he said carefully, his head tilted to the side. "But I'm not just your trainer. I'm your hus..."

"No you're not!" She uncrossed her arms and stood. "And for you to even suggest that is ludicrous. You didn't want a *fucking* wife, remember? The minute you left you..." Stopping abruptly, she took a deep breath. "I'm not doing this. You need to leave."

"Wait," he said, stepping closer the tips of his shoes touched her toes. "I want to know why you're living here and not in the condo? Why aren't you using the account I set up for you and where the hell is the car I purchased?" His hand gestured toward the window as though his precious gift should be parked outside.

Furrowing her brow she looked at him as if he'd grown an extra head. "Are you kidding? Do you honestly think I'd accept anything from you? You're nothing to me so it'd be like taking a handout and I don't take handouts. I've managed just fine on my own."

His eyes narrowing, he stared at her for a long moment. The doubt radiating from him told her he didn't believe her. She didn't care. She just wanted him gone.

Running a hand over his face frustratingly, he said, "Look...we are...we have an agreement. I promised to take care..."

Cutting him off again, she placed her hands on her hips, "I don't need you to take care of me. I need you to leave."

Anger and remorse flitted across his face before his gaze fell to her chest. The fabric had stretched across her breasts. Unbound, her nipples hardened beneath her shirt.

Her very white shirt.

His gaze turned from annoyance to something else entirely. Elizabeth watched the muscles in his neck strain against his tattoo as his chest rose and fell. The look on his face, and the way his eyes subtly turned amber for half a second made her heart leap to her throat.

Covering herself, he continued to stare, his nearness overwhelming her. Reading him, she felt the heat coursing through him, sensed his arousal. She could only stare back in shock, her breaths coming out short and the room suddenly became unbearably hot. Sweat trickled down her back.

The energy surrounding them both confused and angered her. He couldn't be attracted to her. He didn't want her. And she shouldn't be feeling anything for him, at all. He'd only been here a couple days and already she was undone.

This time when he spoke, his voice was no longer soft and pleading. Instead, he sounded as if he were giving her orders, his mood darkening with every word. "You and Owen...I don't care what you do in private, but do not flaunt your relationship in front of everyone. I'm not going anywhere and you both need to show me some respect. Like it or not, I *am* your husband. The situation may be different, but that fact still remains."

Stunned, she stood there at a loss for words. Was he seriously making demands?

Striding to the door he said over his shoulder, "I'll see you Wednesday. Wear comfortable clothing." And then he was gone.

****

Ramo slammed the car door shut and drove off down the street with no particular destination in mind.

Cursing, he thought how that could not have gone worse if he'd planned it.

What the hell was he thinking? Did he actually order her to not flaunt her relationship with Owen? He didn't mean to say it. In fact, he'd stormed out because he'd been pissed at himself for acting like a territorial idiot. But when that flimsy shirt stretched across the ample breasts God had granted her, it was like a kick in the gut. In that second, when her nipples hardened from the fabric, he pictured his mouth on those beautiful mounds and he'd hardened like a sixteen-year-old boy.

Then, the image of that fucking alpha touching her

caused his vision to alter. An unfamiliar sensation sliced through him and his skin actually vibrated with what he could only describe as anger. Before he could stop himself he was making demands.

Why? Why did he care? He shouldn't care; had no right to care. And he didn't really. He hardly knew her, and he'd left all those years ago to allow her to live her own life, so she was free to do what she wanted.

Besides, this was exactly the reason he'd left. He didn't want to feel jealousy. He didn't want to feel territorial. For years he'd watched his family and friends go through emotional turmoil falling in love and he didn't want anything to do with it. Watching his grandfather waste away after the death of his wife was heartbreaking.

He remembered how happy and funny his grandfather used to be; the jokester of the family. Then in a flash, the light had gone out of his grandfather's eyes. He had to be the one to tell his grandfather his wife had passed. It was one of the worst days of his life. His grandfather, his idol had become a shell of a man. For years he and his parents tried to cheer him up, bringing him to live with them in Wilmington, but no matter what they did or said he was never the same. Years later, when the pain was too much to endure anymore, his idol shot himself in the head.

From that moment on, he refused to fall in love, vowing to never marry or mate with a woman. He'd been furious when Adam ordered him to break that vow. His alpha had reassured him that it would be in name only and that he didn't have to love the girl, just marry her. But then, he'd looked upon the stunning woman coming down the aisle and he knew he was in trouble.

He was out of the city now, which meant he was free to roam in his werewolf form. He pulled alongside the expressway and got out, yanking his clothes off and tossing them on the hood. Jumping over the metal rail, he heard cars honking at him as they sped by. Ignoring them, he phased at the same time he began to run along the wide stretch of grass that ran parallel to the road.

The wind smacking his face and watering his eyes was a welcome relief, but it didn't erase the image of those dark eyes glaring at him. Were they black? He didn't think he'd ever seen black eyes before. And those lips...Jesus Christ.

Damn it, he needed to stay away from her.

Why the hell did she volunteer for training?

At first, when she'd offered up her name, he'd been momentarily proud at her bravery. Then, realizing she may do well and become a Fighter terrified him. Then, being scared for her terrified him even more. He was going down a slippery slope. There was no reason to feel so much for a person he didn't really know.

Now they'd be working together, and he'd have to see her several times a week. He should tell her to quit. It was obvious she was always busy anyway. He didn't know how she was going to manage it all. On the other hand, seeing how she lived alone and depended on public transportation, it was essential for her to learn how to defend herself.

And there he went again...caring and shit for the girl. It was his Fighter's impulse, a Were's need to protect, which had him all messed up right now. The fact she was technically his only drove his compulsion to look after her go through the roof.

He needed to stay away and avoid her dark eyes as much as possible. As he pushed himself harder, listening to the sharp whistle of the wind in his ears, it was like a voice whispering to him, *Good luck trying, Dipshit.*

****

The night of their first training session, Elizabeth raced up the steps to the gymnasium they were using at Wells Park District. Wednesday nights she had class in the evening, so she hoped Ramo alternated the days of the week for lessons or she'd be too exhausted to lift a finger, let alone practice fighting.

Bursting through the door, she cursed her lack of finesse and set her things on the floor by the door.

"You're late, Vitale."

A tremor ran through her at the sound of his voice and the use of her surname, but she hid it by rolling her eyes and joining the group. She took a spot next to Owen who gave her a soft smile but refrained from touching her. Everyone was gathered in the center on the shiny hardwood floor facing Ramo who was talking to them about committing to a workout regimen.

"…along with the diet plan," he looked pointedly at her when he said *diet*. She rolled her eyes again. "I'll be sending you a workout schedule. You'll need two days of cardio, two of weight training, and two days of core workouts."

Shit!

When was she gonna fit all of that in? Ugh.

"We're starting with basic hand to hand combat, then we'll get into hand to claw, and later…claw to claw. We'll squeeze in weapons once a week as well."

Her gaze followed him as he paced back and forth

while he spoke. She wanted to feel disgusted with the guy, but the way he spoke with such authority and power made it hard for her to keep up her façade.

"We'll meet four times a week, but they will not always be the same days or the same location. For security reasons, I think it's best if we stay mobile. People talk and it wouldn't be safe for a group of Weres to return to the same place on the same day or at the same time."

For the rest of the class they practiced different punches. As they were still waiting for clearance to phase during sessions only, they could only practice in their human form. Ramo had spread everyone out in two rows so they could practice without accidently hitting anyone.

"Uppercuts are especially effective in close quarters...Don't forget to turn that foot, Kylen." He moved around the room, helping people with their swing.

Once they had perfected the different punches, he showed them the different ways to block them. For this, they got into pairs for what he called a "soft lesson". "The real sparring will come later."

She partnered with a friendly man who ran the gas station on Division and Ashland. Sharjeel was a good foot taller than she was, but scrawny. They each took turns throwing "soft" punches and blocking them.

She had to admit it to herself she was having a good time. She didn't even feel tired anymore. Her body rarely got this much exercise and throwing each punch sent a rush of adrenaline through her limbs. Every time she threw a right hook, she just imaged Ramo's face as her target.

The few times he'd come around to check on their progress, he never met her eye and simply said, "Good form, Vitale." A few feet away she saw Owen's lip curl at his comment.

She didn't know why, but the way he addressed her by her last name made it seem more intimate than if he'd used her first name, which was weird.

After two hours, he ended class. "I'll message the group with the location and time for the next class." He took out his phone and started scrolling, but not before giving her a lingering gaze under his lashes.

She couldn't help but ponder what that look meant. Was he staring because he found her attractive? Was he giving her a silent warning not to go jumping in Owen's arms? Just thinking about his audacity last night incensed her. Who was he to make demands on her? She ought to say something to him. Tell him he was being ridiculous, and he couldn't tell her what to do.

So why didn't she?

"Are you ready to go?" Owen's voice came from behind her and she jumped slightly.

"Yes," she said, nervously. Damn Ramo for making her feel nervous around her boyfriend. Without meeting his eyes, she put on her coat and grabbed her bags. She kept dropping things with the two sets of eyes on her. They were the last ones left again so she didn't feel too bad when Owen placed his hand on her lower back as they left the gym.

But those brown eyes still burned the back of her head the whole way out.

****

The next few sessions went as the first did. Ramo spoke for a few minutes on what they'd be doing and then they'd dive right in. The only difference from their first lesson was the long email Ramo would send the night before. He didn't introduce a new move unless the trainees studied it up first.

As hard as it was to work around training, she really did enjoy it. Other than Grayson, the other trainees were respectable Weres who were easy to work with. She'd even begun going to the gym after work. Although, she hadn't gone six days a week, she figured four was enough. Ramo was crazy if he thought anyone had time for all that.

Weapons lessons were not going as well for her. It was the only time during training where they were just sitting down and listening to Ramo drone on and on about calibers and double action thingamajigs. Guns just weren't her thing. She was terrified of them really. And when this particular weapons lesson landed late on a Friday night after a grueling week, it took all her strength just to sit upright in her chair.

Tonight Ramo wore another one of his novelty t-shirts. In big caps it read, *Do Not Read The Next Sentence*. In tiny caps below it read, *You Little Rebel*.

What was with this guy and his shirts?

As she sat next to Owen, Ramo blabbed on about what was the best handgun caliber for general self-defense in front of a fold out table laden with different guns. Usually, when he spoke, despite her efforts to avoid prolonged interaction with him, she took these opportunities to simply stare and marvel at his masculinity. She would go through a circus of emotions, fighting her irritating attraction to him, wondering what he'd been up to the last ten year, to imagining herself kicking him in the face.

Thankfully, as she sat so close to Owen now, her feelings were dulled with exhaustion. Her mind was nearly blank as her eyes followed Ramo's thick forearms maneuvering the guns on display, his smooth, deep voice sounded like a television, the volume on really low in a dark room.

Owen's fingers squeezed her elbow and she jerked awake. Her sudden lurch caused Ramo's eyes to flick to her for a moment before going on.

Giving Owen a small smile, she adjusted herself in her seat to pay attention to the lesson. Trying to focus, she watched Ramo load a 9mm. After a while, she thought she was awake enough to sit back in her chair, and she folded her arms in front of her to listened to his instruction.

His voice was so smooth and deep, the tone level like a book narrator. He really needed to speak up.

It was like some invisible force was yanking her eyes closed. They felt so heavy. Taking a deep breath, she fought to tune in again, but his voice was like a deep, hypnotic, lullaby...

"Vitale!"

This time, she jerked awake so hard her arm flew back, slapping Owen in the chest. Embarrassed, she sat up; placing her hands on her lap and gave Ramo a wide-eyed expression.

"See me after class, please," his voice intoned.

Her shoulders slumped as she gave him an incredulous look. Ugh! Really? Now she was in trouble with her instructor/husband? She restrained from rolling her eyes and just nodded.

"I'll wait for you," Owen announced when the lesson ended.

She tensed. She didn't like interacting with Ramo in front of Owen. Their relationship didn't need the added stress so the less he saw the better.

"It's fine. I'll meet you by the car." She slipped on her jacket as she gave him a reassuring smile.

He only glared at her, one hand in his pocket as the last person left behind him.

"Are you going to babysit her for the next few months?" Ramo stood at the fold out, putting each weapon away carefully into black cases. "Because she needs to be able to walk and talk on her own when we begin field training."

Putting a hand on her hip, she let out a loud sigh. Yeah, their relationship reeeeaaallly didn't need *that*.

Ignoring Ramo's comment, Owen turned without a word to either of them and left.

Scowling at him, she said sarcastically, "Thanks for that."

Glancing up from lifting a rifle bag off the table and onto the floor, he responded, "What? He does baby you and you know it."

"No he doesn't."

"He definitely hovers."

"Well, we're dating. I don't mind him hovering," she said almost snidely.

He froze in the middle of zipping up another case, his eyes hard on the table. Then, slowly he nodded. "Whatever floats your boat, *wife*."

"Do not call me that!" she seethed.

Slamming a case shut, he sneered. "Every time you throw your boyfriend in my face, I'm going to throw our marriage in yours. Got it."

"Why?"

"Because I can," he answered spitefully.

She stared at him, dumbfounded. "Why the hell do you even care?" she nearly shouted.

Glaring hard, he came around the table toward her. "I don't care. It's about...about..." he stammered.

"What? Respect? For you?" She asked scathingly as her chin rose the closer he got. "Do you honestly think you deserve my respect?"

Chest heaving as though he was containing a roar, she felt suffocated at his nearness. He smelled of aftershave, of raw male musk, and damn dryer sheets. It made her mind go fuzzy. "No," he murmured resignedly. "I don't deserve it." Running a hand over his jaw, he let out a sharp breath. She smelled spearmint and her eyes darted to his perfectly sculpted mouth. His hand froze at his chin.

Glancing up she saw a look of confusion flash through his eyes. Why oh why did she have to stare at his lips?

Dropping his hand, he said, "Look...this is weird okay. I don't know how to act."

She placed her hands in her jacket pockets, feeling them become moist from the tension. "Just be normal," she said with a shrug. "I don't want to argue with you, but I'm sure you were doing just fine for ten years. Why be different now? I mean...you have no idea what I've been doing..."

A growl escaped him and they both stiffened. Shock stretched across his face.

"Why?" she asked, staring up at him in amazement. "Why did you just do that?"

Surprise still filling his features, he shook his head. "I don't know." Looking away, he rubbed his skull trim. "It must be…just being here is fucking with me."

Not knowing what to say to that, they both stood quietly, absorbed in their own thoughts. The longer she stood there, the more confused she became. How had they gotten on this topic? Her mind seemed to scatter when he was around.

"I'm sorry," he said, quietly. Then he cursed and walked away, obviously frustrated.

"I don't know what the hell is going on…" she said, staring at the floor. It was as if they'd forgotten how to communicate properly.

He'd walked to the window, his broad back to her before he spoke again. "I'm trying lamely to apologize for leaving and it sounds stupid."

"I don't want your apology," she said, softly.

He turned around, crossing his arms in front of him as he gazed at her.

"Truthfully, I want you to leave."

His temple flinched at her words.

Swallowing she went on. "I know it isn't an option, so I'll accept it. I handled your leaving just fine. We…we didn't even know each other. So we signed a paper that basically linked our names. Fine. Whatever." She met his stare full on. "I got over it. I did. But you're coming here now has…"

He was nodding as if he knew exactly how she felt. "I know," he said under his breath.

She inhaled deeply then let out a long shaky breath as he walked back to the table to gather his things.

"I didn't ask you to stay behind for this. I want to know if you're okay and what I mean is, are you okay with the training? You're a good fighter. You pick up the moves like a champ, but then half the time you're asleep." He paused for minute as though he were nervous to speak more. "I know you work all day and you're going to school...it's admirable, really. But I also know you're taking care of your grandmother and..."

"How do you know that?" she asked, her brow furrowing.

He was quiet for a moment before saying, "Small town."

Grabbing her purse from the chair she'd fallen asleep in, she said sharply, "I'm fine. I'll drink more coffee before weapon lessons."

The corner of his mouth lifted. "I don't think your jacket can withstand another mocha spill."

She felt her cheeks flush. Was he teasing her? Grabbing the lapels of her jacket, she stammered, "I don't...I'm a little..."

"Clumsy? Yeah, I know." He slipped his phone in his pocket and grabbed the rest of the bags, heaving the larger one over his shoulder. "Pretend the mocha is an opponent. It seems to be the only time you're on form." He smirked as he walked past her and out the door.

Owen was silent the whole ride home. She knew he was dying to ask her what they'd talked about, but if he did, she'd be honor-bound to tell him. This was something he was working on, learning to phrase questions so they didn't come out like a command.

She could have offered to tell him, but the whole conversation left her more perplexed than she'd already been.

Walking her to her door, Owen was determined to leave her with only his lasting kiss on her mind. He was especially vigorous tonight. She allowed him this hearty goodbye, knowing he was feeling emasculated by Ramo's presence. Fighting her nerves she gently pulled away with a smile, when her phone chimed. "I'll see you tomorrow okay." She gave him a quick peck and stepped into her apartment.

Owen glanced down at her pocket where her phone was. "Night," he said.

She closed the door and hurriedly took out her phone.

Ramo had texted only her and not on the thread with the other trainees. The message was only of a GIF. Opening it, she let out a loud laugh. It was a clip of a meerkat falling asleep. The headline on the top read: *When you can't stay awake in class.*

For some reason, she watched the quick video, giggling to herself…over and over again.

Chapter Six

Once they finally received permission from the mayor to phase indoors for lessons they began training in their wolf forms. This was exciting for Elizabeth as she felt she had the most energy when she was in her wolf form.

They were practicing the pincer movement, a maneuver which flanks the enemy, when the Grayback's adjudicator stepped into the gym with a police officer in tow.

With a non-supernatural in the room Owen ordered all the trainees to phase back except for her. "Stay as you are Elizabeth."

The adjudicator walked straight to Owen. "Every werewolf will need to phase."

She towered over everyone now that they were back in human form. Ramo strolled away from her to the side of the gymnasium where his sweatpants and shirt were. The sight of his tanned, muscled ass took her breath away. She'd seen many a werewolf naked, compared to the perfect form of his wide back, his angled hips… Looking away, she felt Owen's emotions grow angry and she didn't know if he'd picked up on her lusting after Ramo or the fact their adjudicator was making them all phase. Grayson smirked at the situation whereas everyone else tried to avoid what was happening by getting dressed.

Not being able to communicate, she stood in the middle of the room waiting for Owen to tell her what to do.

Owen glared at the adjudicator before tossing a look at Ramo. "Turn around Perez."

Dressed now, Ramo leaned his back against the wall and folded his arms. "You're not my alpha, Hunter."

She joined Owen in growling at Ramo.

Smirking, he said, "You can growl all you like, Vitale, but if you attack me in wolf form, you'll be arrested. Am I right officer?" He asked the uniformed cop, his eyes never leaving her.

The poor cop looked nervous as hell as he stared at her. "Mm...Mam...phase immediately or I'll have to detain you."

Without thinking, she stepped forward as though she could actually say something in her defense, which spooked the cop. He reached for his gun in his holster, but snarls from Ramo and Owen stopped him.

Cursing, Owen ordered, "Phase back, Elizabeth."

Glancing briefly at Ramo, who still glowered at the cop, she turned toward the wall and willed herself to transform. She felt the tightening in her limbs as they changed shape, her body vibrating as she shrank to human size.

When she was fully phased, she reached quickly for her clothes. As she threw on her shirt, she looked over her shoulder where Owen and the adjudicator were talking and then to where Ramo stood. He still leaned against the wall with his arms folded. And sure enough, his eyes were on her, his features expressionless.

Asshole!

Did he have no respect?

Of course he didn't.

Every other Were in the room had had the decency to duck their eyes, but not Ramo. He continued to stare boldly, and her skin tingled as though his gaze could physically touch.

She hurriedly dressed, heat flooding her cheeks, trying desperately not to imagine what he thought of her body. Although she'd completely ignored Ramo's diet tips, she had noticed her body becoming a bit more toned from their workouts.

Slipping on her yoga pants, she turned to listen in on the conversation being held at the door. She brushed her hair with her fingers and ignored Ramo's stare from the other side of the room, then she heard the cop say, "We have reason to believe one of your pack members has been in contact with a rogue Were…"

Her heart dropped to her stomach. *Please God. Don't mention my name. Please.*

From the corner of her eye, she saw Ramo's head pan to the trio by the door, then back to her. He was reading her and what he was picking up made him straighten. Uncrossing his arms, he spoke. "Are you sure your source wasn't talking about me? I'm not a Grayback, but I'm also not rogue."

The adjudicator spoke for the cop. "No Mr. Perez, Mr. Hunter made us aware of your presence in the city weeks ago."

The cop scrolled through his phone. "I just need to question one of your pack members and I'll be out of your way. Uhh…Ms. Vitale?" He looked around the room. All eyes turned toward her, leaving no question who she was.

"You must be mistaken," Owen began as Ramo slid his shirt on over his head and walked toward them. "What's this about?"

She tried to calm her racing heart as the adjudicator spoke up again. "As he said, there have been reports of a rogue werewolf in the city. We just need to question Ms. Vitale to see what she knows."

"She knows nothing," Owen said at once.

"Let us be the judge of that," the adjudicator said putting out a hand so that she could follow them out. "We will have to speak with you alone, Ms. Vitale."

Before she could nod her head, Ramo and Owen simultaneously said, "No!"

The man looked reproachfully to the two vocal men. "I'm sorry gentlemen, but only a relative can accompany her." He nodded to Owen, "As her alpha you may join her, but..." he looked suspiciously to Ramo.

"I'm her husband and I'm coming with." Ramo walked to the door and waited for them to step out.

She felt Owen's fury as his nostrils flared and he reached for her hand. Stiffening slightly at the contact, she allowed Owen to walk her out, ignoring the confused look on the adjudicator's face.

Behind her she heard Ramo mutter, "That's how we roll around here dude. Don't worry about it."

Shutting her eyes at how humiliating the whole scenario was, she couldn't help fear Ramo's anger at being cuckholded in front of everyone more than Owen's anger at her fraternizing with a rogue Were. It was this little tidbit that took her confused state of mind straight down to discombobulated.

Owen led them into a vacated office down the hall.

Ramo shut the door behind them and leaned against it, folding his arms over his chest again. His biceps bulged, the thick cords of his neck tensed.

He was nervous for her.

There were no chairs in the room so while everyone made a small circle in front of the desk, her eyes met Ramo's briefly. He couldn't have known what that one look did for her. As scared as she was right now, his look gave her strength, made her feel safe. Before she could process this, the cop spoke.

"Our sources tell us a rogue Were was seen in and around the city. As you know, packless werewolves are illegal…"

She rolled her eyes. It was illegal to be on your own instead of part of a pack. *Such bullshit.* She loved their pack and being a part of a community, but werewolves should be given a choice.

"Ms. Vitale, have you been in contact with this lone Were?"

"Who's your source?" Ramo asked.

The cop merely eyed Ramo, but didn't answer.

She held her answer as she thought of Jordan. Could she sell him out? The right thing to do would be to bring him in and see if they could help him, perhaps induct him into the Graybacks if he was willing. But he'd been so nervous when she'd suggested it. What if his pack came looking for him and tried to kill him? Could she bear the weight of his demise on her shoulders?

The men stared at her and she felt like a mischievous child. Now she knew how her students felt when she interrogated them. The feeling was horrible. They all glared, waiting for her to answer. Before she could think more on it, she decided to go with half the truth.

"Yes."

Owen let out a frustrated growl, stepping away as he ran his hand through his hair. "Jesus Christ!"

She ignored Owen's reaction, knowing she'd have to face the consequences of her actions later. With a quick glance to Ramo whose grave eyes never left hers, she tried to explain. "He…"

"He?" Owen and Ramo said simultaneously, which was becoming a silly habit of theirs.

"Yes, *he* came looking for me and asked for my help. His father knew my father years ago. He had nowhere to go and I helped him. I gave him some money and told him to be on his way. I don't know where he is now."

The adjudicator continued the line of questioning. "What pack was he from?"

"I don't know. He wouldn't tell me," she lied. Although he hadn't told her, she figured it out when he'd slipped and told her he was from Savannah.

"What's his name?"

"Jordan. He wouldn't tell me his last name," she answered, and this was true.

"Why would he go to you and not your alpha?"

Pushing her thick hair back over her shoulder, she said, "As I said, his father knew mine. I was the only person he knew of in the city." Looking to the cop, she reiterated, "I don't know where he is right now." Truthfully, she didn't know. He could be out to eat for all she knew, so that wasn't really lying.

"Can you tell us anything else he mentioned that might clue you in to where he was going?" the adjudicator asked.

"No, he just seemed really scared. I'm sorry. There's not much else I can tell you."

The officer gave her instructions to contact them if she heard anything else. As they were leaving, the adjudicator looked to Owen. "Mr. Hunter, I trust you'll deal with Ms. Vitale?"

Ramo straightened, looking from the adjudicator to Owen. "What do you mean?"

"We'll leave you to it then." The adjudicator said, ignoring Ramo as he and the officer walked out.

"What does he mean?" Ramo repeated, glaring now at Owen.

The Grayback alpha stared at the floor. "Perez, I need to speak to Elizabeth alone."

"Fuck no. What's going on?"

She sat on the edge of the desk and closed her eyes. "I disobeyed orders."

"No," Ramo said automatically.

"I did. I should have mentioned Jordan to Owen. It's the first thing I should have done." She looked at Owen but for once the alpha wouldn't meet her eyes.

"No," Ramo said again. "He never said it."

She looked to Ramo, incredulous.

"Owen, I doubt you ever said, 'Hey babe, love you in that dress. BTW…in case a lone Were shows up in town, don't mess with it, okay?'"

Owen finally spoke. "It's not that simple. It's against our laws and the human laws. You should have told me he was here, Elizabeth. Better yet, you should have run the other direction when you spotted him and come straight to me," he seethed.

Despondently, she nodded her head. "I know. I'm

sorry."

Stepping closer to her, Ramo said, "But she didn't disobey orders. Just because it's a law doesn't mean she disobeyed orders. You didn't make the law, Hunter. I know how this works. You have to say the order. You didn't."

"It doesn't matter. She withheld information, which could have jeopardized the entire Grayback community. FUCK!" Owen kicked a chair, upending it. The bang of the chair hitting the wall silenced them.

They all stood motionless, no one saying a word. They heard the other trainees' voices and footsteps as they left the gym and headed down the stairs. The sky outside had turned a deep blue as dusk descended on the city.

Owen stood with his back to her and in the quiet of the room, she and Ramo staring hard at each other. The realization of what Owen must do washed over them like an avalanche, numbing them.

She hardly knew this man, but his eyes were the only ones she wanted to see. His face held more for her in this moment than anything in the world ever had. In his eyes, she saw her own fear for he felt every emotion she was going through, if not more. He was terrified for her.

Why?

Why did he care so much? Why did he care so much now, when he didn't give a damn for ten years?

She realized the hurt and anger she felt when she thought of his leaving didn't feel as strong. It wasn't as if she'd forgiven him. Somehow, in the time they'd spent together, the time apart didn't sting as much, especially when they were facing so much. Aside from

Nightwalkers, now she had a punishment to endure. Jesus, what did she get herself into?

"What are you going to do?" Ramo's voice was deep and penetrating. His grim eyes were on her, but the question was for Owen.

Owen turned to face them, "I need to speak to her. Leave."

She watched as Ramo's eyes altered to a gleaming yellow, his lip curling as a guttural snarl escaped him.

This was why she wasn't afraid. He carried the worry she ought to be feeling.

"It's okay, Ramo," she soothed. It was the first time she said his name aloud. She felt Owen stiffen as something flashed in Ramo's eyes. The two men noticed it too.

Owen strode to the door and held it open for him. "You know I won't hurt her. Please, just leave us alone." His voice weary, he waited for Ramo to leave.

She stood in front of Ramo her gaze locked with his. She knew he didn't want to leave her. His face was taut as though the internal battle he was waging was nearly killing him.

Suddenly, Owen muttered, "I love her. Please. Give me a minute with my girl. I don't usually ask for anything, so you know this fucking sucks for me."

Pain twisted her heart at the words 'I love her'. It hit her at the same time Ramo's eyes doused and returned to their normal shade. He stared far off at something over her shoulder and she knew Owen's words echoed in his mind as much as hers.

"Okay," he uttered, his voice hoarse. Then, with his back to Owen, he mouthed *Call me.* She didn't respond as he turned and left, but they both knew she'd call him, and her traitorous heart was looking forward to it.

Owen shut the door and leaned against it, his hands balled at his sides. "Were you ever going to tell me?"

For a second, she didn't know what he meant. Instantly, her guilty heart thought he was speaking of Ramo. Was he referring to Ramo visiting her the other night? How can he possibly know?

"Elizabeth?" he prodded. "Were you ever going to tell me about the rogue?"

Oh.

"I wanted to. I really did, but he was so scared, Owen."

"What if he'd attacked you? Did it ever occur to you he was trying to use you to get to me? His pack could have sent him to infiltrate our pack and ambush us. Does he know about the Fighters we're forming?"

"No! I would never share something so critical to our pack. Owen, I only tried to keep him safe. He wasn't lying. I could tell..." She let out a deep breath, feeling guiltier by the second. "I'm so sorry Owen. I am. I'm even sorrier that you have to punish me. Believe me, I'll accept anything you do, and I won't hold it against you. I promise."

Bounding forward, he reached her, gripping her arms. Speaking through his teeth, he said, "You think I want to hurt you?"

Her hands fell to her chest as she stared pityingly at his expression. "I know you don't."

His voiced was strained, "I'm so pissed at you. How could you put me in this position?" He squeezed her arms, his face contorted in pain. "I have to, Elizabeth. I have to punish you."

All she could do was nod numbly.

****

An hour later she stepped into her apartment, dazed by the turn the day had taken. She could only utter a goodnight to her grandmother when she opened the door to see if she wanted anything to eat as she passed her door. She prayed she'd have the energy tomorrow to tell her what she'd done. By tomorrow, the entire pack would have an email about her impending punishment.

She could just imagine the gossip about how the alpha's girlfriend disobeyed orders. She didn't know what to expect tomorrow evening, but she knew the punishment would be severe and completely legal under werewolf law.

Her phone vibrated as she lay down on the sofa. Seeing Ramo's name, a thrill came over her. She was surprised she could feel any measure of excitement at the moment.

"Hello," she answered.

"Hey. You took too long." He sounded so different. His usually cool tone sounded tense and desolate. "What did he say?"

There was no reason to ask who 'he' was. As guilty as she felt for putting Owen through this, she felt horrid for doing this to Ramo. Now he'd have to watch his wife being tortured for being stupid enough to defy her alpha.

"Tomorrow night," she said. There was no point in defending Owen to Ramo. She was sure he didn't want to hear it.

She heard him curse and exhale a deep breath.

"I'm sorry," she said.

100

"For what?"

Pushing her head back further into the pillow, she stared at her ceiling, "For being stupid."

"I don't want you to be sorry. I want...I want to help." He paused for a moment before going on in a cool voice. "You know where this rogue is and you're going to tell me. But first, we're going to get through the punishment. I'm not a Grayback so I won't get the notice. Where is it going to be?"

It was a while before she found her voice. Somehow, he knew she'd been lying earlier today, and he wanted to know the truth, *and by God she'd give it to him.*

"The 606. Midnight," she said.

"Okay."

"You don't have to watch." She curled onto her side, the phone squeezed between the pillow and her ear.

"I'm going. Just promise me something?" his voice was calmer now. "Don't be nervous. Okay. Just, don't worry about it."

"I'm not nervous. Not really."

"Good." She heard the relief in his voice.

Closing her eyes, she listened to his deep breaths over the phone. It was quiet where he was, and she wondered if he was lying down too.

"What's happening?" she asked suddenly, surprising both of them.

The silence on the other end told her he knew what she meant. Why were they becoming so...close? Why did they both care so much for the other's wellbeing? Did he also feel the pull between them or was it just in her head?

It didn't make sense. She was taken. There was no reason why she should want to stay up all night on the phone with this man like a besotted teenager, but here she was, dreading the moment he'd end the call.

Finally, he whispered, "I don't know."

His answer warmed her insides for some reason, and she felt lightheaded with glee. He didn't know either, which meant he too felt completely baffled at their growing bond. What was more, he felt *something*.

For ten years she felt sorry for herself because the man she'd had an instant crush on when they'd met had left her feeling ugly and unwanted. Now, here he was...feeling things.

Letting out a long breath he sighed, "Bewilderment of the mind often enlightens the heart."

She cocked her head. "I know that quote."

"The Moonlight Chronicles," he said.

"Oh yeah. I read them with my students. We love the series. Are you a Moony?" she joked, referring to the name the series fanbase goes by.

He laughed. "I kinda have to be. J E Hernandez is my mother."

Her mouth hung open as she sat up. "Your mother is J E Hernandez? You're joking?"

"Nope."

"I've been reading the series since I was a kid. Oh my God! Will she sign my books? Is that weird to ask? Wow! I can't believe this." How did she not know this?

She could tell he was smiling as he said, "I can definitely get you signed copies. She'd love to do it."

"How did I not know this about you?"

"I'm not the author. She is."

"But...your mother's famous. They made all those

movies. Wait...you must be loaded. Holy shit."

This time his laugh came out loud and hard, the sound of it did funny things to her insides. "Uh...you can say that."

"So do you write too?" she asked, lying back on the cushions.

"Nah. Words aren't my thing. Aside from books I read in High School my mother's series were the only books I ever read."

"I guess you don't really have to, but do you work?" she asked.

"I'm an architect. I do a lot of jobs for my cousin's construction company. I'm taking a bit of a hiatus though to train you meat heads."

She shook her head, smirking at his name-calling.

They talked for nearly an hour about his family and she told him about her grandmother and what she was studying in grad school. He sounded genuinely interested in everything she said, asking the appropriate questions and laughing at her dumb jokes. It was easy to talk to him. There was a level of comfort around them, especially as he was so relaxed and cool. It was nice to talk to someone and not feel her awkward anxiety build up.

"All right, Vitale...I'm about to ruin this conversation" he said, his voice tired. She was positive he was lying down and couldn't get the image out of her head.

Frowning she said, "Why?"

"Because I have to ask about your boyfriend."

She sighed. "Is it really vital to ask about him?"

"Yes, it's *vital*, Vitale." He laughed. "Ha. I just got the meaning of your name."

She rolled her eyes. "Okay. What about him?"

The line went quiet for a moment before he asked, "Is it serious?"

"Ramo…" she began.

"Don't tell me it's none of my business because I have a piece of paper, which says otherwise."

She let out a frustrated breath. "Boy, you love to throw that in my face, don't you?"

"Yes. Now answer the question."

Squirming she said, "It's serious enough."

"What does that mean?"

"It means…it's been a few months and we're invested."

There was a pause before he asked, "Are you in love with him?"

"I'm done with this," she replied.

"I'm not."

Groaning, she said, "Why do you want to know?"

"I'm nosey. I like to know everything."

"Well, considering I'm about to be punished for disobeying my alpha, I'm going to pay him some respect by not discussing this with you."

There was a long pause before he said, "So you're not in love with him."

"What?"

"If you were, you'd have said so. Weres who are in love shout it from the rooftops," he said, a matter of fact.

She had no response, and they were both quiet as his statement hung between them. Listening to his measured breaths through the phone sent chills down her back and she wondered what he was wearing or if his arm was draped over his head or rested on his chest…

"One more question and I'll let you sleep," he said. His deep voice tickled her ear.

"Yes?"

Clearing his throat he asked, "Does he make you happy?"

Surprised by his question, she thought about it for a while and could not think of a single answer. She guessed she was happy. She wasn't unhappy. "I think so."

"Mmm…" he purred.

"Ramo, why does this matter to you?" she asked.

Sighing, he answered, "Because I did the unimaginable to you and I hope you've found some happiness to drown the hurt I caused."

Damn.

He was wrong. He *was* good with words.

Speechless, she closed her eyes, wanting to tell him again she was fine, no harm done. The truth was, though, he had hurt her and she was sick of carrying on with her façade.

"But that's a topic for another night, Vitale," he said.

Thankful she didn't have to talk about it, she told him goodnight and hung up.

Under the covers in her bed, she didn't think of the torture she'd have to endure tomorrow evening, but of the man who would stand by her.

If only her traitorous heart would think of her boyfriend and not her husband.

Chapter Seven

The next day, Ramo mulled over the shitty coincidence of going through another werewolf torture in such a short amount of time. When this was over with, he was going to campaign against torturing Weres as a method of punishment.

Switching his phone to his left ear, he said into the receiver, "Are you sure? Please tell me you're absolutely fucking sure man."

Adam's voice replied, "Yeah Ram, I'm sure. I'm emailing the document now."

Ramo ran his hand through his hair in relief. Unable to sit, he paced the living room.

"Thank God."

Adam's voice said through the phone, "I'm CCing Danny. He'll need to be there to represent the pack." Hesitating, he continued, "You know I'd be there for you man, but…"

He waved a hand in the air as if his cousin could see him. "I know. Two alphas in the same vicinity is madness. Don't worry about it."

After hanging up, he stared at his phone. The urge to call her was so damn overwhelming, but something held him back.

No. Not something. Someone.

What if Owen was with her? Even worse, what if Owen answered her phone? Would he do that?

Considering she'd been in contact with a lone werewolf, who knew what her alpha would do to ensure she still wasn't in communication with him.

He found the last message she'd sent him, which wasn't on the trainee thread. It was a simple, LOL with several exclamation marks.

Wanting nothing more than to make her laugh again, he texted her and he didn't give two shits if her alpha saw his message.

—I think your punishment should be to bang erasers together. Serves a teacher right. That shit sucks.—

Waiting for her to text back, he sat at his desk near the window and fired up his laptop to print out the document Adam sent.

When her text came in, he reached for his phone way too quickly.

She responded with a laughing emoji and,

—Schools haven't had chalkboards in years, grandpa. Whiteboards.—

Letting out a hearty laugh, he responded back.

—Ah. I take it you don't slap books against their hands either, huh. Shame.—

He didn't turn off his phone but stared as she texted him back.

—Nope. We make them reflect on their behavior.—

He smirked as he responded with an emoji rolling its eyes.

—What if he makes you reflect on the wonder that is Owen? Now that's torture!—

—Be nice.—

—Nah. It's more fun to be an asshole.—

—You're so good at it.—

—You know it. ;)—

Ramo left his condo close to midnight and walked to the nearest entrance of the 606. The 606 was an elevated path where Chicagoans rode their bikes, ran, and basically took in a beautiful day in the city. Never having walked the path as it was fairly new, he had to admit how neat it was to enjoy a long path through the city, overlooking neighborhood rooftops.

His senses told him a large group was gathered about a mile down. Heading west along the path, he shook off the bitter cold, trying to pick up Elizabeth's scent. Finding it instantly as he was more aware of her scent than his own, he detected her anxiety and a cold pain ran down his spine.

The feeling was foreign to him and without a doubt, totally and completely frightening. There was no reason he should care so much about her; so much he couldn't stand it. Balling his fists, he felt his muscles contract as pure wrath radiated from him.

She should not be here. She should not be enduring this fear just because she tried to help out some dumb shit.

And Owen…how the hell could he go through with this? Could he really watch her suffer?

As he neared the crowd, his heart rate accelerated as he honed in on Elizabeth. Her back was to the metal railing and Owen stood beside her as the other pack members spread out along the path. Some were huddled together clearly gossiping while others simply stood with their arms crossed sporting solemn expressions.

Elizabeth's eyes rose as he drew closer and his stomach knotted like his insides were arm wrestling. She didn't purse her lips or roll her eyes per usual.

There was no upturned nose or hard look his way either. Instead, her features were soft, her eyes locked on his. Without reading her emotions he could tell she was relieved to see him. And was that longing lurking behind her gaze? He bit down hard, reeling at the way her gaze made him feel.

Damn it. He wanted to go to her and hug her. Never in his life had he wanted to hold a woman just to soothe her and not for other reasons.

Pausing a few feet away from them, he barely spared Owen a glance as he said, "So what's it gonna be?" Looking around, there were no visual torture devices.

Kicking a black bag pack on the ground by his feet, Owen said, "In here."

Glaring at the bag like it offended him, he asked scathingly, "What fits in there?"

Owen just frowned at the concrete.

You've gotta be fucking kidding me! "A whip? Seriously?" Feeling his blood boil, he looked to Owen then to Elizabeth. "She's your girlfriend. You couldn't find something less severe?"

"The only thing for miles was the Pillory and your alpha burned it to the ground," he snapped.

Ramo's head cocked back in surprise. The last werewolf to be tortured in the Pillory was his fellow Fighter, Jason. It had killed Adam to do it, so it made sense Adam had destroyed it, but now Elizabeth's punishment would be worse.

For centuries, werewolves tortured those who disobeyed their alpha with medieval devices. Thankfully, there weren't a lot left or being remade. A whip however was pretty common and easy to find.

Ramo looked at Elizabeth. Her beautiful face was pale, her eyes dead on the ground. Without thinking he reached for her arm, but before he could make contact, Owen's growl stopped him.

Flinching, he balled his fist, irritated as fuck that this man was keeping him from touching his own wife.

WTF! How did he let this happen?

He would have been better off not coming back to Chicago, but the fact was he was here, in her life. He didn't know how this whole thing would end up, but he was beginning to think he couldn't leave no matter what happened.

The other Graybacks started to snarl, some pacing side to side as they sensed another Were coming toward them.

"He's with me," he called out, taking his eyes off Elizabeth to nod at his fellow Fighter, Danny Amato.

Danny strolled toward him in his detective gear including duty belt and bulletproof vest. Clasping hands, he thanked his friend for coming as the other pack members seethed around them.

"What is he doing here?" Owen asked, regarding Danny as if he were dirt on his shoe.

"Don't worry about him. He's here for me." Ramo answered.

"Why?"

"Because a Blacktail must be here to witness a pack member's punishment."

Owen narrowed his eyes. "Elizabeth isn't a Blacktail."

Ramo reached for the bag on the ground and took out the whip. Shoving it into Owen's hand he said, "Elizabeth isn't getting punished today. I am."

****

What?

Elizabeth gaped at Ramo as though she didn't know who he was. Had she heard him right?

Fisting the whip, Owen glared at Ramo. "What are you talking about?"

Reaching into the back pocket of his jeans, Ramo took out a folded piece of paper and handed it to Owen. "According to our bylaws, a werewolf is permitted to take the punishment in place of a spouse. So..." He held out his hands and smiled. "Let's do this."

She shook her head mutely, not believing for one second this man, the man who'd left her would willing do this for her.

He gave her a boyish grin, "I told you not to worry about it."

Finally, she found her voice. "No." Stepping closer to him, she said, "You're joking."

He gave her a sidelong glance. "This would be a terrible joke, Vitale. Give me some credit."

"Are you crazy? You can't do this."

His eyes blazed as he looked at her, but he said nothing.

"Owen! Tell him this is ridiculous." She pleaded.

Her alpha finished reading the document and folded it, relief and annoyance emanating from him. "He's right," he said, resignedly. Turning, he walked a few feet away to a spot on the other side of the path. "Let's get this over with."

"No!" she shot back at Owen. "This was my doing. I should be the one to take the punishment."

Owen merely glared at the ground, slapping the whip against his thigh in agitation. She was surprised to

111

feel envy radiate from him. He wanted to be the one to take the punishment for her, not Ramo. But once again, their marriage stood in his way.

Swinging her gaze to Ramo again, she tried to get him to understand, but the look he gave her told her he was not going to budge on this.

Taking off his t-shirt, which read, *Surely Not Everybody Was Kung Fu Fighting*, she watched his tanned torso elongate as it slipped over his head, his thick biceps rippling as he slid his forearms through the sleeves, his piercing gaze locked on hers.

Shoving his shirt into her hands, he said. "Hold this." Underneath the shirt, his fingers squeezed hers and she almost latched onto him. It was the first time he'd touched her in ten years and her heart rate accelerated, her fingers still tingling when he let go.

Shaking her head in astonishment, she whispered, "Why?"

The corner of his mouth curled up and he whispered back. "You really think I was gonna let anyone put their hands on you."

Her heart slammed against her chest. Hugging his shirt at her midriff, she said, "You're insane."

Laughing, he winked at her before turning and strolled to where Owen waited. Over his shoulder he called to her, "Now don't go sniffing my shirt, Vitale…"

Owen snarled at him.

"…And don't spill anything on it either. I like that shirt."

She let out a harsh breath. How could he joke at a time like this?

A light, cool breeze hit her face and she fell back

against the railing as if she were pushed, squeezing his shirt in her hands.

She watched as he gripped the metal railing with both hands, his broad shoulders flexing. Her gaze roamed over the sinewy muscles of his back, his intricate tattoo, the dark skin so perfectly smooth she bit back a moan at the thought of it being marred because of her.

Feeling eyes on her, she glanced around at Danny Amato who was staring at her. At first, she thought he stared with contempt, but was surprised to feel understanding. Giving her a clip nod, his expression told her he agreed with his pack member and to just deal with it.

If possible, she shrank further into herself, hating she was the reason Ramo would suffer tonight. Suddenly angry she shouted, "Everyone leave!"

Owen and Ramo looked around in surprise.

She only had eyes for Ramo as she spoke, "Ramo is not a Grayback therefore they don't need to be here. Please. Leave."

From her peripheral vision, she saw Owen nod then gesture to everyone to clear the area. No one uttered a word as they trudged along the path in both directions.

"Thank you," Danny uttered to Elizabeth, his focus on Ramo as well.

When it was just the four of them, Owen cleared his throat. "You can leave too, Elizabeth. You don't have to watch this."

Shaking her head vigorously, she said, "I'm not going anywhere."

Ramo's chest swelled as his eyes bore into hers. "Go," he said, softly, cocking his head to indicate she leave. "I'll tell you all about it later."

A tear slipped down her cheek, "I can't."

God she wanted to rush to him, but it would only prolong the inevitable. She realized then, *she'd* never touched *him*. It was he who'd placed his hand at her back on their wedding day; who'd gripped her hand just now.

Jesus, the urge to feel him beneath her fingertips was so overwhelming she thought she might burst from the agony of it. The need to touch him, smell him, taste... Why was she overcome with such desire at a time like this?

Undoubtedly sensing her need, the bastard winked at her before turning around again. Hoping Owen mistook her need for Ramo as a need to comfort, she held her breath as her alpha placed himself in position behind him...

...raised his arm...

...and swung the whip onto his perfect back.

The tears were unbidden now, a torrential river down her cheeks.

The whip struck again, and his muscles flinched, but he didn't utter a sound.

The next swipe cut through his beautiful tattoo and fury laced through her for ruining the design.

Again and again, Owen struck; each hit shattering a piece of her. *His beautiful skin*, she chanted, over and over in her head. Trembling as she watched, she didn't notice she cried out till he called to her in weak voice. "Shut up, Vitale. I'll heal."

She knew he was trying to make her laugh by being crude, but it didn't work. She took his insult as an endearment and only ached for him more.

Owen struck again, adding another harsh crimson line across his back.

Hugging herself, she bent forward as her wails of grief echoed around them. When had she fallen to her knees? The moment felt so surreal. How had this all begun? She was crying for her estranged husband who she hated and couldn't remember how they'd gotten here.

Owen struck again, this time, bringing Ramo to his knees. His hands turned white as he gripped the railing with all his might, struggling to stay upright.

The sound of cracking bones filled the air and she vaguely felt her limbs stretching. She didn't know how it happened, but one minute she was curled into herself on her knees and the next she was crouched on all fours, staring at Ramo's battered skin.

"Elizabeth!"

The sound of someone shouting her name barely registered.

"Elizabeth! Don't do it!"

Don't do what?

"I swear to God, Elizabeth. This will only make things worse."

Owen. It was Owen speaking to her. What was he talking about?

From the corner of her eye she saw Danny take a step back. Whipping her head around she saw that the cop held his hands up, glaring at her. "I can't phase on duty, Elizabeth. If you attack me, it'll only make more trouble for you."

Attack? What was going on?

She looked to Owen to see if he could explain, then saw him recoil. "Stand the fuck down, Elizabeth! That's an order!" he shouted.

Whimpering, she bowed her head to him, trying to understand what was happening.

"Don't hurt her," she heard Ramo say in an agonized whisper.

"Hurt *her*? She almost mauled us," Owen said, his eyes watchful on her.

Try as she might, she could not recall the last few minutes. The last thing she remembered was Ramo hitting the ground...

...And the second he fell to the ground, her vision had altered, then...Well she could piece together the rest. As she was in full werewolf form and her throat hurt, she could deduce she'd gone all beast mode on Owen and Danny.

But the torture had stopped. She didn't care about anything else, as long as Owen had stopped hitting Ramo.

"Can you phase back?" Owen asked quietly, already knowing the answer.

She shook her head, taking a cautious step forward.

"Hey!" Owen shouted.

Shaking her head again, she forced her emotions to scream the fact she was okay now. She just needed to check on Ramo.

Understanding dawned on Owen and he nodded his head in permission.

She walked to him on all fours, as he lay on his side facing her. "Well look at you," he said, his half-lidded eyes on her. "Jesus, you really are a stunning wolf!"

The compliment threw her, and she hesitated as she approached him. She was bigger than him in her Were form, but despite this, he did not cower from her. In fact, his eyes brightened as he gazed at her.

His hand twitched and she knew he wanted to touch her but didn't dare around Owen. She didn't care, however, if Owen despised her for what she was about to do. Her only thought was of taking the pain away for Ramo.

Gently, she nudged his shoulder down with her snout so that he turned onto his stomach. Ramo's cheek lay on the ground, his jaw tense and waiting. Ignoring the rising growl from her alpha, she began to lick the wounds from his back.

He hissed at first contact, then groaned as her touch alleviated some of the pain. Every cut she touched was her apology, her gratitude for what he'd done. As she worked her way around his marred skin, she listened to his strained breaths, watched the rise and fall of his shoulders, knowing this intimate gesture was affecting him as much as he was affecting her.

"That's enough!" Owen ordered.

Instantly, she stopped, but did not back away.

Sitting up, gingerly, Ramo leaned back against the railing. Bending one leg at the knee, she noticed his cheeks were flushed. Eyeing her through his lashes, he said, "Thanks." He'd heal faster now that she'd helped him.

His eyes roamed around her and she knew he wanted to run his hands through her mane. The wanting overwhelmed his pain.

Her head spun in Danny's direction as he approached. The cop froze when she bared her fangs, snarling.

Ramo's deep chuckle calmed her. "Damn, that's

hot." He winced as his laughter must have caused him pain. "Down girl," he joked. "Danny won't hurt me. He's just gonna take me home."

Standing to her full height, she towered over him as she offered her paw, helping him up off the ground. He stretched out a hand to lean against the railing, panting at the effort it took to stand. Looking up at her, he smirked shaking his head. The jerk was loving the attention. "Never thought I'd feel intimidated and turned on at the same time." He bit his bottom lip as he watched her.

"Take him home," Owen ordered, his voice hard and cold.

Danny gave Owen a hard look over his shoulder. His features softened as he turned to her. "I need to take him now and you need to phase back. It's against the law. You'll be able to once he's out of here."

Nodding, she stared at Ramo, not too keen on him leaving her with an irate alpha.

"Lessons are still on for tomorrow," Ramo said wearily as he draped an arm over Danny's shoulders. Eyeing her he added, "Don't be late." Then, the two men walked together down the path heading east.

The further he moved away from her, the less worried she became, knowing he was in good hands. Without looking at Owen, she phased back.

Wrapping her arms to cover her chest she looked around at her torn clothes scattered all over the path.

Owen came up behind her and slid his shirt over her head and down her torso. It reached to just above her knees. Turning, she finally met his eyes.

He stood before her, shirtless and seething, but did not say a word. He was a cyclone of rage, jealousy, and lust. She stared blindly at his chest waiting for the onslaught. Would he punish her privately? He could if he wanted to. No one would know. It would be the end of them, but if he demanded she stay with him, what choice did she have?

No. Owen was better than that. He wouldn't force himself on her. He was just hurt right now. Her alpha had watched as she cried over Ramo and then almost attacked him. What was worse, Owen allowed her to heal Ramo when she'd licked his wounds. Guilt oozed from her and she met his eyes.

Owen was staring at her mouth and the look of disgust on his face terrified her.

She flinched as he brought his hand to the side of her face. Cradling her cheek, his thumb pressed roughly over her mouth, rubbing back and forth as he tried to wipe away Ramo's scent.

Tears stung her eyes as his other hand curled around her hair at the base of her neck, pulling her head back.

"I'm sorry, Owen. Please. I'm so sorry. I couldn't…" she didn't know what she could say to make him feel better.

"Shhh…" he whispered, menacingly. "I'm not going to hurt you Elizabeth."

"You're angry," she said, stupidly, stating the obvious.

He nodded, both hands massaging her head, his fingers laced in her hair. If he wanted, he could crush her skull in second.

Despite the fact she trusted him, he was still scaring her.

His eyes traced her features as he bit his bottom lip.

"I don't know if I can take it anymore." Bringing her flush against him, he hugged her in a painful embrace. Whispering in her ear he said, "I can't fucking stand that he's here. I hate the way he looks at you. I hate the way you look at him. The son of a bitch actually had a hard on when you put your precious mouth on his back. Do you have any idea what that did to me?" Trembling now, he added, "Tell me you love me, Elizabeth. I need to hear you say it. Tell me now."

"I love you, Owen. Please. I'm sorry. I love you."

Too consumed with Ramo's sacrifice, she said what Owen needed to hear, but she didn't know if she said it with genuine love or fear.

Chapter Eight

Owen drove her home in silence. Too frightened to speak, she gazed out the window, begging her traitorous emotions to remain silent. She kept her mind blank, noting the snow had completely melted off the ground. Weather. *Focus on the weather*, she told herself.

When he walked her up to her apartment, she was surprised he followed her in. Quite frankly, she thought she sickened him at the moment. When he headed down the hall to her bedroom she froze.

"Get into bed, Elizabeth. It's late."

Heart hammering, she followed him into her room.

He sat at the foot of her bed, hands clasped with his elbows on his knees. Head bent, he said, "Nothing's going to happen. I just need to be here for a bit."

Calming some, she grabbed a change of clothes, went into the bathroom and turned on the shower. Her head hurt from crying all night and her body was exhausted from being up so late.

She sighed heavily as she stepped into the shower. Ramo's scent wafted around her and her stomach muscles tightened. Squeezing her eyes she fought not to think of him. She couldn't. Not with Owen in the next room. Her alpha was hurting too much. She'd obviously not hidden her growing feelings from her boyfriend very well.

Throwing on a black tank and gray pajama bottoms

pants so as not to flaunt too much skin around Owen, she brushed her wet hair then turned out the light.

He was in the same position at the foot of her bed.

Slipping under the covers, she lay on her side, facing the window and the waxing moon.

They listened to each other's breathing as each was lost in their own thoughts.

Owen finally broke the silence. "Do you know how troubling it is to feel gratitude for someone you hate?"

Understanding what he meant, she tried to put herself in his shoes. How would she feel if she had to hurt him and some other woman stepped in and sacrificed herself for her boyfriend? As hard as she tried, she'd never be able to grasp how he really felt, but it had to be all kinds of fucked up.

"I'm so relieved you weren't hurt. I am. Christ, I didn't sleep last night, thinking of every possible way to get you out of this and here comes Ramo with the perfect plan. Shit. He doesn't even know you and he was willing to go through physical pain for you. You can't help but admire someone like that and yet my hatred for him has only deepened."

He really needed to stop talking about Ramo before her emotions gave her away. With her eyes locked on the moon, she thought of the upcoming full moon and where she would run that night.

Owen broke into her thoughts again. "I need you," he said softly.

Stiffening, she looked at his back hunched over his knees.

"I can't wait much longer. Especially now. I just can't. I seriously want to piss all around your damn room right now, that's how territorial I'm feeling."

She licked her dry lips. "I know this isn't fair to you. I'll understand…"

He cut her off. "No." Getting up he came to kneel on the floor on her side of the bed. "This will not be the end for us. I'll wait. But not long. We'll go slow. I promise."

He pulled her to him and kissed her gently. Pressing his forehead against hers he said, "I need to go before I completely lose it. I'll pick you up tomorrow for training." He kissed her again. "I love you, Elizabeth."

She lay in the same position as he left her room, then her apartment. She listened as he walked down the stairs, toward his car and then off down the street. As the sound of his car faded, she leapt from the bed, threw on a sweater and gym shoes and ran out the front door.

Ramo's condo wasn't too far from where she lived. She'd walked halfway before finding a cab. The condo was a duplex up with wide front windows. The lights were off in his duplex, but she could sense he was there. Ringing the doorbell with trembling hands, she waited.

A buzzer went off a moment later and she let herself in. Walking up the short steps to his door, she opened it and closed it behind her as she took in the beautiful home that could have been hers.

To her right sat an espresso wood desk with a laptop and printer set on top in front of huge bay windows looking out onto the quaint street. Along the wall facing her hung a flat screen television much bigger than hers at home. An old black and white movie was on, but it must have been muted because she didn't hear any sound coming from it. Facing the television was a gray sectional with tons of pillows.

"Vitale?" Ramo's weak voice came from the other side of the couch. The sectional was so large she couldn't tell he was on it from where she stood.

Coming around to face him, her eyes took in everything. He lay on his side, still shirtless and in jeans, his cell phone in his hand. He must have buzzed her in from an app on his phone. His arm not hidden under a plush pillow was the tattooed one from shoulder to wrist and down his side to his hip.

"What are you doing here?" he asked, trying to look amused, but it was clear he was still in pain.

Seeing him at home in his element was doing things to her brain. Hadn't she wondered what he did in his spare time? What his home looked like? She didn't want to wonder what it would have been like to live here with him, but here she was, standing in the home he'd bought for her.

"Let me have a look at your back," she said, taking off her sweater and throwing it over the ottoman in front of him.

"Uh…if you're going to lap at my back again, I will take no responsibility for what I'll do to you," he smirked.

Her heart leapt at his words and for the first time in God knows how long she felt very warm between her legs. Trying to ignore his devilish grin, she sat on the ottoman and reached for his arm. Pausing before she touched him for the first time, she fought the building excitement fused with apprehension. When she gently gripped his shoulder to turn him around his warm skin tensed beneath her fingers.

Bending forward to take a look at his wounds she

inhaled his heady scent and the heat boiling inside her made her stomach clench. She held her breath and focused on his wounds.

"Are you in pain?" she asked, breathily.

"It's not bad," he said, giving her a sly wink. "Thanks to you I'll heal completely by morning."

"Do you have any Tylenol?" she asked.

"Yeah. In the kitchen cabinet by the microwave." He gestured over his head to the spotless kitchen with brand new appliances and shiny black granite.

Getting up, she busied herself in the kitchen, getting him water and two Tylenol. When she handed them to him, he thanked her and took them without argument, wincing slightly as he shifted against the cushions.

Taking the glass from him, she set it on the floor.

"Vitale?" Ramo stared up at her, his chestnut eyes glowing from the glare of television. "Why are you here?" he asked again, his gaze tired but watchful.

Staring at the elaborate tattoo on his arm, she shook her head. What did one say to their estranged husband after he'd sacrificed himself for them? "I can't believe you..." She let out a shaky breath. "You have no idea..."

"Hey." He forced her to meet his eyes. "It was nothing. I'd do it every day if it kept you from getting hurt."

"Don't say things like that."

"I'll say whatever I want," he raised an eyebrow mischievously at her.

Taking a deep breath, she looked at his tattoo again, which flanked his broad side, going over his shoulder, up to his neck, and down his arm. "What is this?" she asked pointing at the elaborate tattoo,

"It's Polynesian. I was stationed at Pearl Harbor for a few years. It was my first tattoo. It represents rebirth." He pointed to the arm under him. "The ones on this arm represent our unit rank during World War II."

"You were in the Navy?"

"Yes mam," he smirked, the dimple on his right cheek making an appearance. "Twenty years."

Tilting her head she reached for his other wrist and turned it to look at his forearm. "And this?"

Adjusting himself carefully on his side he said, "All the Blacktail Fighters have a moon tattoo on their forearms. The alpha on his neck."

"Do you have any more?"

He gave her a roguish grin.

She looked at him reproachfully.

"Kidding." He pointed to his calf he couldn't reach. "I have an anchor on this leg." Then, he drew his jeans up to the leg he could reach to reveal another large tattoo. It was a pretty cool image of an open book. Taking a closer look she recognized the words from the Moonlight Chronicles.

"Is that a page from your mother's book?"

"Of course. Proud of her."

"That's the quote you mentioned the other night." She read the words written in bold down his leg. *Bewilderment of the mind often enlightens the heart.*

"Yeah." He dropped his jeans down his leg and draped his arm over his head. She had a great view of the elaborate tattoo on his side, running over his sinewy muscles. She took a deep breath as he went on.

"My mother was Buddhist for a time in the seventies. Buddhists believe we create our own cyclical existence. We operate out of basic misunderstanding or some shit like that. So, in order to understand the suffering of our bewildered mind, we have to have had enough of it. In order to say enough is enough, we have to go on a journey before we can see clearly." He shook his head and smirked. "My mom was a big hippy back then."

She smiled back.

"I'd been rereading my mother's books after my grandfather died. It always made me happy to read them and that line resonated with me." He eyed her curiously, then, taking a deep breath he went on. "My grandfather killed himself shortly after my grandmother died. We were really close. I started meditating at my mother's insistence and reading her books and their underlying message...I thought it would help me understand what he'd been going through, but till this day, I still don't get it. I said the same to my mom and she said I'll understand when I go on my journey and lose my heart." Rolling his eyes, he shrugged.

"So you got a tattoo of something you didn't understand?" she smirked.

He laughed. "Yeah."

The boyish grin on his face was really distracting. He must have sensed what he was doing to her because his smile faded, his eyes becoming dark and hooded.

"I should go."

She made to stand, but he stopped her, reaching for her hand. "Don't."

Utterly frozen by his touch she watched as he locked their hands, his eyes on their fingers as he caressed her skin slow and agonizingly sweet. Her heart rate quickened. She wondered how a simple touch could feel so amazing.

"Can I ask you something personal?" he said.

Not understanding what was happening she watched him study their fused hands, his strong fingers gentle on hers. "Sure," she whispered.

"Have you and Owen..." His fingers squeezed hers, his jaw hardening.

"No," she answered immediately.

His eyes shot to hers, taking in every feature and she wished she could read his mind. "Why not?"

Looking away, she felt embarrassment rush through her.

"Elizabeth?"

Her given name on his lips was her undoing. It was as though he were the one to name her, not her parents and her name finally had meaning. Before she knew it, she was spilling all to him. "I have anxiety attacks. Pretty bad. Every time we get close..." she eyed him nervously, but Ramo's expression remained impassive. "I don't know. It triggers my anxiety."

"We're close now. How do you feel?" he asked, his face genuinely curious.

She furrowed her brow. "I feel fine. I've never felt that sort of panic with you. Well...when I first saw you on the street, but nothing after that." She didn't want to delve too much on this particular fact.

His head shifted over the pillow to get a better look at her. "Do you get this only with Hunter?"

"No, it's happened before." She stared at their hands and let him figure out what she meant by that.

"Elizabeth, are you saying you haven't been with anyone intimately since your anxiety started?"

She shook her head.

"Why?" his voice was tense, his eyes so eager on hers.

"I have a theory."

Pulling her hand, he held it in both of his, tenderly messaging her palm. "Tell me," he demanded.

Taking a deep breath, she said, "Every time I'd let a guy get too close to me after you left, I felt...guilty. Like I was betraying you. After a while, it would cause this feeling of anxiety and then progressed into full on panic attacks."

He frowned, his brows pinched. "Have you ever been with a man? Ever?"

"No." She released his hand, overcome by their indecent conversation.

He wasn't done with her hand and yanked it back. "Look at me."

Rolling her eyes, she said, "I don't need to see you gloat that I've remained faithful to my deserting husband."

"I'm not gloating. I'm...mesmerized."

She gave him an exasperated look.

"Elizabeth?"

She stiffened.

His eyes were glazed over all of a sudden, his tone different now. She waited on bated breath as he uttered his next words in the huskiest, sexiest voice she'd ever heard.

"I want to kiss you."

Her body hummed with desire at his words, and as much as she wanted to straddle his huge body and have her way with him, she did not move.

Do it. Don't do it. God, please, do it.

"But if I kiss you, I won't be able to stop, and your

intimacy problems will be a thing of the past."

She could only gape at him.

"Thank you for checking on me, but if you want to remain a virgin, you need to leave."

"Ramo…" she uttered.

"I mean it, Elizabeth." He nodded toward his waist and she saw the thick bulge straining under the denim.

Nodding, she stood and grabbed her sweater pausing at the door, she was just going to say goodbye, but he said, "Goodbye, Vitale."

She left.

****

Training the next day went fairly smooth. No one mentioned the night before although a few people snickered at Elizabeth when she wasn't looking. Ramo only pushed those pricks harder.

There was a tense moment when Owen showed up to the gym twenty minutes early to thank him for what he'd done for Elizabeth, then gave him a subtle warning to stay away from her.

Aside from the fact his wife was in a relationship with an alpha to another pack and said alpha was in love with her, (cue the nausea) he couldn't stop thinking about her confession to him. No way in hell did he ever expect her to stay faithful to *him*.

Jesus Christ! She was still a virgin. When she'd admitted this colossal truth last night he wanted to tear her clothes off and fuck her raw. What saved her from his losing it was her virginity, his injury, and a tiny fraction that gave a rat's ass about the Grayback alpha.

He tracked her every movement from the minute she walked in the door; on time for a change. Elizabeth always walked into a room in a rush with a sheepish smile. Her smile brightened as Sharjeel greeted her. She was always so welcoming with others.

Her eyes shot to his over Sharjeel's shoulder and he knew she was remembering last night and his arousal for her. Although the most intimate thing they'd done last night was hold hands, he felt like it had been so much more.

Shaking his head at his girlish thoughts, he focused on the hand to hand combat they'd be covering tonight.

An hour into their lesson, Owen got a call from a state trooper friend who'd spotted some unusual movement off of the 90 expressway.

Putting his hatred for the guy aside, Ramo stepped up. "I'll come with you." About to call a halt to the day's lesson, Owen cut him off.

"No," Owen said. "Finish the lesson. This is more important. I'll take Joe." His eyes met Elizabeth's concerned face. "It's fine. I'll be back as soon as I can."

After the Grayback alpha left, Elizabeth looked at him nervously, but not to worry her, he scrunched up his face and shook his head at her as if it were no big deal.

In all honesty, Ramo didn't like the idea of Owen and his beta going out there alone. As a trained Fighter, Ramo had more experience. He had half a mind to take the trainees out there for a field exercise, but they weren't ready. Truth be told, he didn't want Elizabeth anywhere near danger, especially around Nightwalkers.

As hot as it was to watch her fight with the other trainees, every time her partner knocked her down or managed to deliver a hit to her flawless skin he wanted to smash them into a wall. When she'd get hurt he had to turn his head so the others wouldn't notice the rage in his expression. Even now, her partner just swept her leg and she fell hard on her side.

He took it out on an unsuspecting trainee who'd stopped to drink some water, keeping Elizabeth in his peripheral vision. This insane part of him wanted to pick her up and cradle her in his arms till the pain went away. Hell if she got a paper cut, he'd shred the piece of shit paper and then light it on fire. Thank God they worked on mats or he'd rip apart every trainee that touched her.

Without Owen glaring at him, he felt free to ogle Elizabeth as she continued to spar with Kylen, delivering a nice push kick, which gave him a perfect view of her glutes in action. The yoga pants she wore hugged her round bottom and luscious thighs impeccably. All of a sudden, he wanted to be holding her for another reason.

Rubbing the back of his neck in utter sexual frustration, he ended class, letting them know he'd email them with the new location and time for the next lesson.

Elizabeth walked to the window, peering outside. She must have been checking if Owen was there to pick her up.

"I can drive you home if you want." Ramo said, hoping she'd say no.

Spinning around, she looked surprised to see they were the only ones left in the gym. "Thanks, but I should wait for Owen." Turning back to stare out the window, her racing heart and heavy breaths were not lost on him.

Nodding, he let his eyes roam over her back and her voluptuous ass, remembering how beautiful it looked when he'd brazenly watched her dress the other day. He seriously wished he were a sculptor because she'd be the perfect model. As though her body were reeling him in, he crossed the hardwood floor and sat on the windowsill close to where she stood; his back to the glass.

"You don't have to stay, I can wait alone," she said, her voice trying to cover her nerves.

"I'm not leaving you here by yourself." He crossed his arms and looked around the room. "I don't mind waiting with you."

She nodded. "Thanks."

He had an odd feeling he was on a first date or some shit and he scrambled for something to talk about. "So when do you graduate?"

She looked at him oddly. "May. I told you this, remember? I'm not going to the graduation and you scolded me about walking on stage."

"Oh yeah." That's right. He sucked at small talk.

They were quiet for a while as he searched for something profound to say to her. He felt like every private moment should be filled with more...just...more.

He came up with, "Why don't you want to walk on stage?" He was a fucking waste a space. *Seriously?*

As if she knew he was reaching, she looked at him pointedly, "I don't know. Why did you leave me at the altar?"

Ouch.

He sooo deserved that.

Shaking her head as if she were trying to shake off the sudden anger she was feeling, she said, "Sorry. I don't know why I... Just forget it."

Chewing the inside of his mouth as he nodded at the floor, he knew they'd have to talk about this sometime. He owed her an explanation, but how could he put what he felt into words; words, which would undoubtedly hurt her.

"You were eighteen, Elizabeth. I had been a bachelor for over eighty years and all of a sudden, I'm married to a kid." She flinched at the word 'kid'. "I know how it sounds but put yourself in my shoes...I didn't know you. You were...are from another pack and when I saw you, standing there terrified next to your dad and so young, I thought...How could I do this to someone so beautiful?"

The way she gazed at him pulled at his wicked heart.

Before he could stop himself, he kept going, spilling way too much truth. "I didn't like the way I felt when I looked at you. It felt wrong, ugly. Here I was several years your senior and I wanted to tear off your dress and do things that would make you call out my name."

Closing his eyes, he tried to block out the image of how incredibly gorgeous she looked on their wedding day. "I couldn't do it. I'll never be sorrier, but I just couldn't live with myself if I took your innocence, your life away just for a contract. I should have explained, but it was easier to have you hate me. If you hated me, you'd forget me."

"I never forgot you." Her black eyes seared into his before she ripped them from him to gaze out the window. She didn't say anything else, but what did he expect?

Her words echoed in his mind, over and over. *I*

never forgot you. Those four simple words carried so much weight. He wanted her to say them again.

Watching her every move, he waited for something, some telltale sign of what was going on in that beautiful head of hers, but her face was emotionless. She didn't need to say anything, though. He would gladly sit here and stare at her for hours and not say a word.

She continued to stare out the window, her generous breasts rising and falling rapidly. "How's your back?"

Sighing quietly, he was thankful she switched the subject. "Good, the scars are almost all gone," He told her, staring at her profile, her arms, hips, those curvy thighs. Never in his life had he not taken what he'd wanted. He spoiled himself, taking every beautiful thing life had to offer. Here was a true beauty, with a body that was made for him and he couldn't have her. "I'm sorry about last night."

She turned to him. "For what?"

"For making you leave…" He fixed his heated gaze on her face, daring her to look away.

Shaking her head, she said, "It's fine. It was late and I shouldn't have been there anyway."

There was a long stretch of silence between them as he continued to watch her carefully.

Tenderly, he said, "I didn't want you to leave."

Closing her eyes, her forehead creased, and she inhaled deeply. "Why are you doing this?"

Without hesitating, he said, "The more time I spend around you, the greedier I become."

She looked to him. "I'm not yours."

Ramo's gaze never left hers. "Do you want to be?"

She shocked him by not answering. He was sure she was gonna shout 'hell no' in his face.

"Come here," he whispered.

Again, she surprised him. Slowly, she crossed the two feet that separated them. As he was seated, they were at eye level and he gazed at her beautiful, flawless skin itching to caress it.

Instead, he reached for her hands again, this time, running his up her forearms and back down, squeezing her elbows. Goosebumps rose on her skin and he smirked. "Your heart's beating pretty fast."

"So is yours," she countered.

"Is this too close? I don't want you to get anxious."

"I told you, I don't feel anxious around you. I feel...I don't know." She pulled in her lips, her eyes following his strong hands caressing her skin. "Why do you want to touch me?"

Breathing in the scent of coconut lotion on her skin, he said, "The same reason you want me to." Interlocking their fingers, he pulled her closer to him. She was now standing between his muscled thighs.

"Ramo...don't" she sighed.

"Why not?" Biting his bottom lip, he let her hands go and gripped her hips, squeezing gently.

Her sharp intake of breath nearly made him come in his pants and he growled low.

Shutting her eyes, she gripped his forearms. "Please Ramo, don't do this to me."

Their foreheads nearly touched as he inhaled her scent. "You're aroused, Elizabeth," he whispered.

"Please..." she breathed.

"I'll stop if you can tell me you don't want me."

She stared at his biceps, his chest, her gaze

roaming over his thighs. "Why are you doing this to me?" she pleaded again.

Leaning closer, he whispered in her ear, his mouth grazing the sensitive lobe. "Because you are all I think about and I want more than just holding your hand."

Pulling back to gage her reaction, he watched her lick her lips invitingly as she stared at his. He couldn't have mistaken the asking in her expression.

Just then, he picked up on Owen's scent.

Fuck!

Quickly, he said, "I like to kill puppies," Then pushed her away from him.

She stumbled slightly, a baffled look on her face.

Two seconds later, Owen strode through the open gym door.

The alpha faltered, taking in Elizabeth's expression. "Everything okay?" he asked her.

He spoke up for her, his arms folded over his chest, legs crossed at the ankle to cover the lasting evidence of his arousal. "I just described the mercy kill we saw at the Sweetin Home. Pretty gruesome."

She seemed to come out of her trance, staring dumbfounded at Owen. "Yeah. Horrible," she breathed.

Owen narrowed his eyes, looking from Ramo to Elizabeth.

God, he felt like a piece of shit, bastard. "Did you find anything?"

Shaking his head, Owen said, "No, but it wasn't one of us." Stepping closer to Elizabeth, he took her hand. The hand Ramo had just been holding. "Can you drive by?" he asked Ramo. "See if you recognize the scent?"

"No problem," he nodded, trying to ignore how

Owen's thumb caressed her skin.

"You ready?" Owen asked her.

"Mmmhm. Let's go." She didn't look his way as she grabbed her coat and purse and headed for the door.

He didn't know if he should laugh at having to tell her he killed puppies to cover her erotic emotions or punch his fist through the glass for her asshole boyfriend coming in and spoiling the moment.

Standing there with his hands on his hips, he stared at the floor, trying to figure out just what the hell he was doing. Why did he feel the need to touch her, to be close to her? Why now? She had a boyfriend. He, Ramo had left her alone for ten years. He had no business trying to stake his claim now. Could he really be that guy? The kind of dick to go after a girl who was taken?

All he knew was he could not stay away from her. The more he saw her, the more he had to be close to her. Hell, his body ached for her right now.

Rubbing his hand roughly over his face, he stared out at the darkening sky. What if he hadn't picked up on Owen's scent? How would the alpha react if he saw how close they had been together? Ramo didn't care if he'd try to hit him, but would Owen hurt Elizabeth?

He stalked out of the gym, telling himself he was going to stay away from her, knowing he was full of shit.

Chapter Nine

The next evening Elizabeth worked on a paper she'd put off for too long when her phone buzzed.

Her heart leapt when she read Ramo's name.

—Hey. Need the rogue's contact info.—

Furrowing her brow she replied,

—Why?—

—He needs help right? Where is he?—

Guilt ran through her knowing she was going to give Ramo what he wanted. She thought about giving Jordan a head's up, but what if he ran?

Trusting Ramo knew what he was doing she wrote back.

—YMCA in Old Irving.—

—Thanks. Don't worry. I'll take care of it.—

—I know you will. :)—

—What are you wearing?—

—Bye Ramo!—

—;)—

She stared at his name at the top of her phone screen for entirely too long. With a sigh she tapped to read Owen's last text to her that morning.

—Miss you. Can I come by tonight?—

She'd texted back letting him know she needed to work on this paper, but she couldn't put him off forever.

Why was this so hard? She was a grown ass

woman. Probably the only virgin she knew at her age and she couldn't picture herself having sex with Owen without losing all her faculties in a panic.

Ramo's searing eyes as he grabbed her waist slithered into her mind and a leap of fire shot straight to her core.

Why couldn't she be this hot for her boyfriend? Owen was handsome and powerful, any girl would kill to sleep with him.

Tossing her phone onto the kitchen counter, she decided not to pick it up again until her paper was done.

The next night she had class, which didn't let out until nine. Her friend Sophia was taking the class with her, so they walked to the train station together on those nights.

"Honestly, I don't know what you're waiting for." They walked down the stairs to the Division Blue Line. The subway was nearly empty at this time of night. "Seriously, you're making it a bigger deal than it is," Sophia admonished.

Regretting instantly telling her friend how persistent Owen was being, she rolled her eyes. "You know damn well why this is a big deal to me. It always has been."

"Yes, but you're not really married. The guy left you for ten years. Hell, I would have been sending his ass snap shots of me and different men every year on our anniversary." Sophia's face flushed. Her best friend, a human still hated the fact Elizabeth had married at such a young age.

She let out a laugh. It had been a long time since she'd had anything to laugh about. "Sophia!"

Laughing too now, Sophia said, "What? I would."

She mimicked taking a selfie of herself with sultry expression. "Happy Anniversary, Dirt Bag!"

Elizabeth laughed so hard, wishing she'd had the guts to do something as ballsy as send Ramo a picture of her and another man. Alas, the only thing she did was date here and there.

Their laughter died down as they waited for their trains. Sophia was headed eastbound as her apartment building was downtown and she was going in the opposite direction.

"Look, if you're ready and I'm sure you are then take a Clonie." Sophia dug in her bag to fish out her phone. "I know you take one during the moon heat, but I think it'll help you out when Owen's trying to…you know…"

She had never thought of taking medication for her anxiety. She usually drank wine or just avoided intimacy to prevent the attacks. Weres took Clonazepam to keep their bodies calm during the moon heat; the night before the full moon when werewolves were fertile and filled with an extreme sexual charge.

Young and single werewolves would rely on Clonazepam to get them through the night without a heat mate. She'd taken it every moon heat since her first transition at the age of fourteen.

Her heart rate spiked just thinking about being with Owen and not in the excited way Ramo brought out of her, but in the I'm-going-to-pass-out-can't-feel-my-limbs kind of way.

"What's holding you back?" Sophia asked, as they heard one of their trains pulling in.

Before she could stop herself she blurted, "Ramo."

"Ramo?" Sophia scrunched her face in annoyance.

"Why would you...Wait...Do you like him?" she asked, her face outraged.

Letting out a nervous laugh, she said, "Do you hear how juvenile that sounds? He's my hus—"

"—deserting husband—"

"—husband and it hasn't felt right. Especially now."

Her friend narrowed her eyes. "Especially now? What? Did something happen? Do you have feelings for him?"

She tried to avoid her gaze. "Your train's here."

"Shit." She walked backward as she called out. "You better call me tomorrow. I need to hear this." Before she jumped on the train, she called out, "And you better start the convo with 'I GOT LAID'!" Laughing at the look she shot her, she blew a kiss as the doors closed.

She only had to wait a few minutes till her train arrived. Picking a window seat, she didn't bother scrolling through her phone. She had so much on her mind: school, work, training, Nightwalkers, the torture on the 606, and Owen's need to consummate their relationship. Over clouding it all was Ramo.

He was right. The more time they spent together, the more she needed him. Her stomach lurched at the thought of Owen ever finding out how she felt about her estranged husband.

She just had to keep reminding herself he'd left her.

But he was back...

"Hey you."

Elizabeth jumped in her seat, knocking her bags to the floor. Spinning around she saw Jordan seated behind her, leaning his forearms on the back of the chair next to hers.

Jordan smiled sheepishly. "Sorry."

"Jordan! Jesus, you scared me." She placed a hand on his arm. "Are you okay? What are you doing here?"

"I followed you," he said, a smile still plastered on his face. "I know you have class tonight and I was going to approach you earlier, but you and your friend were having an interesting conversation, so I just waited till you got on the train."

She shut her eyes, mortified. "Oh no. Did you hear us?"

Blushing he said, "Yeah." Shifting closer to her, he said, "Look, I just wanted to catch you before you went home. I'm leaving the city tonight and I wanted to say goodbye."

"What? Where will you go?"

"Your...uh...friend has a contact in..." he hesitated, looking around nervously. "Well...I can't tell you where. Perez and I agreed not to tell you where I'm going."

"Why not? I want to know you're okay."

Shaking his head, he said, "It's better this way. He knows where I'll be and it's safe. I'm joining another pack."

She shook her head, not liking the sound of this plan. "What pack? How do you know they won't turn you in? Jordan...you can't..."

"Yes, I can, and I will." His face fell and she felt his emotions turn guilt-ridden. "Perez told me what he did for you. Elizabeth...God...I'm so sorry. I didn't think it would come to that. I was stupid and your friend let me have it."

"He didn't hurt you did he?"

"No," he laughed, "But he was…colorful."

She groaned.

Waving his hand dismissively, he said, "He's a good guy. Trust me. I'm going to be okay. It's best you don't know where I'm going in case you're questioned again." He glanced up as the train slowed. "I'm going to get off here. I don't want you seen with me. I've put you through enough already." He stood.

"Jordan, please be careful."

Taking her hand he kissed the top of it. "Thank you for everything you've done for me Elizabeth. I'll never forget it."

He walked around the silver pole in front of her and waited for the doors to open, his young face bright with excitement.

"And Elizabeth…" The door opened. "Don't do anything with your alpha you're going to regret. In my opinion, when a man takes a beating for a woman, *he's* a keeper." With that, Jordan disappeared from sight and out of her life.

She sat open-mouthed, wondering how Ramo had managed to take care of Jordan in such a short amount of time. She worried what would become of him, but the damn kid's parting words still rung in her head.

It wasn't as though she took what Ramo did for granted. She was extremely thankful to be sure, but his reasoning for taking her place still baffled her. If he hadn't left her ten years ago without looking back or checking in on her, she'd think he was acting like a man in love, but that was ludicrous.

Dazed by her thoughts and the encounter with Jordan, she stepped off the train at the next stop. The moment the train took off behind her, leaving an eerie silence on the outdoor platform, she sensed him.

Ramo stood, tall and magnificent on the other end of the vacant platform, his face in shadow.

Shivering at the sight of him, she stood there, waiting, wanting him to come to her.

When he did, he moved steadily, walking toward her in jeans and a bomber jacket, which made his already wide shoulders ginormous. Once every few feet a working lamp overhead would illuminate his skull trim and sharp gaze. When he reached her, they were both cast in shadow as the lamps on this side of the platform were out.

In her flat boots, he towered over her and she had to angle her head back to meet his searing gaze. The five o'clock shadow on his jaw hardened his already rough features. It suited him so well she nearly caressed his cheek.

"The boy say goodbye?" he uttered.

"Yes," she breathed. The two of them should never be alone. It was too much for her little heart to bear. "How did you know?"

"I followed him, following you."

She let out a nervous giggle.

"I knew he'd go looking for you. Wanted to be sure no other Were spotted the two of you together. Was going to intervene if I had to."

"Will he be okay? Tell me the truth?"

His eyes softened at her concern. "He will. Trust me."

Her hand went to her heart. Shaking her head disbelievingly. "I can't thank you enough. I can't believe..." She looked away, biting the inside of her mouth, looking out over the light traffic on the expressway. Her ponytail blew in the wind, covering her right shoulder. He had taken care of everything. He'd taken the punishment for her and now Jordan would be safe thanks to him. She hoped he felt her gratitude and not the yearning building inside her. "Why are you being so wonderful?" she asked solemnly, and she caught him gazing at her hair.

"Is it so surprising?" he smirked.

She raised an eyebrow, meeting his eyes knowingly.

He shook his head. "Don't answer that."

They were silent for a beat and she watched as his expression darkened.

"I heard you," he said under his breath.

The hairs rose on her neck, knowing exactly what he'd heard. "Ramo…"

"Don't Elizabeth," he pleaded.

Confused, she asked, "Don't what?"

"Don't sleep with him," he demanded, his brows lowering.

Embarrassed, she tried to look away, but he stepped closer, backing her into a pillar.

Bending to meet her gaze he pleaded, "I know I have no right, but I don't give a shit. Please."

"I'm not discussing this with you."

'But you're thinking about it, right?"

Her anxious expression gave her away.

He let out a harsh breath and looked off along the platform. It was a while before he spoke. "I don't know what's happening between us, but there is something. I know you feel it damn it. I fucking *feel* you feeling it."

"Stop!" Angry now, she uttered through gritted

teeth, "You can't show up here and tell me not to be intimate with my boyfriend. Who the hell do you think you are?"

"I'm your fucking husband!"

Her hand flew of its own accord, but he caught her wrist before she could strike his cheek. Tears welled in her eyes. "You left!" she screamed, trying to push him away with her other hand, but he gripped it too. "You left!" she repeated, trying to hit him and struggling to get out of his grasp. All the rage she'd buried deep inside her erupted in their faces. "You fucking left me!" Her voice cracked and the tears spilled forth. She was so sick and tired of him forgetting that monumental fact.

With a panged look, he pressed his forehead to hers, "I know. God, I know." He held her wrists by the sides of her head, bringing her flush against him. His voice husky, he said, "But I'm here now," and crushed his lips to hers.

Electricity jolted through her as his cool lips met hers and her body froze from the intense contact. All the fight in her ceased, she stood immobilized, her mind reeling at what was happening.

He paused for a moment, as if stunned at the reality that they were actually mouth to mouth. Then, his lips parted, running over hers in smooth yet purposeful moves, kissing her bottom lip, then the top, coaxing them to open. When her lips freely obliged, he slid his tongue across her bottom lip then slipped it in and it was like a ball of fire churned in her stomach, igniting every inch of her body. She tasted her tears on his tongue as he moved skillfully, letting out ragged sighs while his arms wrapped around her.

Unbidden, her faithless hands wandered to his shoulders, his neck, reveling in the feel of him. His muscles were taut underneath her touch.

This was so wrong, but damn if it didn't feel right.

And so fucking good.

It was as though the need inside her turned manic; she felt drugged.

He squeezed her body to him, nipping her bottom lip with his teeth, then burying his tongue inside her once more.

Ahhh...the taste of him made her melt in his arms, his lips driving her on as though kissing them was the only way to survive.

She gave as good as she got, taking in every touch, his scent, his rock-hard body up against her. She never wanted him to let go.

He groaned when she pushed her hips into his and Elizabeth felt his arousal. Pulling back he eyed her carefully. "Are you okay?"

"What?" Her eyes were on his lips, wanting, needing to taste more. She pulled him to her, running her hands over the scruff on his jaw.

Kissing her once softly, he gently pushed his hips into hers again, watching her cautiously. "Are you okay," he repeated.

"Ahhh...yes," she moaned, pulling him toward her, taking charge of the kiss. Why did he keep asking her that? Her muddled brain couldn't decipher a thing at the moment. All she knew, all she wanted to know, was Ramo's body fit perfectly against hers, his lips on hers, his hands...

Wait...How did this start?

What was she doing?

She broke the kiss. "Stop." Placing her hands on his chest, she pushed him away.

Reality, cold and cruel reared its ugly head. She was on the Addison platform kissing her estranged husband out in the open for everyone to see. There was no one around except them, but anyone could step down the stairs at any time. Oh my God! What if Owen showed up to meet her?

Looking around nervously, she avoided his gaze. "I have to go."

"Elizabeth..."

"No!" She picked up the bags she hadn't noticed she'd dropped on the ground, then looked him straight in the eye. "Don't ever do that again."

"Elizabeth, you kissed me back..." he straightened up, watching her with a grim expression.

"It doesn't matter. I shouldn't have..." With a shriek, she placed her hand over her nose and mouth and sniffed. "Jesus, I smell like you. What if he's there? Shit..." Rambling she stormed off toward the stairs, Ramo keeping pace with her. "Please, just leave me alone, Ramo."

"Notice how you only started panicking when you thought of Owen?"

She flinched. "Of course I'm panicking. I was just making out with another man."

"You were fine while you were in my arms," he uttered softly, as they turned onto Addison, heading toward her apartment.

Shocked, she faltered, only just realizing why he kept asking her if she was okay, because he thought she was going to have a panic attack. Only, she completely fine. Utterly aroused, but her anxiety hadn't been triggered till she thought of Owen catching her.

Owen.

Her heart rate accelerated so fast, it knocked the wind out of her, and she stopped dead on the sidewalk. Taking a deep breath, she began to pace, her hands beginning to tremble.

Ringing blared in her ears and the world around her blurred, her peripheral vision going red and distorted. She tried to say something to Ramo, but she couldn't speak, her tongue leaden in her mouth.

She couldn't breathe.

"Elizabeth!" a concerned voice sounded from somewhere, but she couldn't answer.

Before she knew it, she was being carried; the night sky came into view, then brick buildings on either side of her. Whispering tickled her ear, but she couldn't make out what was being said.

Closing her eyes, she breathed deep, begging her heart to slow.

She didn't know how long she'd checked out, but the feeling in her limbs returned, the trembling slowing. Steadily, her pulse calmed and Ramo's voice hummed in her ear. "Easy, baby. You got this. That's right." His hand caressed her cheek, gliding through her hair. Goosebumps fluttered over her skin at his touch, but her heart rate maintained its steady beat. "Good..." he whispered.

Opening her eyes, she took in their position. She was in his arms, cradled like a baby. Somehow, he'd sat on the ground and she was in his lap.

"How are you doing?" Ramo murmured, his eyes studying her features.

Taking another deep inhale she said, "Mortified..."

She met his anxious eyes, which were entirely too close. "I'm good. It passed." Standing carefully, she looked around for her things.

"Here," he said, his face so grim you'd have thought she died in his arms.

"I'm fine. I'm used to those, you know." She shook herself, gaining control of her faculties.

He narrowed his eyes. "It was pretty scary. You just checked out. I don't even think you heard me. For a moment you just stopped breathing. "

"It's not a big deal…"

"Elizabeth, he makes you panic just thinking about him. Yes it is a big deal!" Ramo uttered through gritted teeth.

Putting a hand up when it looked like he was going to follow her, she said, "Please. Drop it. I need to go."

"Let me walk you home…"

"No, please. He might be there. I'll be fine."

Ramo didn't look happy as she turned to walk to her apartment. Even though he'd nodded, she knew he was following her, making sure she was okay. It was fine with her. She just couldn't stand being with him and thinking of Owen at the same time.

Trying to shut out all thoughts of Ramo, she walked up the front steps. Her chest always throbbed after an attack, her nerves on end. She rubbed at her chest, thankful Owen hadn't been waiting for her. Before she could ascend the stairs leading up to her apartment, her grandmother opened the door, her sharp eyes honed on her. She waved a wrinkled hand, beckoning Elizabeth inside as if there were some big secret she needed to spill.

"Nonni, I can't right now. I need…"

Standing in the doorway in khaki shorts, slippers and an old Washington DC t-shirt Elizabeth had given her in the eighth grade, her grandmother gave her a look, which brooked no argument. Crossing her arms over herself to cover Ramo's scent she walked past her into her little living room. Her grandmother's house was always warm and cozy and smelled of antique wood and meat sauce.

Although her grandmother spoke perfect English, she only spoke to Elizabeth in Italian.

"Don't bother hiding his scent. I smelled you down the street." She came forward, her little head bobbing around, sniffing her neck and face. *"I hope he was a good kisser because it may be the last one you'll ever have."*

"Stop. I know it was stupid."

"I didn't say it was stupid. He is your husband after all. If anyone kisses you it should be him." Her grandmother spoke over her shoulder as she walked into the kitchen and began making her a plate of whatever she'd made.

"I don't recall you being on Ramo's side all these years." She sat at the kitchen table, feeling a hundred times better, ready to eat her grandmother's famous eggplant parmesan. She wondered what Ramo would think if he knew she'd ignored his diet plan.

"I'm on your side." She set the plate in front of her and sat across from her. Ancient eyes glared as though she were trying to read her mind. *"Are you going to tell Hunter?"*

"No!" she said immediately. "He'll freak out. He already thinks I have feelings for him."

"You do." Her grandmother said, candidly. Then,

in a grave voice, which didn't help her frantic nerves
she said, *"Be careful, mimma."*

Chapter Ten

Sitting in his car, Ramo stared at the steering wheel, flipping his cell phone in his right hand, over and over again. He didn't know how long he'd been parked there, but since the sun had set and he was listening to a song on the radio he'd heard three times since he'd shut off the car, he guessed it was way too long.

He had no reason to drive to her place and park where he could see her front door, but he was sure he was entering stalker territory with no end in sight.

The fact was…he was worried about her. So worried he couldn't see straight, couldn't think straight. Seeing her break down the other day nearly killed him. Why would someone as strong as she was panic the way she did?

He'd googled anxiety attacks and learned shit, really. There were no hard facts as to why people experienced them. There was some thought they may be hereditary or stem from stress or life changes. Considering Elizabeth was a public-school teacher, in graduate school, struggled to pay the bills, and most likely worried over her grandmother, it boiled down to what specific stressor she was dealing with at a given moment.

Despite her explanation, Ramo couldn't get the idea out of his head it was Owen's doing. For the past couple days, he'd wondered if the guy was hurting her and ordering her to keep it quiet. Would the Grayback alpha use his authority over her in such a way?

The more he thought about it, the crazier and scarier his theories became. He'd had to down an entire bottle of whiskey the other night to calm his nerves.

The alternative solution to alcohol?

Keep a watchful eye on her.

And if sitting in his car outside of her apartment for hours on end made him a stalker then fuck it. He didn't care.

What was scarier than him sitting out there like a creep was his attachment to her. As he stared at the black leather on the wheel, his vision blurring from lack of movement, all he could think about was the fucker's hands on his wife.

His wife.

His...

Ever since he'd kissed her a sense of ownership had taken root. He knew he didn't *own her,* but hell if he didn't want to mark his territory. He couldn't help it. He was a wolf for Christ sakes and the woman he was falling for was with someone else.

He'd struggled with this from the minute he'd found out about their relationship, but now...

Now they were getting closer. Too close. And his emotions were a chaotic electrical current on the verge of a shortage.

He sensed her before he saw the car and took steady breaths to contain his mood so her date wouldn't pick up on it.

Her date.

The SOB had picked her up earlier to take her

somewhere. She'd stepped out of the apartment building looking hot as hell in black leggings, knee-high boots and a gray leather jacket. It took everything to not rip the alpha's throat out for looking at her.

Owen parked in front of her place…

Ramo's lip curled

…got out of the car…

His chest rumbled as he growled, a searing pain entering his chest.

…and walked into the apartment after her.

His body screamed as he squeezed the ever-loving shit out of his steering wheel.

"FUCK!" His shout was more like a growl, cutting his throat.

He was parked far enough away he wouldn't be detected. Not that he really gave shit at the moment since he was stepping out of his car and slamming the door as if he were going to follow them inside.

Shit.

What was he doing? He couldn't go in there.

He paced and rubbed his skull trim, then ran his hand roughly over his face.

What if Owen tried to…

Before he could finish the gut-wrenching thought, he punched his hand through the car window, shattering tiny pieces of glass onto the passenger seat.

She wouldn't.

Elizabeth wouldn't let Owen touch her that way. Especially since they were feeling this…whatever it was. Would she?

Jesus Christ. This feeling sucked. He wondered if he was on the verge of a panic attack.

Taking out his phone with his bloodied hand he

opened their thread and began texting her without even thinking.

Why the fuck is he there?

He paused before pressing the send arrow.

His raging emotions told him to send the message because she was his wife. Another part of him told him he had no right and not to be stupid.

Which part did he listen to?

If he sent it, there was every chance Owen would read it and know something was going on between them.

He drew in a ragged breath. If he was a sensible guy, he'd leave now and leave her the hell alone.

Too bad for all of them he was a crazy motherfucker.

****

Her grandmother's ominous warning rang in her ears the next couple days. What had she been thinking letting Ramo kiss her? And dear God, why did she replay it over and over inside her head?

Without warning, she'd suddenly relive the moment and her body would become flush with excitement. Walking up the stairs to her classroom, in the shower, eating a cheeseburger... It seemed everything she did reminded her of their kiss, and she'd daydream about his incredible scent and the feel of his strong lips for hours on end. It was certainly a distraction she couldn't afford to have when she was on a date with her boyfriend.

Elizabeth had been thrilled when Owen received a call from Joe reporting a huge fight had broken out at the bar and the police were there. He'd cursed and given her a swift kiss before racing out of her apartment. She knew he'd been hoping to get a little further tonight and was glad for the reprieve, but she couldn't evade him forever.

Sophia said if she dressed sexy, she'd feel sexy and hopefully it would put her in the mood. Borrowing Sophia's knee-high boots had made her feel hot and she'd even put on eye shadow and lipstick, but she wondered if Ramo would like the way she looked. Not Owen.

Stepping into her bedroom, she sat on the bed and kicked off her boots, trying not to check her phone again. Every chance she had tonight she checked her cell, dying to receive a text from Ramo. Anything. She'd even wished he'd send her a stupid meme or one of his goofy jokes, but he hadn't contacted her in days.

Did their kiss mean more to her than it did to him?

God, she felt so stupid.

Her phone buzzed as an incoming call came in. Ramo's name shown on the screen and the excitement she felt terrified her to her very core.

"Hello?"

"Is he there?" His voice came out somber and curt.

"No," she muttered weakly, a thrill running through her. A very small part of her thought she should feel guilty for telling him she was alone, but for some reason her first instinct was to do what he wanted. That wasn't good on sooo many levels.

She listened to his short breaths through the receiver as though he was struggling with what to say next.

"Did you..."

"No," she answered immediately.

He let out a harsh breath then coughed. "Will he be

back?"

"I don't know." The silence on the other end unnerved her.

"Ramo…"

"Don't say anything," he cut her off.

Squeezing her eyes shut, she gripped her bed cover, wishing they weren't going through this agony.

"Go to the window," he demanded.

"What?"

Slowly he repeated. "Go to the window."

Holding the phone to her ear, she walked mechanically to her bedroom window.

"Lift the blinds."

Curious, she did as she was told, again. "Where are you," she asked, breathlessly.

"Not far," was all he said.

"Okay, they're open." Her eyes traveled over the empty lot next to her building, the street, and apartment buildings, but she couldn't pick up where he was.

"Too dark. Turn on the light."

Her heart rate increased its tempo. Blushing, she reached to the side and turned on the light next to her couch. The instant the light was on, she hitched in a breath. "Can you see me?"

His deep voice was hypnotic. "Step to the right," he ordered.

She did, squinting as it was harder to see with the light on. As her eyes adjusted she scanned all around outside, the gangway, every window… Where the hell was he?

"Take off your clothes," he said, smoothly.

She froze, staring at a dark window, her voice caught in her throat.

"I need to see you. Take off your clothes and lay back on the chair."

An old armchair was stuffed into the corner of her bedroom by the window. It was where she usually read or threw her laundry.

Heart pounding, she couldn't speak. Her body felt more alive than ever before and a rush of excitement warmed her belly.

Could she really do this?

Men had seen her naked before since she was a werewolf, but she'd always tried to shield herself somehow and she'd never paraded her body like he was asking. She didn't exude confidence the way he did. God, he was probably used to beautiful, thin women. Why was he doing this? She was too curvy. It was embarrassing enough the first time. Why the hell would he want to see her naked again?

"Do it, Elizabeth," he said, breaking the unbearable silence.

Damn his compelling voice. Unable to resist temptation, she placed the phone down on the arm of the chair and grasped the hem of her top. Pressing her lips together, she slid it up over her head and tossed it on the floor. Her pants were next. And as she peeled them down her legs, she cursed her thighs.

Trembling now, she reached behind her to unfasten her bra, then pulled the straps over her arms. She felt the heavy weight of her breasts and her nipples harden from the cool air at the same time a growl emanated from the phone. Goosebumps covered her skin as she felt his gaze on her chest and the corner of her mouth curled wickedly.

She added her thong to the heap on the floor a

second later. Then, there was no looking back. Every hair stood on end as she felt his eyes roam up and down her body. She was never so aware of every single inch of her as she was right now. Her toes curled on the carpet and she shivered from the cool air in the room. Her eyes fell to her hardened nipples and it was then she felt his arousal. It was all around her. Glancing up, her lids low, she smirked as confidence ran through her, surprising the hell out of her. She let him get his fill before grabbing the phone again.

There was silence on the other end. Then, in a low voice she didn't recognize, he said, "Wow." He paused, "You're beautiful."

Smiling, she gazed in the direction his emotions were blaring from. Every instinct told her he was in the dark window she'd spotted earlier.

"Lay down."

She turned to the couch, putting her back to the window and he moaned in her ear.

She almost giggled as she imagined the look on his face, staring at her ample bottom.

Laying back against the plush pillow, she placed her free hand over her belly, attempting to hide the little bump she hated.

"Don't cover yourself. I want to see everything."

His husky voice melted her insides.

"Move slightly to the left," he said. "Perfect."

She'd never thought she'd be so turned on by a man she couldn't see, but somehow she felt his gaze as though fire shot from his eyes, scorching up and down her skin. Her body radiated with unimaginable desire. She began trembling and squeezed the side of the couch to hold herself in check. The moment was all too much.

Without thinking she blurted, "I need you."

There was silence on the other end, then he answered warmly, "Soon love."

"I can feel your eyes on me."

"Good," he said. "Open your legs. Let me see you."

With a wantonness she didn't know she possessed, she widened her legs, giving him an eyeful.

He hissed in her ear. "God, Elizabeth. I'm so hard right now."

Her stomach leapt, picturing his swollen length and the image sent a jolt through her body, right to her center.

Closing her eyes, she tilted her head back. Never in a million years would she believe she'd be doing something like this. What was it about him that turned her into putty? Her palm slid across her skin, roaming over her thighs, belly and up over her breast. She arched her back, writhing as she squeezed her nipple, breathing shakily.

"Fuck," he whispered. "You're killing me."

Her hand continued its journey of her body, traveling low as she gyrated her hips back and forth in a slow rhythmic motion.

"Yes, Elizabeth. Make yourself come," he ordered, roughly. His soft moans sending shivers down her spine.

Utterly lost in the moment, she opened her eyes to gaze with heavy lids out the window. It was the most erotic moment of her entire life. Even though she couldn't see him, it was as if his hands and mouth were all over her. She could feel him everywhere.

"You're so fucking hot," he moaned deep in her

ear, his breaths coming in fast.

She wanted to see him; to see what he was doing; what she was doing to him. Was he pleasuring himself as she was? Was he as charged as she was from the powerful need to be together?

A fierce energy urged her on, wanting him to see how much she wanted him. Pinching her nipple as she plunged her fingers inside herself, her body undulated on the chair.

"Ahhh…," he uttered in an unrecognizable voice as she felt him reach his peak.

His moans ignited a fire inside her and her stomach tightened. Her body spasmed with an earth-shattering climax, sending her over the edge. Her eyes rolled back, head digging into the cushions. The phone slipped from her shoulder as she floated back down to earth, her cheeks burning crimson.

His silky chuckle told her he was still watching her every move. "Why are you blushing?"

Lifting the phone back to her ear, she countered, "Why do you think?"

"Don't be shy, Elizabeth. You're beautiful. Jesus, you have no idea what you do to me."

She pictured his eyes roaming over her with a satisfied grin and she covered her face, fighting the urge to giggle.

"When can I see you?" he asked huskily.

Tensing at his question, she ducked her head, reaching for the sheet on the bed to cover herself with. Panic spiked through her.

"What's wrong?"

Elizabeth couldn't answer him. What could she say?

Everything told her there was nothing to be ashamed of. He was her husband. They were getting to know one another and building a bond she could not explain. If Owen wasn't in the picture then she'd have no cause to worry. They'd be free to examine...whatever this was.

But did this mean she forgave him for leaving her all those years ago?

Shit. Her emotions were going haywire. There was too much she had to think about. And she just wasn't ready to face the fact she was falling for her estranged husband while involved with another man.

When she didn't answer, he sighed. "Elizabeth...I'm sorry."

Frowning she asked, "For what?"

"I need to leave you alone. I don't know what got into me. This isn't fair to you. It isn't fair to..." He cursed.

Her stomach knotted at the thought of betraying Owen.

"I try you know," he said, softly.

"Try?"

"I really try not to look at you or text you when I'm not with you." He coughed. "Well...I try enough. I know it's wrong, but fuck, Elizabeth." he inhaled deeply. "I can't stop thinking about you."

She squeezed her eyes shut and choked back a sob, forgetting he could see her.

"I'm sorry. I guess...I guess that doesn't help."

There was a soft thud as though he pressed his head against the glass. Staring at the dark window she thought she could see his outline.

When he spoke, his voice was muffled and tired.

"You're killing me, Elizabeth. And I know I deserve it."

There was silence for a moment, then the phone went dead.

Chapter Eleven

St. Patrick's Day in Chicago was a celebration that left its mark. Either you came out of this day in one piece with a slight hangover, ended up on a social media newsfeed in a compromising photo/video, or, worst case scenario, you wake up in jail or in the hospital. Which was why, Elizabeth avoided going out on this day for the last four years. The few times she braved the holiday in college, she'd wound up making out with a stranger one year and losing her shoe the next. The last time she went out on this day, she'd fallen on her knee and ripped her favorite pair of jeans walking home in the wrong direction.

When Sophia begged her to go out the Saturday of the parade, however, Elizabeth jumped at the chance. If anyone needed to step out of reality and get shit faced, it was her.

So after watching the city dye the river green and catching the last couple minutes of the parade on television, she met her friend at O'Donovan's on Irving Park to start their drunken mission.

Knocking back green beer, they laughed at the lewd shirts worn by bar goers and chatted with the people around them, feeling relaxed and carefree. When the bagpipes paraded through the bar, they took out their phones and took videos and selfies, uploading them to Facebook to regret the next day.

After hitting up the next bar, McNamara's, Elizabeth couldn't avoid Owen's constant texts to go to his bar. She knew he worried about her and wanted to make sure she was okay, especially since he knew Elizabeth was on a mission to get trashed.

Glossy-eyed and reeking of beer, they Ubered to Owen's bar where they managed to squeeze into a spot at the corner of the bar.

As every bar in the city celebrated this holiday, it was the same here as it was everywhere else. The smell of beer-soaked floor was potent in the air and the music and chatter drowned out any thoughts she may have had.

Elizabeth had to admit she was having a great time not thinking of work or school and just enjoying the moment. She couldn't remember the last time she'd laughed so hard, or even when the last time she'd socialized period. With all the work they did in training, it left little time to catch up with her pack members.

Sipping her beer and toying with the beads some stranger had thrown around her neck, she pointed out a cutie eyeing her friend.

"Elizabeth, that's my cousin!" Sophia yelled at her over the blaring music, spitting beer in her face, and giving her cousin a noncommittal wave.

Squinting as though the guy were a mile away and not a mere two feet, Elizabeth giggled. "Oh. Sorry."

"We know pretty much everyone here so it's not like I can hook up." Sophia rolled her eyes, not too happy coming to this bar when half the Graybacks were in attendance and Sophia's family lived in the neighborhood.

Her friend didn't look like she could last long

anyway as she swayed back and forth, mean mugging the whole room.

She was about to ask Sophia if she wanted to have one more shot before heading out, when Ramo strolled through the doors.

Elizabeth didn't know if it was the alcohol or her ordinary reaction to him, but she gasped then hiccupped.

"What?" Sophia asked, looking around.

"Ramo," Elizabeth whispered. At least, she thought she whispered. She could barely hear herself at all over the music.

Looking around the crowded bar, she couldn't see where Owen was and assumed he was in the back.

"Oh damn." Sophia said. "He's gorgeous." Her friend's hand slipped off the bar and she stumbled slightly as she ogled Ramo making his way toward the back.

The two of them must have been obvious since Ramo panned his head in their direction as if they'd shouted his name. Shit. She hoped she hadn't shouted his name. His eyes met Elizabeth's, taking in her appearance and he smirked, then he disappeared down the back toward Owen's office.

Turning to meet her friend's wide-eyed expression she laughed.

"You're screwed, girl." Sophia laughed and ordered a round of Irish car bombs.

The sea of green was doing a number on her vision. The room was becoming blurrier and blurrier. Was blurrier a word? It sounded funny.

Shaking her head when Sophia's cousin offered to buy another round of shots, Elizabeth asked for another beer, insisting those were safer since they quenched her thirst.

She couldn't be sure, but either she was swaying to the music or just swaying. All she knew was if she let go of the bar she was going down.

People watching was part of the fun, and she was surrounded by them, knocking into some on all sides of her. She stared a bit too long at a couple making out, thinking perhaps they should just go home and do it already, which made her think of Owen and what he wanted to do so she drank some more.

At the end of the bar, a girl was crying hysterically to her friend, which made Elizabeth laugh. Then she thought that was mean and felt bad for the girl, wondering why she was so sad at an exciting place like this and on such a fun day.

When she turned to Sophia to point out the sad girl, she realized her friend had been talking to her this whole time and she hadn't heard a word. Not that Sophia noticed because her friend kept going.

A familiar tingling trickled up her neck and she knew Ramo was back in the bar area. Determined to feign nonchalance, she started laughing at whatever Sophia was saying as she followed Ramo's every move through her peripheral vision.

He ended up at the end of the bar next to the sad girl and ordered a beer, deftly avoiding her as she was him.

His shirt was green and read, *Oh For Lucks Sake*.

She didn't get it, which meant she was two sheets past the wind. No…Three sheets past the wind. Or was it *to* the wind? What the hell did that even mean?

Elizabeth noticed him take in the overly crowded

bar as he leaned his arms over the counter and wondered why he didn't approach her. She had this insane thought he should be standing next to her. Then she remembered this was Owen's bar and she was *his* girlfriend. If Ramo came within a foot of her after what they'd done the other day, they'd be all over each other.

No she wouldn't. She couldn't. Why had she thought that? Of course she'd be able to control herself right?

"Who's the blonde?" Sophia asked, squinting in Ramo's direction.

"Mmm…" Wrapped up in her thoughts, Elizabeth hadn't noticed the short-haired blonde who'd sidled up to her husband… No. Not husband. Ramo.

Not bothering to hide her glare, she watched as the girl smiled and flirted drunkenly with her husband…uh…Ramo.

Dread burned her insides. Since Ramo's return, she never once considered if he was currently dating someone. She'd heard rumors about his extra-curricular activities throughout the years, but it just hadn't occurred to her he'd still date now. And why wouldn't he? She had a boyfriend. He had every right to date. Why had she been so naïve to think Ramo would be single while he was here, let alone celibate?

Elizabeth clenched her teeth as the blonde laughed at her own joke apparently and Ramo chuckled too, shaking his head at her. The sight of him giving his devastating smile to another woman made her sick. Then, the little slut leaned her perky breast right onto his shoulder, whispering into his ear.

Fury.

Red, hot, scorching fury seared through her. Like a

backdraft, it burst from her stomach, shooting through every limb. Her body hummed, her mind going fuzzy from the red haze.

Ramo's eyes shot to hers, evidently feeling her sudden rage. Standing up straight, he looked around the room quickly, then pointed to his eye.

Confused, Elizabeth looked to her friend who'd been watching Ramo too.

Swiveling her gaze to Elizabeth, Sophia hissed, "Oh shit. Elizabeth, your eyes are yellow." She glanced around too, as if nervous someone would notice a Were on the verge of phasing. "Are you gonna turn?" she asked, wide-eyed, taking a step back from her.

Elizabeth didn't answer, she just glared at the blonde who had no idea Elizabeth was about to rip her throat open.

"Calm down. Go splash some water on your face before you beast out on the whole bar...*Jesus!*" Sophia said, shoving her away from the bar.

Giving Ramo what she hoped was a death stare; she walked on surprisingly steady legs to the bathroom. Her rage must have steadied her because, thankfully, she didn't fall.

Opting for the employee bathroom past Owen's office, she closed the door behind her, and went straight to the sink. Turning on the faucet, she let the water run as she calmed her irises. She watched in the mirror as they returned to their normal dark shade. Despite her eyes, her body was still buzzing with jealousy. She'd never felt the emotion before, and it was clear she didn't like it. Not one bit. It was a horribly, icky feeling.

The door to the bathroom flung open behind her

and she saw Ramo's reflection standing in the doorway behind her.

"Get out," she demanded, glaring at him.

"What the hell was that?" he asked, closing and locking the door behind him.

"What are you doing? You need to get out."

"No. I want you to tell me what the hell that was out there."

"Nothing," she said with a false smile, feeling the rage flush her face. "I was just enjoying the show you and your little friend were putting on."

He narrowed his eyes as he stepped slowly closer, his wide shoulders crowding her. "I wasn't putting on a show. I wasn't doing anything."

Pursing her lips, she wished her buzz would go away, knowing she was going to regret every word spilling out of her stupid mouth. She leaned forward for emphasis and lost her footing, bumping her head on his chest. She righted herself quickly. "Didn't look like nothing. Looked like the skinny bitch was gnawing on your ear."

"Whoa! Easy, Elizabeth. She didn't even touch my ear."

Rolling her eyes, she scoffed and pushed past him. "Whatever. I don't care. Do whatever the fuck you want."

"Hey!" He followed her, spinning her around and backing her into the door. "What's your problem?"

"You're my problem. Leave me alone!"

They glared at each other, their noses nearly touching as he bent down toward her. She could see his mind at work, and hated she was being so obvious. Why couldn't she just keep her mouth shut?

"Jesus, you're jealous." It was a statement, but it came out a question.

"I seriously don't care what the hell you do, Ramo."

"Yes you do," he said immediately.

The look in his eye was all too knowing, too intense. She had to look away, trying to calm down. "I don't care," she whispered, again, his heady scent coiling through her senses and down to her very core.

Nodding his head as though he was sure he was right, he forced her to meet his gaze, his eyes burning into hers. "Now you know what it feels like," he hissed bitterly.

"What?"

"You know exactly what. You think I like watching you with *him*?"

Shaking her head dumbly, she said, "It's different…"

"How the fuck is it different, Elizabeth? How?" he shouted in her face.

"Because you're mine!" she shouted back.

His head jerked back as if she'd slapped him.

The look on his face, the flash in his eyes before he smashed his mouth to hers would live in her memory forever.

Ramo's brutal kiss was a warning, a threat, a claim on what she already knew was his.

She. Was. His.

And she was tired of fighting it, fighting him.

Pressing himself against her, his mouth moved over hers roughly, sucking her bottom lip, nipping it with his teeth. His tongue delved deep and she moaned, needing more of him, all of him.

She couldn't get enough.

His hands gripped her waist and back as his thigh spread her knees apart. Holding onto his massive shoulders she pulled him to her, relishing the feel of him and what his every touch was doing to her. Never in her wildest dreams could she imagine it would feel like this. How could she want more even when he was this close to her?

Ramo's hand gripped the back of her head, angling her neck back to run his mouth over her skin, his hips driving into her over and over again. There were layers of clothing separating them, but if he continued this, she was going to orgasm. A part of her would be embarrassed, but another part wouldn't care as long as he never stopped this sweet torture.

Pulling back he gazed down at her body. Then, as if he were unwrapping a fragile package, he pulled down the strap of her dress to expose one full breast. He closed his eyes and sucked in a sharp breath through his teeth, his head falling back. He looked as though he were thanking the heavens for what he was seeing. The expression on his face as he bowed his head to see her made her shudder.

"Fuck, you're beautiful." His hand massaged her breast, his thumb kneading the nipple till it hardened. Ramo's eyes yellowed as he took her in his mouth.

"Ahhh…" Elizabeth moaned.

She dizzied from the feel of him. Bunching his shirt in one hand, her nails dug into the back of his head, keeping him exactly where she wanted.

The beating of the music became a distant drum, eclipsed by their heavy breathing and the pounding of their hearts.

She needed to taste him again. Grabbing the sides of his head, she brought him up to her mouth. He smirked before their lips met and she moaned again. The combination of his heady scent, the intoxicating taste of his tongue, the hard muscles beneath her fingertips, pressed up against her breasts were too much and too little.

This man was everything and she never wanted to let him go.

Easing back, Ramo gazed at her body as he squeezed her waist, her thighs. She'd never seen a man like this before. It was as if he were possessed by something feral. His face darkened, his eyes seeing nothing but her. If it wasn't so incredibly sexy she would have been scared.

"I am baby," he whispered, his voice hoarse as if he'd been shouting. "I'm yours. I've always been yours. I'll always *be* yours. Jesus, Elizabeth, I worship the very ground you walk on." He bit his bottom lip as he continued his exploration of her, and she nearly passed out.

"Let me take care of you. Just you."

Confused, she just nodded, not understanding what she was agreeing to. Ramo could ask her to make him a sandwich right now and hell if she wouldn't do it.

Ugh. This is where men got women. *Damn we're suckers!*

His body slid down hers till he was on his knees. Stupidly, she thought he was literally going to worship the ground she walked on till he raised the hem of her dress. Stiffening, she gripped his shoulders in question.

"Let me Elizabeth. You have no idea how long I've wanted to do this."

Do what?

Something told her she knew what he was about to do, but he wouldn't do that right now would he? *Here?*

Lifting her left leg, he positioned it over his shoulder, and she had to reach for the door handle beside her for better support.

Her heart pounded in her ears as a yearning like she'd never felt before squeezed low in her belly.

She felt Ramo's fingers move her thong to the side and the growl emanating from him made her smile satisfyingly.

Then, he touched her.

She froze. Not from nerves, but from pure desire. No one had ever touched her there.

Ever so gently, Ramo's fingers rubbed over her folds, then without warning, she felt his tongue glide over her, warm, hot and slick. Her body bucked, pushing herself further into his mouth.

"Ramo," she cried out, her head thrown back, taking pleasure in the foreign sensations he was igniting in her. How the hell could this feel so damn good?

His tongue continued to do wicked things to her, lapping, probing that she nearly lost her footing. With both of his arms wrapped around her thighs, she moved with him as her body tightened and she begged him not to stop. Ramo's ministrations became more vigorous at her words and when he began flicking the hidden bud in rapid movements, her body burst into flames. As soon as he felt her going over the edge, he slid two fingers in her and her body clenched around them once, twice…four…seven times.

Oh My God!

Never in her wildest imaginings did she think it

could be like this. It was as if her body had been waiting for him. Waiting to explode.

Her core still tingled with her release and greedily she wanted more. As her mind and body settled, she took stock of their position. She held onto the doorjamb with one hand, the other on his skull trim. Ramo still knelt before her, his mouth kissing the inside of her thigh gently. When he finally brought himself up they stood there, stunned, neither of them saying a word.

Watching him closely, she saw passion in his expression at first, then concern. Closing her eyes, she tried not to think too much about what was outside the door. Somehow, the noise from the bar got louder, intruding on their erotic seclusion in the back.

A jolt of panic laced through her at the thought of Owen walking in on them right now and she covered her face.

"Don't," Ramo whispered. "You'll just upset yourself."

Shaking her head, Elizabeth said, "I think I'm too buzzed to have an attack. But…"

"I know Elizabeth. I know." He went to reach for her cheek then thought better of it, his hand fisting over his mouth. "Shit. I should be sorry, but I'm not."

This time, he didn't stop himself. Bringing his hands to her face, he forced her to look at him, his breath warm on her lips. "I don't think I can stop touching you. I don't want to stop. Do you understand?"

Before she could let his words sink in, there was a loud commotion in the bar. A fight was sure to break out on a day like today, which meant it was high time she went home. Sighing as the fight escalated and men shouted over chairs being knocked around, she was about to tell Ramo she'd sneak out the back with Sophia, when a high-pitch scream rang out; the kind that left you cold on the inside.

There was no ordinary fight happening out there. Ramo and Elizabeth were motionless for a second, their eyes wide as they listened. Her first thought was of a crazed gunmen, but she didn't hear any shots. They heard it then, an odd snarling at the same time she picked up the strange scent.

"Nightwalkers!" Ramo said. Pushing her aside, he went for the door. "Stay in here and lock the door."

"Hell no! I'm training to be a Fighter. I'm going with you." she spat back, ready to follow him out the door.

"You've been drinking, Elizabeth. Stay here!"

"My best friend is out there. She's human, Ramo. I'm going." She glared at him, daring him to argue with her.

He froze for a second, looking at her. "Fuck!" He opened the door. "Stay close to me."

The instant he opened the door, a crowd of people came dashing past them heading for the back exit, some screaming, others with terrified expressions on their faces.

They fought their way through the oncoming throng as Elizabeth tried to clear her muddled mind to be able to shift. The task was not easy as she worried not just for her friend, but for everyone in the bar. As they neared the main bar area she prayed no one was hurt.

She gasped in pure shock at the sight. People running, girls on top of a table huddled together in fear.

It seemed, every Were in the room had shifted and were trying to catch the Nightwalkers wreaking havoc in the bar.

There were a few humans on the floor covered in blood and she shuttered. God, please let them be okay. Please...

Elizabeth ran straight through the chaotic scene with no thought to her own safety. Heading for the bar where she left her friend, she pushed past stumbling bar goers who were blocked from the front door, hoping to escape out the back. Before reaching the long counter, she saw Sophia wasn't there. Did she pass her on the way out the back? Was she able to escape out the front?

She was trying to pick up her friends scent, but the alcohol all over the floor and the Nightwalker's stench were overpowering her senses.

As she searched the dining area of the bar, she took in the two large Nightwalkers, fighting with four trainees and Owen, who'd already shifted.

Ramo had described them perfectly. They were shaped like jackals, but as large as a grizzly bear. Their beady eyes were the most terrifying part of them, glowing as if they were possessed.

Ramo caught up with her, scanning the room for any others. His sharp gaze landed outside where several people were running down the street.

"They're attacking the whole city?" she asked, the image of young civilians, out for a good time, running down the street for their lives burned into her memory. Ramo knew about as much as she did at the moment, but he nodded wordlessly anyway.

"I need to go out there," he told her, already storming toward the door.

Elizabeth glanced at Owen, who'd managed to subdue the two Nightwalkers with the help of his pack members. He only met her gaze for a second before going after Ramo. Shuddering at the thought of him taking on more Nightwalkers, especially if he suspected she was up to something with Ramo a mere minute ago, she followed them both out the door. Did he know? If he got hurt or god-forbid, killed tonight… She couldn't think it. She needed to phase and help them.

The moment she stepped out of the bar to the cool night air something flew at her, landing right in her neck. She felt a sharp sting and something dangling. A dart? Grabbing for whatever was sticking out of her, she noticed Ramo and Owen backtrack as they too saw the flying object.

"Elizabeth!" Ramo twisted her hand around, taking the syringe. Whatever had been in the vial was now coursing through her bloodstream.

Panic surged through her, as her limbs began to feel very heavy. "What is it?"

Ramo crumpled the syringe, tossing it on the ground, gritting his teeth. "You can't phase."

"What?"

Looking around as more Nightwalkers stormed down the streets chasing screaming pedestrians, he said, "There are witches out here too. No Nightwalker would have been able to shoot this."

His hand gripped her wrist, leading her toward the nearest car. "You need to get out of here!"

"Ramo. I have to help."

"They just shot you with a serum that keeps you from phasing. How are you going to fight?"

"Give me a gun."

He gave her an incredulous look. "You fall asleep during weapons all the time. Hell no! Get in the car!"

A growl sounded to her left and she'd forgotten Owen was there, watching their entire exchange. Grunting once, she understood he was telling her to go as well.

Looking to Owen then Ramo, Elizabeth knew she was wasting valuable time. "Fine."

Opening the door, Ramo shoved her into the driver's side, even though there was a man sitting there. With pure terror in his eyes, the guy moved over to the passenger side to let her in. "What the...shut the door! Quick!"

She did and started the car.

"What you are doing?"

"I need to see what's happening. We'll be safe in here." She hoped.

Taking off in the direction Owen and Ramo ran, she beeped the horn at the people still on the streets. Rolling down the window she shouted at them. "Get inside somewhere and take cover." It was obvious it was worse out here. From where they were, she could make out four Nightwalkers ahead of them, claiming anyone in their path.

Her stomach rolled and the man sitting next to her gasped in fear as a Nightwalker jumped onto the back of a human man, knocking him to the ground, his long snout taking in his entire head.

"Christ! What the hell are those?"

Elizabeth glanced next to her, noting the man was hardly a man. He looked to be about twenty years old.

"Nightwalkers."

"How many are out there?"

"I don't know."

Where the row of bars and restaurants ended, the street cleared, and she punched down on the accelerator heading East on Division toward downtown.

A huge furry blur whipped across the street and she slammed on the brakes. A werewolf and a Nightwalker were tumbling on the ground. She didn't recognize the Were as a fighter, which meant other Graybacks were joining the fight.

"No!" she shouted when the Nightwalker sank its teeth into the Were's back leg, then turned to take off.

"It's okay…it's okay… He's leaving." The boy said next to her, sighing breathlessly.

"Oh God, no. She's…she's going to die," she uttered, stunned. How could this be happening? She wanted to go to the female Were on the ground, but she had to know what was going on. She had to see if Ramo and Owen were all right.

"It was just a bite. They'll be fine."

Shaking her head, she squeezed her eyes shut for a moment, then took off once again to catch up with the rest of the Fighters. "Their bite is poisonous to us. She won't live." Her voice cracked. The pain in her chest was insurmountable as she recognized the Were as the mother of those triplets who'd been scared at the first meeting Ramo had attended.

Elizabeth was going back for her if her mate didn't. After she checked on Owen and Ramo, she'd go back to her. She was a Fighter. At least, learning to be one and she had to stick with them. If she could only phase…

"Just a bite to the leg can kill us?" The boy was hanging on to the dashboard with one hand and the oh-shit-handle above the passenger window with the other, his wide-eyes looking all around for more Nightwalkers.

"Not humans. Werewolves."

"You said, 'us'."

"Yeah. I'm a Were."

The boy snapped his neck as he faced her. "What the…"

Pursing her lips at the look he was giving her, she caught the sight of a trainee leaping onto a condo complex and hanging there for a moment like King Kong, searching for the nearest Nightwalker ahead. After a few seconds, he jumped higher onto the next building as he headed east. She kept him in her sights as she drove on.

"You're a…a…" The boy let out a sharp breath. "Why aren't you out there?" he asked nervously.

"I can't phase. Don't worry. I'm not going to hurt you." She was used to how uncomfortable some humans were when they discovered she was a werewolf.

"No…it's just. I've never met one…a werewolf."

Giving him a stiff smile she asked, "What's your name?"

"Ryan."

They were in the heart of downtown now where the buildings were taller and closer together. The night sky was cloudless, a clear black backdrop to the towering buildings with their square yellow windows lighting up the street below. She could just make out Nightwalkers and Weres down the street and a few more werewolves who'd jumped onto buildings or gripping the side of them to get a better vantage point. As there were no

Nightwalkers doing this, she could assume they were incapable of jumping that high or hanging on.

"Nice to meet you Ryan. I'm Elizabeth. Thank you for letting me use your car."

Ryan let out a shaky laugh. "Sure no prob...Whoa!"

Owen raced across the street about fifty feet ahead of them, leaping onto a Nightwalker who was headed right toward him. They smashed into each other so hard, she heard cracking bones. As they tumbled onto the sidewalk, Owen jumped up first, grabbing the Nightwalker by the neck and smashing him into a bank vestibule window.

"Holy shit! That was bad ass," Ryan said, breathlessly.

Elizabeth let out a long breath she didn't know she was holding as Owen disappeared right down another street.

She was about to turn right onto the street he'd gone onto when something fell onto the roof of the car. Ryan and Elizabeth both jumped at the same time.

"What was..." Ryan began, but a second later the large black face of a jackal burst into their line of vision, it's snout upside down as it glared at them from the front window.

Without thinking, Elizabeth slammed on the brakes, sending the filthy shit flying across the hood and twenty feet into the air. It landed on his side, but leapt catlike back onto its feet, crouching menacingly as it glared at them in the middle of the street.

Slamming on the accelerator, she hit it with the front end, knocking it back several feet ahead. Hitting the breaks they watched to see if it got back up.

A row of tiny, round lights emerged from behind the fallen jackal and she realized it was more Nightwalkers, their glowing eyes honed in on them.

"Oh. Fuck." Ryan said.

Before she could react, a dark brown Were leapt from a building on her left straight to the street in front of them, facing the Nightwalkers. The headlights on Ryan's car shone bright onto Ramo's dark fur at his back. He was standing tall, his arms outstretched, claws out, daring them to attack.

A trickle of sweat fell down her back as her heart raced. He was outnumbered. She needed to help him.

Sensing what she was about to do, Ramo spun around, his razor-sharp eyes on her as she went for the door.

Ramo's massive claws seized the front of the car, his nails screeching across the hood. Hunching over he pushed Ryan's compact car with all his might. Their bodies propelled forward as the car sped backward down the street, parked cars zooming past them. They were both screaming as they flew, knowing Elizabeth had no control of the car.

The line of Nightwalkers and Ramo were tiny shapes in the distance as the car finally idled to a stop.

She and Ryan were both breathing hard, squeezing the dashboard with all their might.

"Are you okay?" she asked, when she could finally speak.

"Uh uh. You?"

"Yep."

She tried to make her eyes shift so she could see better down the street, but it didn't work. What she could make out was other Weres leaping down from buildings to help Ramo. The scene in the middle of the street became a blur of massive wolves and jackals bunched together as they battled it out.

Ryan reached for her hand and squeezed. "Don't."

She looked to him in confusion.

"That werewolf obviously wanted you out of harm's way. There's nothing we can do. You'll just get us killed."

Her eyes went to their clutched hands. She hadn't noticed she'd put the car back in gear, ready to drive directly to Ramo.

Ryan was right of course. She was useless in human form.

Nodding silently, she reached for her phone in her crossbody purse as Ryan craned his neck in every direction searching for another onslaught of Nightwalkers, but all seemed quiet over here.

There were several texts from Sophia.

Are you ok?

Liz?

Answer me!

I hid behind the bar. We're ok.

Please answer me!

Elizabeth sighed in relief. Remembering Sophia had been standing next to her cousin, they must have both ducked for cover.

I'm okay. Do you need a ride home?

Her friend answered instantly.

Thank fuck! I'm at my cousin's house.

Elizabeth responded quickly.

Good! Stay there. I don't know if they've captured them all. Please. Stay there.

Ok. What about you?

I'll be fine. I'll text when I'm home.
Please be careful. Love you!
Love you too!

"Helluva meet cute, huh?" Ryan said.

She stared out the front window. As she'd been texting, the fight had moved on. There was no one in the street up ahead.

Were they okay? Please let them all be okay.

And what was that look Owen gave her before he ran out of the bar? Did he know she'd been with Ramo in the bathroom? Could he smell her on him? It was hardly important at the moment, but if anything happened to him...

"Elizabeth?" Ryan interrupted her thoughts.

"Yeah?"

"So...Can I?"

What the hell was this kid talking about? "Can you what?"

She felt embarrassment ooze out of him. "Can I get your number?"

Elizabeth glanced at him disbelievingly then slammed her forehead into the steering wheel.

Chapter Twelve

"Three humans and two werewolves were killed on St. Patrick's Day when an attack of mutant jackals erupted near downtown…"

Elizabeth turned away from the television. CNN had been reporting the attack since last night with no other update except for the twelve wounded humans and two Weres. They weren't too concerned with the Weres who'd been hurt in the attack since they would heal quickly, but it was all she could think about considering one of them was Owen.

She'd gone back to where they'd seen Destiny, but her husband had carried her to the nearest hospital where she died in his arms. Elizabeth's stomach dropped for the umpteenth time, the image of the mother frightened at the meeting… Why did she join the fight? Why didn't she, Elizabeth do something to stop the Nightwalker? She kept thinking about everything she could have done. If Destiny hadn't been in the way she could have tried to run it over; shoot him if Ramo had given her a gun. It made her sick to think of her three children growing up without their mother.

What was more, Sharjeel, her happy go lucky friend and fellow Fighter had been killed downtown. She didn't know the humans who were dead now, but it didn't matter. Their deaths will forever live in her memory.

When Ramo first talked about what they were facing, it had been alarming to be sure, but it did not prepare them for what happened yesterday. How in the world could they foresee animals and witches going against, not just werewolves, but defenseless humans as well?

As hard as it's been having him here, she was never more thankful for Ramo's help than she was right now. She didn't care if she never slept again, she was going to practice her battle tactics and choke it up and learn how to handle every piece of weapon Ramo had. She wasn't the only one feeling vengeful. Pack members were blowing up Facebook, vowing revenge. Joe, the Grayback beta was seething in Owen's kitchen as he punched his thumb across his cellphone. She didn't know who he was texting, but it seemed important. She could understand his fierce need to be doing something. It was how everyone was feeling right now.

Owen's bedroom door opened, and Dr. Moros came down the hall. He was a handsome man in his mid-thirties who specialized in the supernatural anatomy. As a vampire, his help wouldn't have been welcome in a werewolf home, but as soon as he'd heard of the attack, Dr. Moros teleported straight to the city from the east coast to do what he could to help. Quite frankly, Elizabeth didn't care what he was, as long as he did what he could for Owen.

"How is he?" She asked, getting up from the sofa where she'd been perched for the last few hours. Owen had refused to go to the hospital, insisting the humans who were hurt needed all the attention.

"I've given him something to help him sleep. He'll

need a lot of rest for the next couple days. The abrasions on his chest and stomach will heal, but there may be scarring." He nodded at the look Elizabeth gave him, raising his hand in the air for patience. "He'll be all right, but the cuts the Nightwalkers inflicted were incredibly deep. Had he gotten stitches sooner, he'd be on the mend, but since it's been several hours since the attack, the skin had begun to close over infected tissue. I had to reopen some areas to clean the wounds. He's lucky he didn't die of infection."

Closing her eyes, she shook her head mutely.

"Are you all right? I can examine you if you're hurt..." Dr. Moros began, taking a cautionary glance at Joe, then down the hall. If Owen were awake right now, they'd all hear his snarl.

"No. I'm all right. Thank you doctor."

He took out his card and handed it to her. "Please, don't hesitate to call." Turning, he eyed Joe again who was now standing two feet behind him. "I'll get out of your hair."

Joe followed him out the door, evidently not trusting the vampire doctor in a house full of werewolves.

Elizabeth watched the doctor climb down the front stairs of Owen's townhome. Turning, he said something to Joe and then disappeared right on the spot. She jumped, knowing this would happen, but it was still frightening to watch someone teleport right in front of you.

Her phone chirped on the kitchen counter where she'd plugged it in to charge. She realized she hadn't slept all night and was still wearing the same green t-shirt dress. The thought of sleep didn't even occur to her, but she could use a shower and something to eat.

The text was from Ramo and her heart kicked as it always did when she saw those four little letters on her screen.

—*How is he?*—

—*He'll be ok. You?*—

—*All good.*—

—*Where have you been?*—

Wincing after she pressed the arrow, she cringed as she watched the little bubbles go back and forth. Did her text have to sound like a nagging girlfriend?

—*Just had a meeting with my Fighters.*—

Oh, of course. It was weird how she kept forgetting he was from another pack. She wondered if the other Graybacks felt the same way but doubted it.

Staring at his text for way too long, she couldn't think of what to say. Alone in the kitchen, she could still hear CNN in the living room, but other than that, the house was quiet. Too quiet. All of a sudden, she felt like an intruder, as if she shouldn't be there, which was crazy. Owen would want to see her as soon as he woke up.

Perspiration coated her skin as she thought of what he may ask her when he did wake.

Oh no.

Tunnel vision hit her, and she reached out for the nearest stool.

—*What's wrong???*—

Through her blurry vision, she saw his message pop up. How did he…

He was near.

She was on the verge of a panic attack and he was close enough to feel everything she was going through.

Shocked she hadn't had one last night, it was no wonder she would have one now just thinking about the attack and what she and Ramo had done in Owen's bar.

—*Elizabeth?*—

—*Please?*—

Before she responded, she stared at his name and the word 'please'. She stretched her senses out to find him and when she did, she let the warmth of his strength, his love fill her up.

Wait…

Was it love she was feeling from him? Whatever it was it was undeniably strong.

When her trembling slowed, she texted him back.

—*I need you.*—

The words just popped in her head, flowing straight to her fingers. She wasn't embarrassed or nervous; all the things she ought to be feeling. Instead, she felt a huge weight lift from her shoulders. It was good to actually say what she was feeling.

Watching the bubbles across her screen, she thought he was never going to respond.

—*You have no idea how much I need you right now. So much I can't be far from you. I physically cannot be away from you too long or I'll be sick. And the fact you're in his house is going to give me an ulcer.*—

—*Meet me at my place.*—

—*No*—

Flinching at his response, she hesitated before texting back.

—*Why?*—

She didn't have to wait too long for his next text, as if he were typing at lightning speed.

—*Because if I see you, I'm going to be all over you. As much as I want you, Owen needs to be in top form. There will be other attacks like last night or worse and our packs need to be focused on defending our Weres not on what's happening with us.*—

He was right of course, but she didn't know how to hide what she was feeling.

—*He's going to know. If he doesn't already, he's going to know how I feel about you.*—

—*Hide it Elizabeth. We have to.*—

—*I think he may know about the bar. In the bathroom.*—

—*Fuck!*—

More bubbles across her screen.

—*I'm sorry, Elizabeth. This is why I have to stay away from you. Will you be able to throw him off?*—

She didn't know what she would say, but she had to think of something.

—*Sure. I'll say I was throwing up in the bathroom or something.*—

—*I'm so sorry.*—

—*Stop apologizing. Just do me a favor…*—

—*Anything.*—

She smiled at the word 'anything'. Just a few weeks ago she was fighting with him and rolling her eyes every time he was around. And now here he was, her loudmouth husband, acting like a mated Were.

—*Don't stay away from me. If I have to hide it, you do too. We'll have to see each other during training and meetings, and I need you near me. I don't know what it is. I just do.*—

—*I know. It'll suck, but I'll be here.*—

—*Thank you.*—

His next message turned her vision blurry.

—Elizabeth, you're stuck with me. I couldn't leave even if I wanted to.—

It was as though fireworks erupted in her chest. She walked to the window with a smile, trying to put distance between her and Owen's bedroom.

—Careful. If you keep saying things like that, I'm going to fall hard...—

Leaving out the love word, she figured it might scare him away.

—I'm already falling baby.—

Elizabeth burst into tears.

****

The next night Owen held a mandatory meeting for the trainees. Since his bar had been boarded up for the time being while repairs were made, everyone packed into the alpha's townhome.

Unable to avoid the meeting, Ramo held onto the banister as he stepped up the front stairs, his equilibrium on the fritz due to the whisky fest he'd had all by himself the night before.

Head pounding, he wiped the sweat from his brow, wondering if he was possibly still drunk. It was light outside by the time he'd finally passed out and he'd slept till two in the afternoon, but his mind was still too fuzzy to function.

As hard as he'd drunk last night, it didn't take away the pain he felt at the thought of Elizabeth and Owen going on as couple. Knowing he'd been so close to having her, it was a kick in the ass to have her right back where she was.

Funny thing was, he never planned on building a relationship with her. He definitely hadn't planned on stealing the Grayback alpha's girl, but it seems that was his goal all along. The instant he'd seen her on the platform it was as though his selfish subconscious had decided for him. And the deeper he fell into her chaotic vortex of a life, the more he wanted her.

Joe answered the door and let him in. They both gave the other a curt nod, which goes to show they were warming up to each other. He wanted to wink at him to piss him off but didn't have the energy to start with him. Shit, he was losing the will to fuck with people. What was wrong with him?

Making his way into the living room, he faltered at the scene before him. The remaining trainees were seated on armchairs and at a round kitchen table, which was placed in between the kitchen counter and the family area. On the plush sofa, Owen sat bare-chested with his feet propped on an ottoman in front of him. Beside him was his wife.

The two looked like they'd just gotten out of bed. Elizabeth's hair was dry, but the piece of shit next to her looked like he'd just been given a sponge bath, with his wet blonde locks going every which way.

A dull pain hit his stomach at the sight of them together this way and he didn't know how to react. A voice in his head told him to rip the fucker's heart out and feed it to him, but another voice, which sounded like his asshole alpha, Adam told him to chill out.

When he was finished assessing Owen's lack of clothing, he took in Elizabeth's simple white T and yoga pants. Her hair, which was always in a damn ponytail due to their constant workouts was down, blanketing her shoulders and reaching down to just above her waist.

Her black eyes met his telling him everything he needed to hear right now. With her emotions blaring sadness for the loss of Sharjeel, her gaze told him she was his and this was just for show. He knew this of course since he had been the one to suggest it, but *fuck*...

"Thanks for coming, Perez." Owen gave him a grim smile as he reached his hand to Elizabeth and placed it on her thigh.

His hand was on her thigh.

Her fucking thiiiiiiigggh...

"Sure," Ramo replied, giving him a curt nod as he perched on a stool as far away from the couple on the couch.

Jesus, this was going to be hard. In all their meetings Owen rarely showed her affection like this. He was sure it was because it was inappropriate behavior for the rest of the pack, but he was also positive Elizabeth told Owen he didn't want to see public displays of affection. This was why he'd made his asinine demand on her weeks ago. He couldn't take it. Somehow he knew he wouldn't be able to handle seeing Owen put his hands on her and just seeing them sit close together nearly killed him, but now he had his hand on her THIGH!

Miles was giving his report, but he only had eyes for Elizabeth. She gazed down at the floor as if her mind were somewhere else too.

God, she was beautiful. In the months he'd been here, it seemed she became more beautiful with every encounter. He knew he shouldn't stare but holy hell she looked so amazing. He realized he never saw her relaxing on a couch before, with her feet tucked under her in plain clothes.

She was always high strung because he was around, and in her coffee stained jacket laden with ten bags. He found himself wondering what it would be like to cuddle with her on a sofa watching a movie and eating popcorn. As soft as she was, he would be in heaven and probably wouldn't be able to focus on the movie. The more he thought of this scenario, the more he wanted it.

Miles continued his report and when he mentioned a tranquilizer gun, Elizabeth's head shot up.

"...hit me in the back and I felt myself phasing back."

"I heard others were hit with this tranquilizer too," someone said.

Elizabeth's hand came up to grip her neck. "I was one of them."

Everyone looked to her curiously, but she spoke to Miles. "I hadn't turned yet, but I was hit in the neck and Ramo said I wouldn't be able to turn. It felt like warm liquid running through my body, weighing me down and I knew he was right."

"Are you okay now? Can you turn?" Miles asked.

Elizabeth nodded, but it was Owen who answered, giving her thigh a squeeze. "I had her phase earlier today to be sure. She's good."

He ground his molars as Elizabeth's cheeks flushed.

Did Owen make her phase back to human in front of him as well? There was no way he'd been standing there in front of Elizabeth's naked body in his own house and not try to do something. Is this why he looked all refreshed from his shower?

He was gonna be sick.

Jumping out of his seat, he crossed to them. Elizabeth's eyes widen as he glared at Owen. "I have to go."

Owen's narrowed gaze was all too knowing. "What's the rush? You know...you're not looking too well."

Sucking in his lips before answering, he said, "Overindulged last night. It's a habit after a fight to drink to the fallen." It wasn't as if he was lying, his Fighters did do this, but if he didn't leave right now, he was going to kill the Grayback alpha and kidnap his girl.

Owen nodded slowly, removing his hand from her thigh to around her shoulders. "Be sure to email me a report in the morning. I'll be much better by then," he said this as he played with Elizabeth's hair.

"No problem," he turned away from them before his eyes went up in flames. Before he could reach the door, Elizabeth's voice made him freeze in his tracks.

"Ramo?" She was standing five feet away from him with something in her hands and everything in her eyes. "Owen wanted me to give you this. Usually we have a ceremony for an act of valor in the pack, but since you're a Blacktail...well... You'll have to settle with just me."

He closed his eyes briefly, wishing to God her words could be true.

"So on behalf of our pack, thank you." Handing him a small medal pin, Elizabeth placed it in his palm, her fingers lingering on his skin as her eyes glazed over. He took it, closing his fingers around hers.

She jerked but didn't pull away. Biting her bottom

lip, her eyes raked over him as if she wanted him as much as he wanted her.

"Thank you," he said, pulling on her hand gently. His hard gaze glanced toward the family room, then, he brought her wrist to his mouth, giving her a light kiss.

Closing her eyes, she said weakly, "You're welcome."

****

Elizabeth fought the yearning coursing through her as she watched Ramo close the door behind him. Keeping the image of his wide muscular back in her mind's eye, she thought about Sharjeel's corny jokes, hanging onto the grief to cover up her emotions.

Owen was probably reading her now. Never mind the room full of angry, grieving Weres. It was *her* reaction to Ramo he was honed on.

Before Owen woke this morning, she'd decided to center on her sorrow for the deaths of her pack members, which wasn't hard. The devastation of the attack was enough to fill her with enough melancholy there was no chance she'd give away her feelings for Ramo.

She hoped.

"Did he touch you?" Owen had asked her when he'd woken, watching her closely. Anger had risen to the surface, anger at Owen for accusing her, anger at not being able to show her true feelings for Ramo. She'd held on to that rage and lied through her teeth to protect herself and her pack. Ramo was right. Owen would go ballistic if he knew the truth.

It's funny. They'd never been given the chance to be together and yet she felt like she'd lost him somehow. Her heart ached for him now. She'd nearly broke down and cried when Owen put his hand on her leg, knowing just what it was doing to Ramo.

She felt as though she was having an out of body experience. How did she end up here? How could she be falling in love with a husband she despised for so long and technically be with her alpha who could very well punish her for deceiving him?

Folding her arms across her stomach as though she could physically hide the truth of her heart, she walked back into the living room, back to Owen, back to her lies.

Chapter Thirteen

The weekend came to Elizabeth's relief and with it the moon heat. The night before the full moon was an evening of sexual desire, which Elizabeth had never experienced. As curious as she'd always been, it was too dangerous to risk pregnancy when she was a married Were. Mating with another man who was not her husband would have broken the contract between the two packs and she wasn't about to test the fate of her pack mates for a night of pleasure.

Shrugging off her jacket and shoes the minute she entered her apartment, she wiped her forehead with the back of her hand. Her temperature was rising, her stomach muscles tightening. It wasn't sunset yet, but her body was already feeling the effects of moon heat.

Where was Ramo? Was he thinking about her? Was he preparing for the moon heat? Would he take medication, or would he go to someone tonight?

Bile rose in her throat and she fanned herself. Loosening her ponytail and massaging her temples, she stormed into her kitchen, looking for the pills she always took. It was a little early, but something was off tonight, as though the moon heat were affecting her alone.

Opening the orange container she saw there were only two pills left. She usually took four. Would two pills be enough for the whole night?

Popping two in her mouth, she unbuttoned her shirt, fanning herself with the open flaps.

Did he have someone to go to? She'd slept through the last moon heat and it never even occurred to her he'd have someone else. There must have been several girls over the last few years he went to during this night. God, how many full moons were in a year?

She hated where her mind was going, but her emotions were going haywire along with her hormones.

Padding through the living room, she dug in her purse for her cell phone.

Where are you? Sending the text without further thought, she shrugged off her shirt, and tossed it on the couch. Standing in the middle of the room in her white bra and dress pants, she stared at her phone, but the text that came in wasn't from Ramo.

I miss you.

Guilt seared through her as she read Owen's text. They had decided to stay apart again during this moon heat. As tensions were high, there was every chance he could knock her up, if they weren't careful and the way Owen had been feeling lately, condoms would be the last thing on his mind.

The Nightwalker attack and his growing suspicion of Ramo had amplified Owen's stamina. Every chance he had, he was all over Elizabeth. She couldn't hold him at bay for much longer. It was bad enough she let him kiss and touch her every night, sleeping next to him as though they were married. This new obsessive side was both wearying and frightening. Every kiss, every touch, was a knife in the back to Ramo. She cried herself to sleep each night trying not to think of Ramo and what he was going through.

Ramo's text came in on top of Owen's.

On my way to drop off some paperwork to Hunter. You ok?

Sending a quick 'I miss you too,' to Owen, she then answered Ramo.

Yeah. She rolled her eyes at her lame answer, but what could she say? You better not go to anyone tonight. Even though I've been making out with Owen every day, I forbid you to even look at another girl.

??? Ramo's text only heightened her nerves.

Fuck it.

Without another thought, she let it all out.

I know you've had heat mates in the past, so I was wondering if you were going to someone tonight and I just wanted to say that I will rip your leg off if you do.

Send.

As she watched the bubbles on the screen she paced the floor.

LOL. Not a chance.

His response made her want to punch the air with glee.

Heading into the kitchen again, she took out a wine glass and popped open her favorite cheap bottle of red, her heart all a flutter. She stilled when his next text came in.

That goes for you too Vitale.

****

"To what do I owe this honor, Perez?"

Ramo strode into Owen's townhome, his eyes going everywhere as though he were making sure Elizabeth was nowhere near the prick on this day. Waving a file folder in the air, Ramo replied, "Just dropping off some papers."

Owen eyed the folder warily. "Beer?"

"Sure." He followed Owen into the kitchen and parked it on a barstool, placing the folder on the counter.

As Owen popped the cap off, he nodded toward the file. "What is it," he asked, then handed Ramo a LaGunitas IPA.

Ramo was still taking stock of the house, his chest tightening at Elizabeth's lingering scent all over the fucking place. Looking away at the two dirty wine glasses in the sink, he took a long swig of his beer nearly finishing it. Setting it down, he watched as Owen pulled a box of Cheese-It's from his cabinet and lean his hip on the counter.

The pain that seared his chest at the alpha eating Elizabeth's favorite snack no longer shocked him. He pictured her lounging on Owen's couch as she was the other night, eating her crackers and laughing at some shit her alpha said and the need to kill overwhelmed him.

"Wow. Is it that serious?" Owen asked, picking up on Ramo's rage.

Ramo waved a hand in the air as he polished off his beer. "Nah. Just the moon heat messing with me." He cleared his throat. "Speaking of which…"

Owen rolled his eyes as he set the crackers down.

"I'm in no position to tell you what to do…"

"You're damn right."

"But, I can remind you to stay away from Elizabeth tonight." Ramo knocked his knuckles on the file folder.

"This is a copy of our marriage license and the treaty."

Owen's face flushed, glaring at the folder as if it

offended him. "I already have a copy. All files were sent to me when I became alpha."

Rubbing his stubble, Ramo opened the manila folder and slid the top sheet toward Owen. "You haven't seen this one. Our adjudicator drafted it this morning."

Ramo didn't wait for Owen to read it. "It's a contract. States your relationship with Vitale must remain platonic." Ramo watched him carefully, trying to read every expression. "Hold hands, kiss…do whatever junior high kids do, but you are in no way to fuck my wife." His voice was calm and cool, projecting what he sure as hell wasn't feeling. He hated having this conversation, but there was no one to blame but himself. If he'd stayed all those years ago to be real husband to Elizabeth, he wouldn't be sitting in front of her boyfriend right now demanding them not to have sex.

Owen's eyes gleamed yellow, the vein on his forehead ready to pop. "Platonic? You're kidding me right?"

"Nope. Can't risk the chance of pregnancy when she's married to me. It'll break the treaty and with everything going on, both our packs would suffer."

Owen tossed the sheet on the counter. "She can't get pregnant unless it's the moon heat and we've never been together on those days, so this is shit."

Ramo shrugged. "Still can't risk it." He pointed to the contract. "Elizabeth's great-grandmother was human, which means she has human blood. She can very well get pregnant on normal days." Ramo knew they were reaching with that one, but stranger things have happened in the supernatural world.

"I'm not signing it."

"Yes you will. If you don't, the treaty is null. You want to explain to your pack why you don't have our backing at the worst possible time?"

Growling, Owen leaned over the counter, pointing a finger in his face. "This is bull shit! You're staking your claim on a woman who doesn't want you."

Ramo smirked as he stood. "Whatever, Hunter. Just keep it in your pants." Turning he headed for the door, but Owen's next words stopped him dead in his tracks.

"Is it a breach of contract if I've already fucked her?"

A stab of pain pierced his chest, burning his insides as though he'd been shot by a firing squad. He saw red. Blood. Red. Before he knew it, he had Owens throat in his hand and the alphas' back against the wall. "You're lying!" Ramo's voice was animal-like, his wolf side mere seconds from coming out.

Owen's smug smile taunted him. "Come on. You're close enough." Licking his lips he said conspiratorially, "You smell that?" He jutted his chin out. "It's her. She's all over me."

The blow to Owen's right temple did nothing to dull the fury. Shaking out his hand, he left the piece of shit knocked out on the floor and stormed out.

Fuck!

He was lying. He had to be lying. Either he was or Elizabeth had lied to him.

She wouldn't. Not now. Not when they'd become so close. He'd believed her when she'd told him she was a virgin. There was no way she'd sleep with Owen when he knew her heart belonged to him.

Fear spread throughout his body and he felt like a little bitch. He'd been reduced to a jealous schmuck. Incredible dread squeezed his heart as he thought of the unimaginable.

Owen could have commanded it.

If he had simply used the right words, she would be powerless to stop him. Hell, Owen was a smart guy. He could have said the right things to make it seem she wanted it.

Ramo brought his fist to his mouth, trying not to vomit the beer he'd just had as he sped down the street.

Elizabeth and Owen.

Elizabeth in his bed.

His wife in Owen's bed.

Her dark hair sprawled across his pillow as he pumped into her.

Smash!

Ramo ignored the shards of glass in his hand from punching the window. It didn't hurt. It felt like kittens licking his skin compared to what was going on in his head. And now he had two smashed out windows on his new car and he didn't give a shit.

She would regret it. He was going to make her regret she'd ever laid eyes on Owen Hunter.

Then, he was going to fuck the ever-loving shit out of her.

Chapter Fourteen

"Not now Nonni," Ramo didn't spare Elizabeth's grandmother a glance as the nosey old lady cracked her door open the instant he'd busted the hinges off the building door, too impatient to wait for someone to buzz him in. Elizabeth's grandmother uttered something quick in Italian and shut the door.

He treated Elizabeth's apartment door with the same indifference he'd had downstairs. Her cry of shock irritated him. How dare she be shocked right now? He was the one who was stunned beyond measure.

His eyes followed her every move as she came toward him from the kitchen. She was in a long t-shirt and nothing else. Her hair was gloriously loose, and she held a wine glass in her hand. Some opera was playing on her tiny wireless speakers and all the lights were turned off.

She was trying to calm her body from the heat's effect. The dim light of dusk washed over her perfect face and he didn't know if he wanted to kiss her or slam his head into the wall.

"What are you doing here? It's almost sunset." Elizabeth glanced toward the window.

"So?" He didn't trust his voice yet, his body was still shaking from fear and anger. Walking along the small island and into the living room, his yellow eyes searched for something.

"What do you mean, 'so'? We can't be near each other right now. It's too dangerous. What's wrong with you? And what are you looking for?" Her body turned, following his movements as he circled the room.

He messed with the pillows on her sofa. He honestly didn't know what the hell he was looking for, but a little voice in his head told him he needed proof. Something to show she hadn't betrayed him.

"Signs," he said simply.

"Signs of what? Was there another attack?"

He grimaced, biting down on his molars. "You can say that." He thought about her alpha hitting the linoleum and wished he would of finished the job.

"You're freaking me out," Elizabeth said, backing away toward the windows.

His glare must have been nothing short of terrifying. With his head bent, he stalked her, mirroring the wolf he was. "Did you fuck him?"

Her head jerked back, a crease forming on her delicate brow. "What? No, of course not. Ramo, why are you asking me this?"

"I don't believe you." But shit, he wanted to. He desperately wanted to.

Taking a step back from him, her eyes turned cold. "Well that's your problem because I know what I did and didn't do."

Fists clenched at his sides, he couldn't move. "Your scent is all over him. All over his fucking house. I know you've been staying there. You really expect me to believe you haven't fucked him?"

"Get out!"

He scoffed. "No."

"I mean it. You're pissing me off. Get out!" She pointed at the door, her cheeks flushed.

For a moment he had the decency to feel ashamed, then pure agony washed over him as he fixed his gaze at the woman who would be the death of him. She could hate him and despise him all she wanted, but he would love her till the day he died. She was a part of him, under his skin, in his blood, etched in his fucking heart. He'd tried to avoid losing himself to another for so long and he knew why. Loving this woman was going to kill him.

When he spoke, his voice sounded like an echo of himself, hollow and dead. "I can't...I can't stand by and watch you with him. It's eating me alive. I know I deserve this pain, but it's destroying me. I have no right to ask you these things, but please don't lie to me to spare my feelings. I want to believe you. God, I want to, but the look on that cocksucker's face..."

"Come here," she cut off his desperate rant. She was calm again, the pills she must have taken and the wine helping to control her hot temper.

He stood there frozen for a beat, unbelievably frightened of her.

She held out her hand. "Come here," she repeated.

Taking careful steps to her, he was at a loss for words. For all he knew she was going to kiss him or punch him.

She placed a hand on his chest, her thighs rubbing together as the moon made it's ascent. With her free hand, she took hold of his, bringing his index and middle finger to her mouth. He sucked in a breath as she took his fingers into her mouth, her hot tongue lapping around them.

His cock punched out, straining against his jeans as he stared, dumbfounded.

With her eyes focused on his, she slid his fingers from her plump lips, bringing them down and under her shirt. It took only a second to realize his wife wasn't wearing underwear and his stomach tightened as he slid his moist fingers into her.

He groaned and his lids fell, bending closer to her. She took him in as far as she could and when he felt her barrier still intact, his eyes shot open. He gripped her tightly to him, his forehead to hers.

"See?" She whispered.

He shook his head, his body trembling from the shame, the anger, the insurmountable jealousy.

"I'm yours, Ramo…"

Whatever else she was going to say, he didn't need to hear. Squeezing her tighter to him, he nuzzled his mouth in the crook of her neck, holding her still as he took in the smell of her soft skin, waiting for the trembling to subside.

He held her against him with his arm laced around her back and fingers deep inside her warm body. The relief he felt was extraordinary.

"I'm sorry," he mumbled into her shoulder, feeling like the biggest prick on the planet.

Her chest heaved fast against him, her full breasts pushing into his stomach and her muscles clenched around his fingers. He heard her heavy breaths and knew if he made one single move, she'd come.

"You don't trust me," she breathed.

He shook his head, his mouth still firm in her neck. "I do. I don't trust him. I thought he…" He felt sick again.

"Forced me?"

He nodded.

She slid her hands up his arms and around his back, up his neck and to the sides of his head. She made him look at her. "I need you. Now."

Ramo covered her mouth with his as he expertly pumped his fingers inside her. She came hard, spasming around him, her moans vibrating against his lips. As she settled down he withdrew from her.

She gripped his arm, clinging to him as though she couldn't walk. "Don't stop," she whispered.

Shaking his head, he murmured, "I won't." Then he swooped her up into his arms and carried her into her bedroom and to the bathroom. He set her down gently to run the shower then came back to her. She watched him as he slid her t-shirt up over her head and flung it onto the floor. Biting his lower lip he gazed at her, wanting to bend her over and take her against the sink. But he knew he had to go slow with her.

One hand fell to her waist as he grazed the side of one breast with the other, his knuckles sliding under the plump weight and back up. "Are you sure about this?" He asked, eyeing her cautiously, already knowing what she'd say.

She smiled, one eyebrow arching. "I think we've waited long enough.

He smirked and his cheeks hurt with the effort. "Let's shower first. I need to get his stench off you."

She lowered her gaze but nodded.

He shrugged his jacket off, never taking his gaze off her. He watched her eyes track his every move as he reached over his head to pull off his shirt. His little bad ass did blush when he took off his jeans but smiled appreciatively.

"You like what you see, Vitale?" he crooned devilishly.

"Yes I do, Perez," she countered and turned toward the shower.

His eyes followed every curve as she stepped in. God, that ass! He clenched his teeth as he climbed in after her. They stood under the hot spray in total silence. He was amazed at how natural this felt, as though they'd done it before. The peace surrounding them was nothing he'd ever felt. He was surprised at how calm he was when a minute ago he'd busted down her door. Either the moon heat was playing tricks on them or for the first time in his life he was experiencing how it truly felt to be with the one you loved. He hadn't told her yet. Accusing her of sleeping with her alpha and then declaring his undying love to her seemed tactless. Truth be told, he was terrified of declaring himself. What if she shot him down or told him it was too soon? Having her with him, her wet skin glossing before his eyes, he sure as hell didn't want to lose her.

It took everything he had not to slide himself inside her. It would be so easy. All he'd have to do is lift her and *ahhh...*

He switched places with her so he could rinse off and to keep himself from taking her virginity in a shower. Running his hands over his face, he opened his eyes and saw her staring at him. Not at his face, but at his hard length.

"I love it," she said, glancing up at him through her lashes, her voice huskier than usual. "You're beautiful."

Smiling at her comment, he rubbed the back of his head and neck, his head bent back but his eyes always on her. Never. Leaving. Her. He wanted to cherish the expression on her face for as long as he lived. "You are."

She reached for the bar of soap, lathering it in her delicate hands. She'd didn't meet his eyes and he noticed her cheeks flush. "I've never been in a shower with someone."

Thank fuck! He thought but kept his comment to himself. He'd stuck his foot in his mouth enough today.

She began running the bar of soap over her arms as she spoke. "I wouldn't normally be this slow. I'm always in a hurry and I shower pretty quickly, but now I have an audience so I feel like I should make a show of it." She giggled and his heart nearly burst from the sound.

"I'll take care of this," he said, taking the soap from her. "And if you're in the mood to dance for me, by all means…" he teased.

****

Relaxing some, Elizabeth watched him with heated breaths as he lathered every inch of her body. He began with her arms and back, then down her neck and chest. He lifted each thigh in turn, taking his sweet time, gently squeezing their thickness. Her gaze fixed on his muscled chest and arms, surprised at how a man with enormous biceps could be so gentle with her.

Ramo's eyes yellowed when he reached her breasts, his lids lowering as he cupped them both. "Do you have any idea how beautiful you are?" Running his thumbs over the hardened nipples, he hitched in a breath. "Do you have any idea how long I've wanted to touch these?" He didn't seem to want a response, as though he were talking to himself. "You fit perfectly," he purred, massaging them and she felt how heavy they were in his grasp.

When he pinched her nipple she nearly came again. Crying out she gripped his arms. "Ahhh, Ramo. Please." She watched his taut jaw twitch as he continued to torture her body. Running her hands over his pecs, she pressed herself against him, needing him close.

"Soon," he whispered, then turned her around again. He brought her under the water to wash her hair, going back to the business of cleaning.

She helped him since her hair was so thick and long. When she arched her back to rinse out her hair, her breasts angled toward him and he moaned, bending low to suck one nipple in his mouth as his thumb covered the other. Her fingers stilled in her hair as the feel of his wet, hot mouth over her nipple sent a bolt of fire straight down to her core.

Gripping the sides of the shower, she tried to keep her footing as he played with her breasts, making his way down her slick body.

Kneeling before her, his fingers easily slid into her as his mouth found her sweet spot, sucking and flicking his tongue. Her body bowed as her orgasm rocked her body.

He hummed a soft laugh against her, and the sensation nearly killed her. She brought her hand to the back of his skull trim, keeping him in place. "Do that again," she demanded.

She felt him smile, then, squeezing her ass with one hand and playing with a nipple with the other, he hummed a moan against her, and she came again.

"Ramo. Oh God. Ramo."

He caught her as her legs gave out and carried her out of the shower. He didn't bother with a towel as their bodies were so hot the cool air actually felt like a relief.

Laying her out on the bed, he came up over her, wet chest meeting wet chest and claimed her mouth in a hungry kiss. "You come so fast, baby," he uttered, breathlessly.

Blushing as he ran his mouth down her neck, she replied, "It's the moon heat."

His head came up and he gave her a mock frown. "Ouch."

Kissing him as she held his face between her hands she said, "I took pills, but for some reason I don't think they're working. I can't control myself."

He gently bit her chin, then ran his tongue over her lips. "I took enough pills to sedate me for a month."

"Really?"

Nodding, he said, "I don't think that shit works when we're together." He pushed his hips against her, and she moaned. "Can you imagine if we didn't take them? Fuuuuuuckkk."

"Ramo," she whispered, for no reason other than to urge him closer, her stomach tightening at the need. Her hands ran over his slick, sinewy back. If she could devour him at this moment she would.

He glanced down at their bodies, his hips moving slowly. She barely recognized his voice. "I want to go slow, but I don't think I can... You have to tell me when or I'm going..."

"Now." she cut him off. "Please Ramo."

Balancing his weight with one arm, he spread her legs wider with the other. Positioning himself at her entrance he slid just the tip in. She felt his control, knowing he wanted to make her comfortable. Planking himself on his forearms underneath her shoulders, he kissed her gently as he slid in a bit more, her body stretching to accommodate him. When he reached her barrier he made her meet his gaze. "Elizabeth?"

When she looked at him, her heart squeezed tight, her love for him was too much to bear.

Staring deep in her eyes as though her soul were on fire, he murmured, "I love you," then filled her completely.

Her cry of shock and pain was drowned out by his deep moan. He braced himself, frozen inside her as he panted, his eyes squeezed shut. "Are you okay?"

"Yes," she winced, her voice strained. "It's…it's okay. The pain's going away."

Nodding, he pulled his lips in, biting down hard.

"Are *you* okay?" she whispered.

Letting out a breath he said, "Yeah." He met her eyes. "You're so tight babe and I just… need a minute." Keeping his body still, he kissed the tip of her nose, then stared quietly at her for long while. His features saddened for a brief moment, his thoughts clearly not good. "I wish I could come inside you."

Her heart tightened. "Ramo…" she began, but he stopped her with a kiss.

"I know," he said into her ear, "I'll be careful," then began moving.

Any and all thoughts drifted away as he eased himself in and out of her. She wanted to stop him, to tell him she loved him too. To assure him she wanted to be with him for forever, to lay with him every moon heat and give him a dozen children, but the sensations he was igniting within her wiped away any coherent thought.

She met his every thrust with sure desperation, never wanting him to stop. How on earth had she gone so long without experiencing this? Caught between professing her undying love and slapping him for leaving her when they could have been doing this for years, she felt her body climaxing for the millionth time and tears sprung to her eyes.

When the haze lifted, she searched his gaze and what she saw astounded her. He was not the cool, smug man she knew him to be. He was no longer the angry beast he was earlier either. As he continued to thrust, moving deeper and deeper, Ramo appeared to be in a lethal trance, his dark smolder penetrating her. "Tell me you're mine," he demanded, his voice deep, animal-like. "Tell me."

"I'm yours, Ramo. Yours," she pleaded, her nails digging into his back.

The moan that escaped him as he threw his head back nearly burst the windows. She covered his mouth with her hand before he woke up the entire building. Biting her palm, he came up, slipping out of her and brought his swollen sex between her breasts. Seizing her fleshy mounds, he pushed them together, squeezing his thick cock as he pumped, trembling as he finished. She felt him hot and warm against her skin and pure ecstasy rushed through her.

His moans subsiding, he exhaled noisily, his breaths tickling her hand, which was still pressed to his mouth. She stared at him, mesmerized at his damp skin. He looked so magnificent above her, so powerful and full of lust.

"Shit," he breathed, his chest rising and falling

rapidly. "Let me clean you up."

He was off the bed, in the bathroom then back to her in an instant, lying alongside her. Cleaning her up, she watched the concentration in his eyes, his strong jaw still slick with sweat. She shivered slightly, but not from the cold. She was never more certain of her feelings than she was right then, looking at her husband's beautiful face. It felt so right to be here with him, so incredibly perfect. As soon as the thought came, so did her doubts. She wanted to shove them out of her head, to never think of their time apart again.

"What's wrong?" he asked concern in his eyes. He tossed the towel on the floor and leaned his head in his fist, hovering over her.

"I'm just happy," she sighed, turning onto her side to face him.

He studied her, his eyes going over every feature. "You have doubt though."

Shifting slightly on her white sheets, she really wished werewolves didn't do the emotional reading bit. She pulled her lips in, biting down as she tried to think of what to say that wouldn't ruin their moment. Finally, she met his eyes. "I don't want to."

He nodded, his hand coming up to caress her hair. His jaw ticked as he got lost in her thick tresses. Finally, he whispered. "I was so stupid."

"Ramo, you don't have…"

"Please." He cleared his throat. "Let me do this. It's the very least I can do."

When she didn't say anything, he went on.

"I should have been straight with you. I should have told you I wasn't ready. I should have told you, you were too young to be tied down by a degenerate like me. But don't think for one second I forgot you." He gripped her hair tighter at his last words then sat up to lean against her headboard.

Sitting up to face him, she brought her unmade sheet to cover her chest, her long hair cascading around her.

There was a glimmer in his eyes and the look he gave her melted her insides. "God, you're incredible," he murmured.

The compliment was so real, so heartwarming she almost cried.

"There wasn't a day in all of ten years I didn't wake up and think, I could be waking up to the most beautiful woman in the world. Your hair, your eyes, *you* haunted me every single day. I thought, the longer I stayed away, the easier it would be to forget you, but it didn't happen.

"I did some pretty unforgivable shit. Things I'm not proud of to forget you...I...hope one day you'll forgive me. I'm not dumb, though. I know it will take a lifetime for you to trust me. Fuck, Elizabeth, you are everything. The very reason God tainted this world with my presence. I don't exist without you, *Jesus*, I know that now."

He rubbed his face with his hands, clearly struggling with his next words.

"I'll understand if you never want to see me again, but I'm not going anywhere. I'll stay out of your way, but I'm not leaving you. Never again. I will watch you date, marry, mate..." His swallowed hard, his temple throbbing at the word, *mate*. "But your man will always have to deal with me, because I'm yours. You've marked me in more ways than you know."

Elizabeth didn't know what to say. What *do* you say to something like this? She was still thrilling to the fact he'd thought about her while they'd been apart. It was all too much for her to take in, but he'd said it all.

He loved her.

He wasn't going to leave her.

So help her, she believed every word.

"Say something, Elizabeth. Anything. Tell me to fuck off, but please…"

"I want you in my mouth," she said.

He stiffened, his eyes widening. "What?"

She looked down as his erection swelled magnificently between them. Dropping the sheet, she sat up on her knees, flaunting her ample breasts he loved so much. His eyes immediately shot to her chest and yellowed, a low growl building in his heaving chest. "You heard me, Ramo. I want to do to you what you did to me."

****

"Elizabeth…" he said, hesitantly. She had no idea what she was doing to him. His back pressed against the headboard, he watched this sexy goddess move over him, her dark hair spilling over her shoulders and her amazing tits. Jesus Christ he could come just looking at her. But in the back of his sex-driven mind, he needed to know she was okay. She didn't have to forgive him. He'd work his entire life for that, but he didn't want her worrying he'd ever leave her. There was just no chance in hell that was happening.

"I heard you Ramo. I did. And I believe you. Now let me show you how much your words mean to me."

He watched in awe as she kissed him, running her tongue around his mouth and lip ring, nipping his lip.

Tilting her head, she bent to kiss his neck. He gripped her head as she moved lower, running her tongue along his chest, down to his pec. Shit, she felt so good. He couldn't remember ever feeling so heady, so incredibly aroused and knew it had to be the fact it was Elizabeth, his beautiful wife that was making this so fucking perfect. The feel of his wife, the woman he loved was like no other. She continued to kiss him all over, and when she took his nipple between her teeth, his hips jerked. "Ahhh, Elizabeth. Fuck!" His hands fisted in her hair as he watched her tongue flick over him.

And then she was moving lower, leaving a wet trail as she positioned herself between his legs. She glanced up through her lashes, her black eyes almost teasing him. "Tell me what to do okay?"

Jesus, he was so wound up he was near terrified. If it felt this amazing now and she hadn't even... "Ahhhhhhhh..." he cried, his head angling back as she licked his tip, her soft hand gripping the base of him.

"Is this okay?" she asked between laps.

"Fuck yeah," he grunted, gripping the sheets at his side.

"Can I put the whole thing in my mouth?"

"Jesus Christ Elizabeth. I feel like I'm in the best porno ever. Yes, baby. Do whatever you want," he told her, his voice breathless.

When she took him deep in her mouth, he fought the urge to pump his hips, but she didn't need his help. Every time her mouth slid back down him she took him deeper and deeper, her hand traveling down to grip his tight balls.

"You can kiss those too," he teased.

She smirked up at him, then bent lower, sheathing

both sacs in her hot mouth. Her tongue did this thing…

"*Fuck*!"

Taking her hand, he brought it to his swollen sex, not knowing if he wanted her back on his dick or right the fuck where she was. Her hand fit around him perfectly as she pumped him and sucked his balls. Good lord, he'd never fainted before, but he was sure going to pass the hell out.

His vision hazy, he could see her hips grinding, her arousal as potent as his and she began to moan. Coming up again, she took his thick cock into her mouth, sucking him with more fervor.

His hand gripped the back of her head as his hips punched up, meeting her eager draws. "I'm going to come. Elizabeth…"

His words only drove her on.

"Baby, you have to stop, or I'll come in your mouth."

Slowing, she rubbed his length with her hand. "It'll be less messy. Should I swallow it or spit it out?"

Good lord, was she reading from a script?

"Whatever you're comfortable with my love."

She picked up where she left off in a heartbeat, closing her eyes as she took total control.

Bending his head back, he gripped the top of her headboard over his head as he fucked her mouth, shouting her name when he exploded on her tongue.

His breaths were loud and fast, his chest pumping like he'd just ran up Everest. And what finally killed him? The look on his wife's face as she met his gaze and swallowed.

Chapter Fifteen

—Can I come by?—

Owen's text drove her into a panic. It was seven in the morning. Ramo had only left two hours ago and his scent was all over her apartment. About to jump into the shower, she texted back with trembling hands.

—I'm out the door. I'll come by you.—

Before he could protest she added,

—I'll bring breakfast.—

He only texted with a,

—Ok.—

Taking the fastest shower where she reluctantly scrubbed away Ramo's love making from her body, she got dressed and ran out the door. After picking up a couple skillets at the diner by her house, she jumped into an Uber and headed to Owen's.

The moment he opened the door, he grabbed her, hugging her fiercely.

"Mmmm, I've missed you," he purred.

She tried not to think of anything else, but him. Pulling back she said, "Me too." As he went to kiss her, she noticed a fading bruise on the top of his left cheek. She stopped him. "What the hell happened?"

He looked confused, then rolled his eyes. "Oh. Nothing."

"It's not nothing. That must have been one hell of a bruise if you haven't healed yet. Tell me what happened."

He let go of her with a sigh and walked into the living room. "Ramo happened."

Elizabeth froze. "What?" Oh God. What happened? What did he know? Should she be worried? If Owen knew about them he wouldn't be this calm would he? She was jumping to conclusions. Ramo would have said something last night.

"He came over last night and we got into it. It's fine. We'll get over it."

Relaxing some at his nonchalance, she followed him to the dining room table and set the food down. Carefully, she asked, "What did you argue about?"

He sat down, leaning back as he waited for her to take out the food. "You."

She tried not to let that affect her too much. She knew Owen had told Ramo they'd slept together. She just didn't bother to ask Ramo how he'd reacted. "What about me?"

Crossing his arms, he watched her for a long while, his face expressionless.

"Owen?"

Pursing his lips, he said, "What if I told you, the Graybacks will always honor the pact with the Blacktails? No matter what?"

"Ummm...we have to honor it. I'm...connected," she said with some trepidation, "with a Blacktail."

He waved his hand in the air and leaned his elbows on the table. "Yes, but what if you weren't?"

Elizabeth had no idea where this was going. She sat down next to him at the round table and handed him his Styrofoam container. "I'm not sure I follow..."

He ignored the food and turned to face her,

grabbing her hands. "Hear me out… I think I can get our adjudicator to come up with a new contract, one where you wouldn't have to be bound to Perez."

She shot back, her heart in her stomach. "What do you mean?" The thought of concealing her shock was ludicrous. The only thing binding their two packs *was* their marriage. What was he saying?

"We can still have a union with the Blacktails without the goddamn marriage contract." He squeezed her hands tighter. "Marry *me.*"

OH FUCK!

"Owen…"

"Listen. I'll work out the logistics with our packs. But I'm sick and tired of Perez lording his status over me. You're my girlfriend and I want everyone to know it."

"Everyone does know."

"NO!" He sat back, letting go of her hands. "Everyone knows you're married to *him.* I'm the fucking alpha and this marriage has made a fool of me."

Shaking her head she tried to search for the right words, but they didn't come. She didn't want to marry Owen. She didn't want to be with him. Ramo was her husband. She wanted to admit everything. Now was the time. Elizabeth had to tell him the truth. To tell him she was in love with Ramo and they couldn't be together anymore.

Then, the horrid truth hit her just as she was going to confess everything…

Owen didn't *ask* her to marry him. He had *ordered* it.

No. He must have misspoke. He would never force her hand this way. Owen was always careful with his words *because* he was her alpha. "Owen... We've never even discussed marriage. Are you...asking me to marry you or..."

His look turned passive as he considered her unspoken question. "Eat your food, Elizabeth."

Taking her plastic fork, she scooped up some of her skillet, noting he'd just ordered her to do something, again.

****

Training that day was by far the worst session yet. Try as she might, Elizabeth could not get her head in the game. They were paired with each other in hand-to-hand combat. She was with Grayson who kept smirking and laughing every time she missed her mark.

Images of the previous night kept flashing through her head and her body would flush. To cover these inopportune moments when Owen would look her way, she'd smile at him coyly to make it seem she was thinking about him.

She avoided making eye contact with Ramo even though she was always aware of where he was in the room. His presence was never more pronounced than after what they had shared.

They had parted ways at five in the morning, slowly kissing in her doorway like teenagers for what seemed like hours. Ramo's back up against the doorjamb, she'd leaned into him between his legs trying to get her fill of him.

Her mouth was still sensitive from his morning shadow, her body so deliciously sore. There was so much to be said between them, but neither of them had brought up Owen. Although, Owen was always there, a barrier between them they couldn't quite break.

As horrid as she felt for betraying Owen, she could not summon an ounce of guilt. Making love to Ramo felt so right. She'd wanted to curl her arms around his waist and kiss his gorgeous jaw when she entered the gym. Instead, she'd walked in hand in hand with Owen. As soon as Ramo spotted them he'd turned his back, hands fisted, his shoulder's tight.

What could she do? She didn't want to continue going behind Owen's back and she most definitely didn't want to hurt Ramo this way. What if she came clean to Owen? If she told him she wanted to give her marriage a chance, he would have to let her go. She was Ramo's wife.

But Owen is your alpha who just commanded you to marry him.

It couldn't be true. He wouldn't. Couldn't. Owen would never force her hand, but if he knew what she'd done... A male Were's temper was so unpredictable... On some level he must suspect there was something between them, otherwise he wouldn't have made such a ridiculous order.

Elizabeth would have to make him clarify. Nothing was set in stone. He must...

"Look alive, Vitale." Grayson shouted at her and she shook herself, getting back into position. Ignoring the two men in her life who were only a few feet away, she focused on beating her frustrations out on Grayson.

They parried around the room, warding off each other's blows. When Elizabeth tried a glima move, in which she cupped her right hand around his neck and dug her right elbow into his chest, she was able to stick her leg out and knock him down on the floor. Grayson landed with *huff,* his face reddening with embarrassment.

"Nice, Vitale," Ramo called to her.

Before she could acknowledge him, Grayson swiped his leg across the floor, kicking her feet from under her and she went down, her back and head hitting the hardwood with a loud clap. The air was knocked out of her and she literally saw stars.

Ramo was kneeling over her in a heartbeat. "Shit move, Grayson. She'd already bested you. The rules are to start again, not retaliate."

"It's fine. I'm fine," she said as she sat up slowly, blinking away the wooziness.

Owen came over and knelt on her other side. "Where the hell are the mats?"

Ramo grimaced. "This facility doesn't have any." They looked around at the basketless court. "You okay?" he asked, reaching out to check the back of her head, but before he could touch her, Owen stopped him.

"She'll be fine," he snapped, covering the back of her head with his own hand. "Shit, you have quite a bump there."

Elizabeth had no doubt she had some sort of a concussion. Her head throbbed and she knew she was gonna have a hell of a headache for the rest of the day. "I'll heal," she said, not daring to meet Ramo's eyes.

The moment was incredibly uncomfortable with the two of them hovering over her. Focusing on the pain, she tried not to picture Ramo's hands on her skin.

God, this was torture! He was right there, wanting to comfort her and he couldn't touch her. Not with Owen around. If she felt it, Owen must have too. It was too much. Nausea hit her and she didn't know if it was from the bump on her head or the fact she was cheating on her boyfriend with her husband. Closing her eyes, she bit her lip to stifle a giggle.

"Elizabeth, are you okay?"

Oh God, she had no idea which one of them had just spoken to her. Taking a deep breath, she opened her eyes. "I'm good. Really. Pain's going away." She made the mistake of meeting Ramo's eyes, who smirked at the familiar words from the night before. Despite how awkward and painful this was for him, she was glad he had that. The knowledge he'd been her first.

Just then, Owen's phone went off and he cursed getting up, "Stay right here."

"Stop it, I'm fine. You guys are making a big deal over nothing," she scoffed.

Owen answered the phone and turned away.

"Let's get you up. Are you dizzy?" Ramo asked from behind her as he helped her to her feet.

"No," she lied.

"Liar." His hands lingered way too long under her arms, sliding down to her waist. She felt the back of his knuckles graze her spine tenderly as he whispered, "When can we be alone?"

Stiffening, she held her breath, her blood roaring in her ears. How can his simple question make her body hum with desire?

She knew she was asking for trouble, but there was no way she could tell him no. "Sunrise. After run," she muttered back, and he squeezed her waist before walking away.

As soon as he stepped away from her, Owen turned around with his phone at his ear and an arm crossed over his chest. He stared hard, his eyes searching. He mouthed the word, *ice* and she shook her head, letting him know it wasn't necessary. His gaze stayed on her as he spoke to whoever it was on the phone. Once, his eyes flicked to Ramo and then back to her.

What was he thinking? Did he pick up on her lust just now? She hoped the pain she was in would mask her desire. Giving him a weak smile she turned to listen to Ramo's end of session lecture.

"I've received several emails from your pack members who want to join up. After St. Patrick's Day, I don't blame them. As they will be starting fresh, Danny Amato will be training them. He's asked to sit in with the new trainees to see how we're doing, so we'll have an audience then. Our next class will be in two days. I'll text the time and place after sunrise."

Owen stuffed his phone in his pocket and walked over to them. "For tonight's run, we will be on a soft patrol. The mayor has given us permission to patrol the city." Owen divided the trainees into groups of four with half in the city and half in the surrounding suburbs. "If you run into any trouble, howl out. Do not engage alone."

She gathered her things, looking forward to this evening's full moon run. Taking her time to untie and retie her shoelaces, she peeked at Ramo who was typing something into his phone near the door.

A hand pressed her back when she stood, and she jumped. "Oh sorry," she told Owen who gave her an odd look.

"Ready?"

"Yep." Grabbing her purse, they headed toward the door.

Ramo looked up as they approached.

"Got a minute, Perez?" Owen asked, his hand still

possessively at her back.

She stopped in front of Ramo, holding on to the straps of her purse with two hands.

He glanced at her before nodding at Owen. "What's up?" Joe stood outside the door watching them with his arms crossed.

"Just giving you a heads up...Our packs will be having a summit next week. Our adjudicator is updating Adam now."

Shit! This isn't happening. This. Could. Not. Be. Happening.

Ramo narrowed his eyes. "What for?"

With an unabashed smile, Owen rubbed her back. "To amend the treaty and discuss how we will go forward with the Fighters."

Shifting uncomfortably on her feet, she said, "Owen...Can we..."

"Amend the treaty?" Ramo looked back and forth between them. "There's no amending necessary. It's pretty clear cut." He pointed to Elizabeth. "Our marriage ensures we stay friendly. Without it? No treaty."

"Well now, is it fair for two Weres to be connected in such a way when they're not "acting" as husband and wife? Or mates for that matter?" Owen slid his hand in hers, giving her a firm squeeze.

There was no hiding the sound of her heart rate picking up, just as Ramo couldn't suppress the rising fear within him.

"So the fuck what?" Ramo stood straighter, his fists clenched at his side. "A contract's a contract. As my wife, the Blacktails cannot touch the Graybacks and vice versa."

"We'll discuss it at the summit." Owen frowned and started to urge Elizabeth toward the door.

"No, we'll discuss it now." Ramo stepped to him, getting way too close in Owen's personal space.

Joe growled low, shoulder's hunched. Elizabeth put her hand out to back him off as she placed herself in between the two colossal men. "Ramo, it can wait."

"The fuck it can. What is going on?" Ramo no longer glared at Owen, his eyes firm on hers.

Her heart squeezed at the look he gave her. She wanted nothing more than to hold him and kiss all his worries away. It was suddenly just the two of them, trying to communicate without words. She wanted to tell him the truth about Owen's proposal, but the words wouldn't come out. Please, God this couldn't be happening. Not after last night. Not after Ramo had told her he loved her.

Owen's voice sounded as if he were talking underwater. "We can find another alliance between our packs. She shouldn't have to bear the burden for the Graybacks." Ramo's eyes never left hers as he listened. "And since Elizabeth has agreed to marry me, it's best we start talks now."

She watched Ramo's expression as Owen's words registered. Confusion, rage, fear; his beautiful features marred with her betrayal. "Marry?" His brows drew down over chestnut eyes. "What?" He moved impossibly closer that her neck ached to look at him. "What is he talking about? Did you…"

Owen's hand shot to Ramo's chest. "Back off." He tried to pull her back, but she didn't budge.

"Elizabeth? Did he propose? Did you fucking say yes?" Ramo's breath was hot on her face.

"No...I mean..." Oh God. Blood was rushing to her face, her vision receding. Rage burned through her. She wanted to punch Owen for doing this.

"We're leaving," Owen said in her ear, his hand still on Ramo's pec.

"Fuck off!" Ramo knocked Owen's hand away from him. "Till your cocksucking summit, she is still my wife! Elizabeth..." he grabbed her arm, firmly, but gently, "...What the fuck is going on? Did you agree to marry him or not?"

"What?" The volume in the gym grew so low. She could tell they were shouting at each other, but they sounded so muffled. The room spun around her. "No...I don't know..." She couldn't breathe. Sweat trickled down her back.

"Elizabeth..." Owen warned.

The low rumble of her alpha's warning snapped her out of her stammering. "I mean, yes. We're getting married," she said, although it came out more as a question.

Ramo's face turned excruciatingly deadly. Seething, he growled through his teeth, "You piece of shit. Did you order her?"

"We're done here." Owen shoved her toward the door but was knocked back by Ramo. Joe moved so quickly, she hardly saw her beta jump on her husband.

"NO!" she shouted, trying futilely to track their movements. The room was spinning so fast, it started to close in on her. She couldn't see what was happening. Three massive bodies collided, flashing in and out of her vision. There were low grunts as arms and legs swung about. Suddenly, they were gone. She only saw hardwood floor move as though it had suddenly become a drawbridge, heading straight to her face.

The last thing she heard was Ramo's voice crying her name.

Chapter Sixteen

"Elizabeth? Come on, sweetie. Wake up!"

Ramo's voice was like a beacon to her. Fighting the cobwebs, she forced herself to come to. The feel of a cushion beneath her should have been a relief, but it did nothing for the horrible pain in her head. Opening her eyes, she saw not Ramo, but Owen hovering over her.

"Oh thank God! You scared the shit out of me. Are you okay?"

She squeezed her eyes shut at the sound of his voice. Then, with a jerk, she turned on her side and vomited on the floor.

"Jesus," He cursed. "Get me something to clean this up. And a cold washcloth."

She didn't know who he was talking to, but all of a sudden there was a wet cloth on her forehead. Taking in her surroundings, she realized she was on Owen's couch in the townhouse. "What happened?" she rasped, squinting up at him.

Grimacing, he said, "You knocked your head twice in one day is what happened. How do you feel?"

"Horrible."

She tried to sit up, but he gently pushed her back. "Relax, Elizabeth. You've had two hard falls today."

"Ramo," she said without thinking. Where was he?

Owen sat back on his haunches, his mouth

hardening in a thin line. It was then she took in the deep cut on his upper lip, and two black eyes.

"Ramo and I needed some space," was all he said.

Owen's cleaning lady entered the living room and together they cleaned up her mess, refusing her help when she offered. After washing out her mouth in the bathroom, Owen made her swallow four Tylenol and lay back down as he checked some emails on his phone.

Despite the relief she felt at the much needed rest, she could not get Ramo's expression out of her mind. She wished she could explain, but it seems he'd already figured out the proposal was an order. At least he knew she didn't agree to marry Owen of her own free will.

The sound of Owen tip tapping on his iPhone grated on her nerves. Why didn't he ever put it on silent? If she mentioned this to him, would he order her to mind her business? Anger surged through her and there was no way she was getting any rest now.

Getting up slowly, she leaned back on the cushion to take a steady breath. Feeling marginally better, she glared at Owen who sat at the dining room table, still fixated on his phone. "I'm going."

His head shot up. "What's wrong?"

"Nothing," she stood, slowly, "I have to pick up my grandmother's medicine before she phases."

Standing, he nodded, his eyes narrowing. "Why are you upset?"

Rolling her eyes she walked to the door.

"Elizabeth?" he followed her, placing a hand on the door.

"What? You're going to order me to stay? You know my grandmother can't take her meds in wolf form. She'll…"

"I'm not ordering you. Jesus. Tell me what's going on. Please," he added as he'd just given another damn order.

Elizabeth couldn't look at him, she was so mad. Crossing her arms, she said, "You didn't even give me a chance to say, 'yes'. That is, if you were actually asking me to marry you."

Owen sighed. "I was asking."

"Really? Because you know it sounded like an order. I asked you if it was and you shut me up. Is this how you want me? By force?"

"No…"

"Then rescind it." She met his gaze, hoping her expression looked more stoic than hopeful.

He stared at the door, his features defeated. "Look…I'm not ordering you to marry me. I'm sorry it came out that way. Just…don't give me an answer right away. Give it some thought and let's see how the summit goes."

His knuckles caressed her arm and she almost cringed. It didn't feel right. She wasn't his to touch. Tears stung the backs of her eyes. Why did she have to stay with him? It wasn't fair. She needed to tell him the truth and soon. Tomorrow, she'd talk it out with Ramo and together they'd come up with a plan. There was no way they could all go on this way.

She walked home to clear her head. After picking up her grandmother's medicine across the street, she trudged up the front stairs and through the door. God, Ramo's scent was still in the air. It was so potent it was as if he were standing in front of her. It mixed perfectly with her grandmother's cooking and suddenly she was starving.

Letting herself in to Nonni's apartment, she faltered at the scene before her. She blinked, thinking her mind was playing tricks on her.

Per usual, her grandmother wore shorts, t-shirt and Reeboks standing at the stove pouring marinara sauce over eggplant parmesan. The unusual part of this scene was Ramo, seated at the tiny kitchen table going to town on garlic bread. It was like a bull in a china shop he was so out of place. And yet, here he was, looking so dangerously hot in her grandmother's home. When he saw her, he gave her a wary grin, his mouth full of bread.

He stood as she launched herself at him, wrapping her arms around him and smashing her lips against his. Chuckling, Ramo held her to him, his strong arms wound firm around her middle. He pulled back, his eyes roaming all over her face. "Are you okay? How's your head."

Shaking her head incredulously, she said, "I'm fine. What are you doing here?"

His hands gripped her face as he searched her eyes then felt the back of her head tenderly.

"Ramo, really, I'm okay. How did…what…" she glanced at her grandmother.

"You can ask questions while you eat," Nonni said in Italian, as she placed two plates on the table. *"Quickly before he asks for fourths."*

"I know you're talking about me, Nonni," Ramo warned playfully as he pulled out Elizabeth's chair and took the seat across from her. "I'm going to learn Italian if it kills me and then what will you do?"

"Speak English," her grandmother quipped.

He shook his head with a smile.

Elizabeth watched this exchange with wide eyes, her mouth agape. What in the world was happening?

"When did you two even meet?" she asked, still dumbfounded, but incredibly happy to see him.

His eyes were warm on hers. "She ambushed me the first time I came to see you. I was on my way down and her little nose poked out of the door and she ushered me in."

Elizabeth looked in astonishment at her grandmother. "Nonni! You never told me."

The old woman just shrugged her shoulders as she moved about her kitchen.

Elizabeth rolled her eyes. "So then what?"

Ramo was nearly done with his third plate. Setting his fork down, he continued. "She told me off, which I deserved and then fed me rigatoni. We talked for about an hour, but now the old woman won't speak to me in English," he chastised over his shoulder.

Nonni shrugged again, ignoring them. They both laughed at her nonchalance.

Elizabeth's cheeks hurt from smiling She could not describe the feeling of being in her Nonni's kitchen, eating her splendid food with the love of her life. It was strange to be sure, but it seemed these two got along well and in that moment she forgot about all her troubles and focused on being in her favorite place with her favorite guy.

"Are you going to tell me what you talked about that day?" Elizabeth asked conspiratorially.

He arched an eyebrow with a smirk and shook his head. God, he was adorable.

His smile faded as he regarded her. "Were you going to tell me?" He asked evenly, his deep voice low.

Dropping her gaze, she played with her food. "Of course, but I didn't think it was real and it wasn't. He's not forcing me. He rescinded his order before I left."

His shoulders heaved up and down as he sighed. Crossing his arms in front of him, he leaned back in his chair. "I figured he'd take you to his place. I wanted to take you to the hospital, but I think he was afraid he'd be questioned for domestic abuse."

"I'm fine now. Completely healed."

He nodded, thoughtfully. "I didn't want to let you go. He threatened to call the police if I followed you guys, so I came here. Anything else I should know?"

She shook her head. "Wait...Owen looks terrible. It was two against one. Why don't you have a scratch on you?" she asked, checking him out.

Letting out a smug huff, he pointed to his chest with his thumb. "Fighter."

Her grandmother spoke in Italian again.

Grinning, Elizabeth said, "She said not to be boastful."

"I don't know how *not* to be boastful, Nonni. I'm amazing and you know it."

She loved how he teased her grandmother and oh wow, how she wanted this. She could live the rest of her life happy as a clam as long as she was surrounded by these two.

Looking up through her lashes she whispered, "I don't want to do this anymore. I can't stand to have him..." she glanced at her grandmother's back and mouthed the words 'touch me'. Ramo's jaw tightened, his body seeming to swell before her eyes. She knew he hated this as much as she did, if not more.

"I'll take care of it. I promise." He murmured back,

his eyes riveted on hers. Then, he craned his neck and said to her grandmother, "What's for dessert, veija?"

She didn't know what he'd just called her grandmother, but Spanish leaving those sculpted lips made her insides warm.

Ignoring him again with a dismissive wave of her hand, she went about her kitchen. Then, her grandmother did something extraordinary. Taking a bottle out from the bottom cupboard, she placed it on the kitchen table between them.

"Nonni!" Elizabeth admonished.

Her little gnarled fingers twisted the top off of the Woodford Reserve and she grabbed three glasses.

"A woman after my own heart," Ramo joked and her grandmother smirked.

"My father would toast to the full moon before he phased with a glass of whiskey every month. It is a tradition among Weres, which has died down, but tonight it seems fitting. We will toast to the rising moon and the dawning of a new day." Her eyes seared into Elizabeth's and her meaning could not be clearer.

Elizabeth translated for Ramo and he nodded as if he already knew of the tradition. They all raised their glasses and drank. All the while, Ramo's soft gaze remained on her.

I love you, he mouthed and that was when her heart burst.

Chapter Seventeen

The best part of a full moon was the quiet it inspired. All of Chicago turned in early to let the Weres run free in a ghost town. It was their chance to explore and appreciate their city without restraint or consequence in their true forms. As much as she loved the bustling city, there was something about a sleeping town that made you want to go streaking through the streets, which is what they essentially did these nights.

Owen sent Elizabeth and Kylen to patrol The Desplaines River Trail about twenty miles northwest of the city. Here, she had a chance to beat her paws on asphalt, dirt or gravel; to stretch her legs in an open plain, a thicket of trees or at the water's edge. The space was wide enough so the two of them weren't on top of each other. She could enjoy the solitude of the run to let her mind wander.

And wander it did.

Sometime from St. Patrick's Day and now, she'd fallen in love with her husband. She almost giggled at the thought. Replaying every encounter they'd ever had, she wondered how the arrogant jerk weaseled his way into her heart. No matter how he did it, he was there, and she could not picture her world without him.

They needed a plan. They needed something. She could not keep leading Owen on this way. The truth was bound to come out. Owen had to sense how she felt about Ramo. His ridiculous plan to break up her marriage was a futile attempt at best. He had to know what trouble it could cause both their packs. She couldn't see Adam going for it. Both packs needed to agree for the treaty to hold water.

The early morning sky faded to a dull gray as the sun made its ascent behind dense clouds. Kylen's emotions grew weaker, his pounding footfalls retreating as he headed back to the city.

Ramo's response to her text about where she'd be patrolling echoed in her mind.

—I'll find you…—

She could almost hear his deep, lusty voice murmuring the words in her ear.

Slowing to a trot in a thicket of wood, she watched the sky brighten and felt the morning dew moisten her fur. The sound of crunching twigs and frozen earth calmed her, easing the stress of the previous day.

Her nape prickled, and she detected another Were closing in on her. She froze as the Were grew closer then stopped a few feet from her. The sound of hefty breaths behind her made her heart pound. She turned her head to look over her shoulder. Heat coursed through her body at the sight of her male in all his wolf glory.

She'd seen Ramo in wolf form before, but never alone and never like this. He was magnificent crouched on all fours, his back arched in a perfect angle. Dark brown fur swayed in the breeze as his chest pumped from exertion or from his reaction to her. No matter, it was clear he wanted her, needed her maybe.

He pawed the earth and let out huff, a cloud of smoke dancing from his snout and she understood his request. Ramo wanted her to phase back, quickly.

Standing tall, she willed her body to transform back to woman. In seconds, Elizabeth was standing bare naked in the woods in front of her wolf husband. The cool morning air hardened her nipples and he growled low before her.

Chuckling, she asked, "Are you going to phase?"

In response, he stood tall on his hind legs, his large frame dwarfing the trees surrounding him. He stalked toward her and she smirked, backing away from him.

"Are you trying to scare me?" she asked, playfully as her back hit a trunk of a tree.

He shook his head, his yellows eyes penetrating hers. Towering over her, she barely reached his stomach. He was so beautiful; from his rippling, leathery chest to the smooth hair on his dark snout. She'd never touched another werewolf in true form and the need overpowered her. Holding out her hands, she hesitated. Werewolves were not accustomed to people petting them and she wondered if she should. The deep rumble emanating from his chest, however, told her he approved

Without another thought, she placed her hands on his waist, burying her fingers into the fur at his sides. His answering purr spurred her on and she let her fingers roam over him. Relishing the feel of him, she explored the thick skin of his abs and chest as his shoulders heaved up and down, his heavy breaths feathering the top of her hair. Kneading his forearms as they were the only parts of his arms she could reach, she gripped his paws, bringing them up for a closer look. The padding of his palms were worn and cracked from years of running and she had a sudden urge to feel them on her skin.

Looking up at him through her lashes, she raised an eyebrow teasingly as she placed his paws around her waist. He let out a sharp breath through his nostrils as he spanned his rough fingers around her torso, his claws lightly digging into her skin. Suddenly, she was lifted into the air until they were nose to snout.

She tilted her head to gaze at him, then wrapped her arms around his shoulders, burrowing into his thick neck. It was like a child hugging the largest teddy bear. He felt so perfect she wished she could sleep in his wolf arms for the rest of her life. Her body writhed against his, and her stomach tightened with indescribable need. "Ramo..." she whispered, her hands kneading his great shoulders. "...phase..."

He hugged her tighter to him, and she wrapped her legs around him as best she could. He was trying to calm himself enough to phase, but the fact she was naked and against him probably didn't help matters. After a moment, she felt him shrinking beneath her as she was lowered to the ground, but not by much. When she felt human skin over chiseled muscle she giggled mischievously.

Lifting his head from the crook of her shoulder, he gave her a reproachful look. He murmured, menacingly, "You want to get fucked by a wolf? Keep that shit up."

She licked her lips, her eyes hooded. "You're the one who wouldn't phase."

"I couldn't. Shit, babe, I can barely see straight when I'm around you. I don't know what's hotter, you in Were form or like this." He pushed his hips into her, and she felt his thick length against her sex.

"I missed you," she cooed, kissing his jaw and

down his neck.

"Mmmm… You're killing me." He laid her back against the bark, his hand protecting her skin.

"I need you, Ramo." She squirmed beneath him and he moaned.

Pulling his head back, he eyed her mouth before slipping his index finger inside. She sucked him in, running her tongue over him. Taking his finger out, he brought it between them and slipped it inside her.

Her head fell back as she moaned.

"You're ready for me baby," he hissed.

"Yes Ramo, please." She squeezed him between her thighs.

With his forehead pressed to hers, he placed the tip of his swollen length against her folds, teasing mercilessly until she took matters into her own hands. Reaching between them, she nudged him inside her as she lifted her hips. Biting down on his lower lip, he filled her to the hilt. Moaning in unison, their mouths finally fused.

They kissed for all they were worth, making up for lost time; ten years to be exact. And as their mouths moved furiously, he pumped her up and down, stretching her tightness. It felt different now at this angle as she was no longer sore. But what made it all so incredibly intoxicating was their love for each other. Her need for him was almost painful. If she could swallow him whole she would. She never wanted him to stop.

Their bodies vibrated at their desperate union. Moving into her, he pulled out and in steadily. Gripping her back with one hand as he held onto the tree behind her, his thrusts became stronger, but he was still holding back, afraid of being too rough. She'd only lost her virginity yesterday. But he had to feel how amazing this felt. She only wanted more.

Hissing as he drove into her, he squeezed her ass. "Fuck Elizabeth, you feel so good." His head dropped to her shoulder, his grunts an added bonus to their love making.

"Harder, Ramo. Don't stop." Biting his shoulder, her hips gyrated in unison with his. He complied, pumping harder, faster, grunting with every angry thrust. She felt her orgasm building and closed her eyes. "I'm coming Ram…I'm…"

"Come with me, Elizabeth," his thrusts slowed as heat rushed her body. As it was no longer the full moon, she didn't have to worry about conceiving. Oh, how amazing it felt for him to finish inside her; to feel his wetness moisten her body.

He continued to pump slowly as he drained himself in her, then locked himself against her, his head falling back. "Jesus Christ, I'm dizzy."

Grasping his neck, she kissed his jaw, basking in the heady feel of her husband between her legs, against her breasts. She was loved, safe and there was nowhere she'd rather be than here in his arms. Sweet contentment washed over her. "I love you, Ramo."

He froze against her, lifting his head to meet her gaze. "What?"

Smiling she answered, "I think you heard me."

"Say it again." His eyes were hopeful, but with an ounce of trepidation. Did he doubt her feelings?

Kissing him firmly on the lips, she gripped his cheeks. "I love you, Ramo, only you."

He seized her in a tight embrace as if he were

afraid she'd disappear before his eyes. "I love you too." He pulled back to look at her, his eyes shining with elation just as a tree branch snapped behind him.

****

Ramo knew Elizabeth heard the crack slice the morning silence when her eyes flicked over his shoulder. The sated expression she'd worn one millisecond ago was gone. He watched her face drain of all color and her eyes widened so much he could see the whites all around her pupils.

Fuck!

He didn't have to turn around to see who was standing behind him. Only one person would make Elizabeth look so completely terrified.

Owen Hunter, alpha of the Grayback's stood mere feet away from them and he was still buried inside of his girlfriend.

Screwing his eyes tight, he felt only a spark of guilt for moving in on his girl, but hadn't Owen moved in on his wife first? Still…this was all kinds of fucked up.

Giving her thigh a gentle squeeze, he whispered, "Put your legs down," Wanting to wipe that horrified expression off her face, he felt his jaw tick.

Slowly, with her dark eyes fixated on Owen, she slid her legs down as he slid out of her.

He screwed his eyes shut for a beat, clenching his teeth before turning to face his wife's alpha. As he did, he blocked Elizabeth from view. He felt her guilt, her embarrassment like a hammer to his gut; there was no need to flaunt her nakedness after what he'd just done to her body.

Owen stood in jeans a good twenty feet away, his fists clenched, bare feet planted on the ground. It hadn't even occurred to their lust-driven minds Owen would perhaps show up to where she'd been running. The alpha's face was screwed up so tight; he looked like his head might explode.

Pulling in his lips, he considered what to say. Ordinarily, he'd be an asshole to the guy who'd been pawing his wife for the last few months, but it'd be like kicking a man while down.

"Hunter…"

"Shut up." Owen's voice was raw, his eyes hard.

Holding up his hands in defense, he treaded carefully. "This is happening so the sooner you accept it, the better."

"Fuck you!" Owen spat, his face getting redder and redder. Once the sun was up after a full moon, it took an extraordinary amount of effort to phase back into a wolf. Their human form was at its weakest state. With the sun high in the sky, it was lucky for the both of them they couldn't phase. No matter, he was ready for anything. He could read the guy's anger and betrayal, but if Owen had a weapon on him, he was sure it would be aimed at his head right now.

He took a deep breath. "Let's talk. Me and you." Inwardly, he cringed at his own words. If he were Owen, he'd tell him to fuck off.

Jesus, he hated him on principal, but no man should ever have to see what Owen just witnessed.

The man was visibly shaking now, and he feared for Elizabeth. He could take the alpha down with no problem, but he didn't want him using his authority over her to get back at them.

"I have nothing to say to you," Owen's voice trembled along with his body and he looked over

Ramo's shoulder.

"Owen..." he warned, "Leave her out of this."

The Grayback was through with him as he addressed Elizabeth. "You can't even face me? I just watched you *fuck* him. I just watched my girlfriend let this piece of shit come inside her. LOOK AT ME!"

Elizabeth shuddered as she sobbed. "You don't have to," he whispered to her, but she'd made up her own mind.

With arms clutched tightly over her chest, she stepped from behind him and faced Owen with pitiful eyes.

The strangled sound, which emanated from Owen was so despicable he had to avert his eyes, glaring at the ground. He wanted to hold her to his side, protect her from Owen's accusing stare.

"How...how..." Owen seemed to be falling apart at the seams. He choked on every word. "You...gave him...your virginity? *Him*?"

She gripped her arms so hard she left red streaks across her skin. Her long, dark hair fell all around her and even sobbing she never looked more beautiful. "I'm so sorry, Owen. I wanted to tell you. I tried..."

"Fuck you!" Owen spat, his arms shuddering at his sides.

"Hey!" he shouted, stepping forward.

Ignoring him, Owen ordered. "Come here."

Trembling, Elizabeth hitched in a breath. Then, bringing her arms to her sides, she began to walk toward him.

"NO!" he shouted, gripping her arm. "Don't order her again, Hunter. I fucking mean it."

Owen gave him the ugliest smile. "Elizabeth, get

over here now!"

Glancing pathetically at him, she shrugged him off and walked toward her master, head bowed.

He growled menacingly, reaching Owen before Elizabeth could and slamming him into the nearest tree.

"NO!" Elizabeth shouted. "Ramo, please!" She was at their sides, gripping his straining bicep.

"Back away, Elizabeth!" he ordered.

"No. Please don't do this." She continued to sob, her body a mixture of emotions that were killing him.

He spoke through clenched teeth. "I don't want to fight you, but you need to stop with the edicts. Elizabeth is my wife. I'm sorry you had to find out this way, but we're going to make a go of it. The sooner you understand that the better. "

Angry tears ran down Owen's sweat-ridden face as he stared at Elizabeth. "I fucking loved you."

She continued to cry silently. "I'm...I'm so sorry. I was going to tell you. Please...let me explain..."

"Explain what? I just saw everything I need to know. Why bother now?" Owen swallowed audibly, his features twisting in agony. "You love him?" he croaked miserably, his eyes wide in disbelief.

Sadly, Elizabeth nodded.

"He's a player. He left you and you gave yourself to him and not me?"

Ramo gripped his neck tighter. "I love her too, Owen. I always knew I'd come back for her."

Owen scoffed, pushing him off.

The three of them stood in this locked position for several seconds before anyone spoke. He glared as Owen continued to stare in disbelief at Elizabeth.

Squeezing his eyes shut as if he were in pain,

Owen ran his hands over his face. "Ugh! I can't get the image of you two out of my fucking head." He stalked away from them.

"Owen, wait," Elizabeth gripped his arm, but he shook it off.

Glaring down at her he whispered, "I can't even look at you." Then spun around, probably wishing he could phase and four-foot it back to the city.

"Owen…" she cried.

"Let him go, Elizabeth."

She let out wail, hugging herself. He wrapped her in his arms, murmuring to her. "I'm so sorry. Fuck," he whispered frustratingly as she trembled in his arms. He never wanted this to happen. It was one thing if he'd gone to Owen and told him the truth, but he never wanted the alpha to see them together.

"I have to go to him," she sobbed.

"The hell you do." He gripped her by her arms to look at him. "He's messed up right now. He needs to cool off first."

"I have to make it right."

"I know baby, but now is not the time. He was ready to order you back to him…there's no telling what he'll do."

Wiping her cheeks, she stood; staring in the direction Owen disappeared. "I didn't want him to find out this way."

"I know," he soothed, running his hand over her long hair, caressing her back.

She sniffed, shakily. "I feel awful."

"It's understandable…" He began, but she cut him off.

"No…you don't understand" She inhaled, a fresh

wave of tears running down her face. "I feel terrible for hurting him, but…" She shook her head. "Never mind."

Ramo chewed the inside of his mouth wondering what that *but* meant.

"I can't believe this happened…" her voice cracked.

He held her closer, cursing inwardly. He didn't want her hurting for Owen, but she wouldn't be the woman he loved if she didn't. He wondered if he should leave her alone for a while. Did his presence make matters worse for her? Did she still care about him as much as she did seconds before Owen ruined their perfect moment?

He felt like a bratty kid for thinking this way, but he wanted her attention now. All of it. She was his, and he wanted to start making a life with her ASAP. But now they had Owen's feelings to contend with.

He felt her guilt give way and her shoulders slump. "Can you take me home?" she whispered against his chest.

He closed his eyes, a sharp pain searing his chest.

This was why he'd left ten years ago.

He never wanted to lose a loved one. And if this episode ruined his relationship with Elizabeth, he didn't think he'd ever be the same again.

Chapter Eighteen

"Do you want me to go?"

Elizabeth barely registered Ramo's words. She sat on her sofa, wrapped in a throw blanket, her mind going a mile a minute.

"Elizabeth?"

"Mmm?" She answered distractedly, staring toward the window.

"Do you want me to go?"

Her head whipped around, her eyes sharp on his. He leaned against the door, his hands in his jean pockets. "No. Why?"

Shrugging, he said, "It looks like you have a lot on your mind."

"I do."

He swallowed, the thick cords of his neck undulating as he looked away. "I'll leave you alone then."

"No, Ramo…That's the last thing I want."

He met her gaze and she finally picked up the guilt and fear he felt. What was he afraid of?

"Do you regret it? Being with me?"

A sharp pain pierced her chest. Here she was worried over Owen and her husband was terrified she regretted being with him. "No, of course not. Why would you think that?"

"You were with Hunter for months. I'm not stupid.

I know there were feelings there," he said, again not meeting her eyes.

"Come here," she held out her hand.

Sighing, he made his way toward her, sitting on the opposite side of the couch. She smirked at how large he looked, taking up more than half of the space. She tucked her feet beneath her and faced him.

"I do have feelings for Owen…"

Leaning forward, he placed his elbows on his knees and covered his face with his palms. "Just say it, Elizabeth."

"Say what?"

"Tell me you don't want this; that you want him. Just get it over with. Don't drag it out."

Gripping his thick bicep, she made him look at her. "What the hell is wrong with you?"

He stared, mutely.

"I don't want him. Yes, I'm hurting for him, but I'm in love with you." She took his hands, playing with his fingers as he liked to do hers. "I'm also feeling incredibly awful because a small part of me is relieved he knows." She looked up at him guiltily. "Does that make me a bad person?"

He shook his head. "I'm relieved too."

"I'm going to have to talk to him…" She squeezed his hand at the look he gave her. "It's the right thing to do. Think what you will, but I know he'll do the right thing."

He let out a deep sigh. "After everything we've been through, I honestly cannot stomach you being around him without me."

"He's my alpha. I have to…"

"Then join my pack," he said instantly.

"What?"

"Join the Blacktails. Adam won't mind and I can induct you myself since you're my wife."

Smiling, she continued to play with his hand. "I love that you asked, but you know it will break the treaty if I become a Blacktail."

He leaned his head back against the wall, closing his eyes. "The fucking treaty…"

"Hey! The treaty brought us together." She forced him to look at her. "And I'm not going anywhere. Not to him or anyone else. Well…maybe Zac Efron," she joked, biting her lip.

Raising his eyebrow, he said, "I can step on that kid."

"I don't know. Ever see him dance? He's pretty fast."

"No. I don't watch men dance," he scolded, lifting her from her spot on the couch and onto his lap. "And we'll be avoiding all his movies from now on."

She laughed as she straddled his hips, her t-shirt dress riding high up her thighs.

He moaned, his lids lowering as he caressed her back.

"Hey…" She started as he found her thighs, his gaze following his hands. "Earlier…with Owen…you told him you'd always come back for me. What did you mean?"

"What do you mean 'What do I mean?' Isn't it obvious?"

She shook her head. "Was it true?"

He looked insulted. "Of course it's true." He gripped her back, snuggling her close against him. "First, everything I say to you is true. I'm honest as hell and you know that." He rubbed her backside, glancing down at her lips. He wanted her again and she felt her belly tighten.

"Second, it's true because when I saw you walk toward me on our wedding day in your white dress, I knew I was done for. The whole time you stood there, I could only think about what you looked like underneath that dress. Then your age would ring in my head and I'd feel like a pervert. I told myself, I didn't want to be married, but I knew then, I wasn't ever letting you go. I thought about you every day; with guilt of course, but I did. I told you I wasn't ready and it was true, but I was also scared as hell. You know what happened to my grandfather and I saw how my cousin lost his shit over his mate.

"All this isn't to excuse what I did. It's just…a minute ago I thought I was going to lose you… Call me weak, but I can't handle it. I won't. Like I said, you're stuck with me. Even if you get sick of me and hate me, that's fine. I'm still going to be all up in your life so get used to it."

"How can I ever tire of you, Ramo Perez?" She murmured as she zipped down his jeans, freeing his large arousal.

He inhaled sharply, his mouth falling open. "Promise?"

In answer, she sat down on him, taking him in till the hilt. Moaning, she said, "God yes, Ramo."

He gripped her waist pulling her down on him. Before he ravaged her mouth with his, he whispered, "That's my girl."

Epilogue

"How on earth is a vampire marrying a werewolf?"

Elizabeth sat in the passenger seat next to Ramo looking at her reflection in the mirror of the visor as she did her makeup. Per usual, she had been running late and only had time to shower, blow dry, and throw on the dress he had bought her for his cousin's wedding.

"They had to turn Evangeline after her boys were born. She nearly died. The Vampire King of North America saved her life by making her a vampire."

She looked to him wide eyed. "There's a story there..."

He laughed. "I'll tell you all about it." Rubbing her thigh as he drove, he started, "So Evangeline was engaged to the king..."

As she listened to her husband's version of the story, she laughed at his crass humor and the way he spun tales. He looked so handsome in his suit, reminding her of the rugged man she married almost eleven years to the date.

After months of insistence, she'd finally let him move into her apartment. As much as she felt they should go slow, her husband wasn't having it. And telling him to go slow was like telling a fish not to swim. He pushed and pushed and since she loved it when he pushed in just the right way, she relented.

When the family moved out upstairs, Ramo began

making plans to convert the second and third floors into a duplex up. He knew she wouldn't leave her grandmother and he didn't mind. Their place was currently under construction, so they spent half their time at Nonni's.

She shook her head in disbelief. She knew when he came into town he'd turn her world upside down. And just thinking about what her apartment looked like right now with walls knocked down and no functional bathroom, she'd been right.

Her phone buzzed and she reached into her clutch to check it.

He glanced over. "Everything okay?"

She responded and tossed the phone back in her purse. "Yep. Just another meeting."

His jaw hardened, but thankfully he didn't remark on her alpha. Owen would always be a sensitive topic.

Just as she'd predicted, Owen bowed out gracefully. The days following the notorious full moon were excruciating. Owen refused to speak to her and when he finally did, he was an emotional wreck. After the loooooooongest talk of her life, he understood getting involved with her while she was married hadn't been the best move on both their parts.

He was now dating a Fighter in his and Danny's trainee group as he refused to work with Ramo any longer. She never mentioned the longing looks Owen sometimes gave her at meetings. It wasn't worth the argument. Her heart belonged to Ramo and she couldn't imagine her life without him.

"Here we go…" He said as he pulled up in front of a white mansion with tall columns. A valet opened her door and Elizabeth slipped out looking around the marvelous landscape. "This is Evangeline's parents' house."

She looked around at the old home with its fresh paint and black shutters. They walked in the house where a man in a tuxedo offered them each a glass of something pink. As she took a sip and whispered, "I thought you said her father gambled all his money away. Mmmm...this is yummy."

He whispered back as they made their way down the elaborate hall toward the garden where they could hear a string quartet and hundreds of people milling about. "He did. But the vampire king paid his debts for Evangeline's hand in marriage."

"But she's marrying Adam."

He gave her an admonishing look. "You poor thing. That baby is just sucking all your brain cells isn't he? Gimme that." He took the flute from her and downed it in one swallow. "It has champagne in it."

She rolled her eyes at her husband, rubbing her swollen belly.

They found seats toward the back and nearest the house since she peed twenty times a minute. The sun was finally down, which was the only time Evangeline could be outdoors, which meant the ceremony would soon begin. She wanted to hear more of the Evangeline/Adam/King story, but Ramo said it would be bad luck during the wedding and he'd explain the rest when they went home. They were staying at his place in Wilmington, which was only a three-minute drive from the wedding venue.

Lights twinkled all around them and she gazed adoringly at all the lavish flowers and wedding décor. The aroma of food wafted out to where they sat and she distinctly smelled steak and her stomach growled. Meat was all she craved these days and she couldn't wait to eat.

She gasped when she saw Evangeline walking down the aisle with her father. There was nothing like a gorgeous model-like beauty to make you feel fat and ugly. "She's so stunning she looks fake," she whispered to Ramo. "How's my hair?"

Chuckling, he put his arm around her. "*You* look stunning, baby."

They sat back down when Evangeline reached Adam who wiped his eyes several times, never taking his eyes off his beautiful bride.

Movement off to her right distracted her and she noticed a huge Were with long hair standing in the back, bouncing a baby in his arms. He winked at a woman who sat in the back, her belly as swollen as Elizabeth's..

Werewolves were incredibly fertile. It was a wonder they didn't inherit the earth yet.

As she smiled at the sleeping baby in the man's arms, a woman who looked to be Evangeline's mother walked hand in hand with two little boys in tuxedos. Each held a pillow with rings on them. They made their way, stumbling on chubby legs as they reached their parents.

Ramo smiled, waving at the boys as they took their seats. "My baby cousins," he said proudly, rubbing her belly.

When the justice of the peace introduced the couple as 'Mr. and Mrs. Adam Perez' everyone stood and cheered. She succumbed to tears as she was want to do lately and excused herself to pee, telling Ramo to wait for her to congratulate the new couple.

As she walked toward the house, she froze. A tall man with dirty blond hair stood in the open back door, blocking her way. His hands were in his pockets as he leaned against the jamb, his glowing, white eyes directed at the bride and groom.

Elizabeth knew this must be the Vampire King of North America and for a moment she thought the man was going to attack everyone, but then his eyes doused to their normal shade and he noticed her. The king brought his finger to his lips, mouthing a silent 'shh', then he winked and walked back into the house and out the front door. She looked around to see if anyone had noticed and could only see the long haired Were with the baby, who she surmised was the Blacktail beta, glaring at the spot the king had just stood.

The reception was the best celebration she'd ever attended. The outdoor setup turned into tables and chairs surrounding a makeshift dance floor. Every table had a large floral arrangement along with a bottle of tequila and the Blacktail Fighters knocked backed shots like they were going out of style.

Everyone was in the happiest of moods and danced the night away, including her and Ramo. She was shocked to learn her husband could dance salsa like a *Dancing With The Stars* contestant and by the end of the night, she was keeping up with the moves he taught her.

The highlight of the night? The taco table, which came out just as the drunken guests became rowdy. She was the first in line and made her way to an empty table with Ramo carrying chips and salsa behind her.

She ate while he rubbed her feet in his lap,

watching the bride and groom dance slowly to a fast song in the middle of dance floor.

"Do you want this? A real wedding?" Ramo asked her.

Elizabeth took a chip, dipping it into the salsa. "Our wedding was real and no. I wouldn't change it for anything."

He looked to her skeptically. "Really?"

She swallowed the chip shaking her head. "I got under your skin the day I walked down the aisle and haunted you ever since." She smirked at him. "That's enough for me."

Ramo moved her onto his lap, kissing her tenderly as he caressed her protruding belly. "I'm going to drive you crazy till the day I die, Elizabeth Perez."

And…he did.